Shadow's Fall

T. M. Hart

Shadow Series : Book 4

"No tree, it is said, can grow to heaven unless its roots reach down to hell."

~ *Carl Jung, Aion: Researches into the Phenomenology of the Self*

PROLOGUE

EVERYONE BREAKS.
Everyone.
It is a universal truth. An absolute with no exceptions. The only difference between us is how we break.

And what it turns us into.

This is one such story.

And this will take some telling.

CHAPTER 1

WITH A CRASH THAT FLOODED MY EARS, I slammed into a stall.

My spine snapped, wood splintered, and the surrounding stables rattled. I sank to the ground knowing I had lost the use of my legs. I fought to push myself up, digging my hands into the dirt. I managed to lift my chest off the ground, but my head hung between my shoulders.

"Get. Up." The two words were a low growl vibrating from the shadows before me.

I spat the dirt from my mouth and rubbed my lips across my arm. "I can't." I was barely able to speak. One of my lungs had collapsed.

"Get up!"

After a long pause, I finally raised my head. "You snapped my spine," I gritted.

"Mend it," he commanded.

I laughed at the absurdity of his words. And I could hear the deranged, gasping quality to the sound as it bounced around the abandoned stables.

He was going to kill me.

He stepped out from the shadows then and squatted in front of me. He adjusted the cuffs of his crisp shirt from beneath his suit jacket before settling his cold gray eyes on mine.

While I huddled—filthy, bruised, and beaten on the dirt floor of the stables—Maxim appeared impeccable. There was not a speck of dirt or blood to be found upon him.

"You waste my time." The low timbre of his voice seeped into my skin and filled my veins with his disdain.

I was about to spit in his face. The urge began to rise in my chest. But Maxim held up his finger while giving a tsk.

He stared at me with pity. "Do you really think the Prince of Shadows wishes to be bound to a . . ." He winced, not bothering to finish his sentence. Then he rose inch by inch to his full height, towering before me. And his eyes raked across me, taking in my appearance.

I was forced to bend my neck back, somehow compelled to meet his eye.

Maxim shook his head. Slowly. "If he could see you now. Filthy. Broken. Weak. *Crass.*" He shrugged. "I almost pity him. For this to be his princess . . . what a shame."

I wanted to rise and make him eat his words. To show him how resilient I was. How strong I was. To have him look at me in awe.

But I couldn't. So I said nothing. Did nothing.

And Maxim and I stared at each other. A small amount of muted moonlight seeped into the stables from the filthy windows high above, causing the barest glint in his eyes. He gave nothing. He offered nothing—no warmth, no compassion, just coldness.

Finally, he took a step back and raised one hand, ticking his index finger up in the air. I knew what that meant. I knew what he was about to do. And as cowardly as it made me, I began to shake my head, silently begging him not to.

But he looked at me with that cold glint in his eyes, and those harsh words—the ones that sounded like grinding stones—left his lips. Against my will, my broken body began to rise. Jerkily. Unnaturally. Not of my own will, but of Maxim's.

I stood there before him with every bone and muscle shaking, my teeth rattling, my vision blurred by the excessive convulsions. Finally, he uttered another harsh command, and I was freed. I crashed to the floor.

But this was just the beginning.

Again and again. One command to rise. One to release me. Over and over. And all the while, he looked at me with disdain and bellowed, "Take back your will!"

I tried. I tried to fight the commands. I did. But the longer it went on, the more broken I became until everything turned numb. My eyes glazed over, and my mind began to drift.

At some point, I fell for the last time. Finally, blessedly, peacefully, I was no longer disturbed.

I was left there. Alone.

He hadn't killed me. I would live another night.

I lay in the frigid stables—my face pressed against the cold dirt, my breath wheezing from my damaged lungs—when a

13

swirling barrage of shadows and chaos and rage, such rage, filled the space around me. The wooden structure shook, and the old windows clattered. The barest hint of moonlight which had bathed the dirt floor just moments ago, was smothered in silent wails and screeches . . . in Darkness.

He had come for me. I had known he would. He did every night.

I knew he was particularly maddened when my damaged body was snatched from the floor and crushed against his chest without regard for my injuries.

The icy blast emanating from him cut through my skin and froze my veins. I could feel the Darkness he possessed bleed into my very bones. Calling to me.

I wanted to give in. To let it wash over me. I knew it would offer relief. Strength.

But that, at least, was something I had control over.

I was mastering the Darkness. Even in my battered state, I slammed down on it, not daring to let it consume me.

And faster than it would take for you to put your lips together and extinguish a flame with your breath, I was wisped away from the broken, sagging stables to my quarters high above in the Dark Manor.

**

I wanted him to stay with me.

But he couldn't. Not just then. He needed time.

The constant assault to his psyche night after night was taking its toll. I knew Maxim purposefully left me the way he did just to

14

torture him. And I knew he needed to go after Maxim to satisfy his need for recompense.

So he carried me through my bedroom while he shook and shuddered with suppressed violence. The fire crackled in the oversized hearth offering light and warmth in the lovely, peaceful retreat. And he tried to reel in the rage and desperation. He tried to hold back the Darkness, because—I knew—he did not want it freed in that space.

He carried me into the adjoining bathroom and set me next to the tub with a final shudder. Then in a whorl of shadows he was gone, free to unleash his demons and go after Maxim. Whether they actually trained in some manner or simply fought with one another . . . I didn't know.

I teetered on the edge of the filled tub, balancing with alternating hands while I peeled off my soiled clothes. Somehow, I managed to either pull or tear every last thread from my body. And I shifted to slide into the warm water.

While I sat there, I hoped, I prayed, I pleaded to the gods above that I would be left alone. That *she* would not come for me.

The thought of her—of what she would do to me—made me want to retch, made my skin crawl, made me feel dirty.

Every night I told myself, perhaps she'll be busy with something else. Perhaps she has tired of me.

As I sat in the warm water, hearing only the sound of the fire from the other room, the minutes ticked by. Against my better judgement, I began to relax.

Maybe this is the night she lets me be.

But as soon as the thought had formed, I heard the sound I dreaded. A quiet rustling accompanied by the irregular clanking of metal—a most terrifying noise if I have ever heard one. And it grew louder and louder as it came closer and closer.

I slumped down in the tub and squeezed my eyes shut, wishing I could make myself invisible, wishing I had the strength to fight her off. I should have begged him not to leave me.

The noise came to an abrupt stop. I shivered, digging as deep as I could for courage. And I opened my eyes. Before me was a vision from my nightmares.

The Crone stood in the doorway of the bathroom . . . *with that goddamn bucket.*

The first night, I told her not to. The second night, I attempted to wrestle the bucket from her hands. The third, I tried to get out of the bath. The fourth, I yelled. The fifth, I threatened.

But she always paused, staring at me from the blackness beneath her hood with that crackle of far off power. I couldn't see any part of her face, yet I knew she glared at me with the threat of something truly awful. The force of it always stopped me, causing me to sit and allow her to complete her task.

She shuffled over to me, unable to keep the heavy weight of the full bucket from dragging across the floor. The foul water splashed and sloshed over the sides as she hobbled.

I drew in a breath and braced myself. Without a word, without a greeting, and without hesitation, she began slapping my face and chest with a dirty old rag—each whack a stinging assault.

I fought to keep my hands at my sides. I fought not to move. I knew if I tried to defend myself, she would only pause to stare at me until I wilted into submission. And the misery would be drawn out longer.

It took all I had, but I managed to stay still.

Once she felt I had been tortured sufficiently, she hefted the metal bucket up—much higher than I would have thought her capable—and dumped the remaining frigid water over my head. Then, just as unceremoniously as she had entered, she turned and dragged her empty old bucket, scraping it across the floor as she hobbled out of the room.

With an exaggerated huff, I pushed myself up and did my best to get out of the bath. I had no desire to continue sitting in the soiled water.

I mean . . . if I'm being completely honest . . . whatever The Crone was doing helped in some way. If I had broken bones, they were usually restored to the point of being able to support a limited amount of weight. And in some small way, the physical and emotional battery of the night were somehow lessened.

But still. I would have preferred to be left alone.

I didn't dismiss the improvement in mobility, though. While it was difficult, I managed to wrap myself up in my robe and shuffle over to my bed.

With unfocused eyes, I stared into the fire and brushed out my hair, letting my bones mend.

I didn't know how much more I could take. This was how it had gone every night for the past three weeks. And the nights were starting to blend together.

I was certain we were all sick of it.

I was alone in the manor. Outside of my quarters I could feel only Darkness and shadows and the vast hollow emptiness of that silent place.

With nothing else to do, I grabbed the translation glasses I had from Belcalis and slid them on. Then I settled back against my pillows and opened one of the books from the pile at the side of my bed.

I sat and read, searching for more answers. Another clue. I had read the king's journal entry about the first Prism, Aurelia, night after night until I had it memorized.

But I needed more. There had to be more. Another journal. Some jotted down notes. Something. The king must have written of the Umbra somewhere. There must be some clue as to how he had imprisoned them.

Yet no matter how much I searched, the majority of what I read was tedious reference material. And oftentimes I would end up dozing as my encounters with Maxim left me utterly exhausted.

Yet, at some point before dawn, I stirred. Because there was something big and Dark and powerful. And I could feel it far below.

I was no longer alone.

I found myself sweeping down the main staircase in a dreamy state, slipping through the silence and the blackness. The vast emptiness of the manor expanded all around me, becoming my entire world. Time somehow slowed, and I was aware of each step, each bounce of my shoulder and swish of my hair, each breath. And it all took far too long.

The journey went on and on, stretching through the night. The distance between the top of the manor and the wing hidden deep below elongated, spreading and extending.

There were too many steps to take, too many shadows to pass through, too many little flecks of muted starlight glittering in the chandeliers above, and too many slats of moonlight spilling across the barren floor below.

I traveled endlessly.

But my feet had the path memorized. My skin knew the feel of descending into the depths of his wing. My lungs knew to brace for the cold, dank air. I knew not to fight the ghosts which haunted the underground hall, not to disturb them.

And my chest knew the emptiness and despair which lingered there. My heart was prepared for the way it would constrict around my ribcage.

I didn't think about any of those things, though. I couldn't. All I could feel was the larger than life presence at the other end of the hall. And all I could hear was the sound of trickling water as it echoed down the decrepit corridor.

I stopped myself. I wouldn't go all the way down to the end. Instead, I turned into the one room which wasn't completely full of Darkness. I sat in the one room that also held some vestiges of Light.

And I didn't have to wait long. Moments later, he entered. Wet hair pushed back from his face. Drops of water across his shoulders and chest. Feet bare. Black pants—the button undone.

He didn't say anything. He just stood there in the doorway looking at me. Calmed. Whatever happened each night, he always came back to the manor with his rage eased.

But as he stared at me, his hands clenched into fists at his sides. His chest expanded, causing his shoulders to jerk, and the muscles all down his abdomen and arms tensed.

I stood from his bed, gathering the fabric of my robe as I stepped towards him. "I'm fine," I told him, knowing I had to reassure him. I had quickly learned it was the first thing I had to tell him each night. At those words, his broad chest heaved with a long slow breath and his hands relaxed.

However, I was not fooled. Because I could still see the tension in his eyes. They roamed over me, starting at my feet and traveling up to my hair. I couldn't stop from shivering. I was certain it was the way a predator eyed its prey.

Without a word, he stalked forward, and in one lethal motion, he picked me up in his arms as though I were nothing more than a doll. I couldn't help but release a sigh at the thrill of it, the intensity of it.

"I'm fine," I repeated. "I can walk. Put me down."

He ignored my protest, as he did every night. And in all honesty, I was glad for it. I liked having him carry me. I liked being pressed against him. There was something rapacious in the way he sliced through the shadows as he walked, in the way he carried me with such ease.

And I loved to let my hands, my hair, my nose brush against him as if by accident. I could feel his muscles bunch and tense with each touch.

This was the way it went. I had learned that he would not come to the fifth floor unless it was to return me to my quarters. So, each night I would make my way down to his wing, and each night he would carry me back up.

He didn't say anything. Didn't do anything. But by the time he'd reached my room, I was unable to stop the way my thighs were rubbing together or the way my head rolled from shoulder to shoulder.

I was aching.

He set me down in front of the bed where the light from the moon poured in through the windows. I stood before him, and he didn't waste a moment. His hands were at my waist the minute my feet touched the floor. Yanking free the belt of my robe, he then spread his palms across my collar bone to push the fabric from my shoulders. The skim of his fingers sent a jolt through my veins straight to my very center.

He took one of my hands and placed it on his shoulder, then the other. I knew how much he craved to be in control, and I did my best to give him that. Even though I wanted to twine my fingers along the back of his neck and press my body into his, I stayed as I was.

And I was rewarded for my patience because he placed his hands on my hips and picked me up. I wrapped my legs around him, and he turned to sit on the bed.

With his finger, he traced a line from my bottom lip, down my chin, across my jaw, to my throat. Circling my pulse point.

A flare of energy popped through the room and the dying fire sparked to life.

"Tell me," he growled, rubbing his thumb over my lips.

Instead of saying anything, I took his thumb in my mouth while I pressed my hips into his, knowing I was making the fabric of his trousers wet. He stared at me, and I could see the war raging in his eyes.

"Tell me," he repeated through clenched teeth, his chest beginning to billow.

I placed both hands at the back of his neck and I let my fingers scratch over his nape. I let my lips hover above his for just a moment, about to say the words he needed to hear. Instead, though, I decided to graze my lips over his, softly rubbing back and forth, barely making contact.

He turned where he sat, throwing me onto the bed, covering my body with his own and pinning me under him.

"Violet. Tell. Me." He demanded. His words were desperate, full of ire and torture.

I ran my hands all over his shoulders and back, savoring the weight of him, before hooking my thumbs into his waistband and inching the material down.

Being with him. In the dark. Just the two of us. With the longing. The pull. The want and need. It was something I knew I was lucky to have. And something I would always crave.

I would tell him what he wanted to hear . . . eventually. But for a few moments, I took my time, finding incredible fascination in the way I affected him.

"Don't do this to me," he warned. His eyes were electric, the blue of his irises glowing like neon, and yet veins of black had begun to branch through. The two facets of himself battling, each fighting for control.

"It's good for you," I countered.

"I can't handle it."

"Yes," I told him, "you can."

"I'm going to lose control, and I promise you, you will not like it."

I nipped at his bottom lip. "You're right. I'm not," I agreed, pressing my chest into his. Then I moved my mouth to his cheek, whispering, "I'm going to love it."

A shudder ran through his body. I could feel him begin to shake as he tried to stop himself, to keep himself from driving into me.

I finally cupped his face with my hands. I searched his eyes desperately wanting to understand how I could prove the truth of what I was about to say to him. Knowing he continued to doubt himself. Knowing he still saw himself as a monster, unfit for affection and intimacy. Knowing he wouldn't truly believe what I was about to tell him.

"I want you," I told him, uttering the three words I had to say every night.

"I will never not want you," I added.

Then, and only then, would he stop holding back.

I would find myself in awe of him. Of his strength and power and size. In awe of how much he needed from me, and in how much I was able to give him.

I was strong and powerful. I knew I was. I had to be. And I was glad for it.

But against him, I was everything small and delicate and feminine.

After the room was awash in energy, in the glimmer of Light and the sway of shadows, he tried to pull away from me—convinced he should return to the hole in the ground where he had buried himself for all these years. He may have accepted the fact that I was his, but he still saw himself as a monster. And I was cursed to be bound to him.

I wrapped my arms around his neck and pulled him back down. Then I pushed him to his back and lay on top of him, pressing the length of my body against his. I propped my forearms up on his chest and looked down at him. My hair fell across the side of my face and he reached up to run his fingers over a strand before tucking it behind my ear.

I began to talk to him. Whispering. Secrets in the dark. Anything and everything. Words just for him.

He watched me the entire time, studying my lips, my eyes. Here and there, he touched me, running a finger over my shoulder and watching the path against my skin. All the while, the palm of his hand rested on the small of my back, covering me, holding me there against him.

And the more I murmured, and the more he touched me, the more he relaxed.

When I knew he reached a certain level of comfort, I began to ask him questions. Things that were simple and easy. And I always felt a small thrill when he answered.

Once I was certain he wasn't going anywhere, I grabbed a book. Rolling off him, I arranged the pillows behind us as I told him what I found. Then I snuggled into his side, and I made sure to adjust his arm, placing it around my shoulders so I could lean into his chest.

I read for a little while, going slowly and running my finger along each word, just in case he was interested in following along.

At times, I found his nose grazing my hair or his lips almost touching my forehead.

Our time together was unlike anything I'd ever known before. And I knew I'd do anything to keep it.

To keep him.

When the sun rose high in the sky and hazy light filled the room, I murmured one last thing to him.

"Don't go today. Stay today. Be here when I wake up." I whispered my words, hoping to make them less than what they were.

I made the same plea in the light of every day. But he was always gone when I woke, no matter how tightly I tried to hold on to him as I fell asleep.

He stared at me with those electric blue eyes, and for the first time . . . he nodded.

CHAPTER 2

"YOU KNOW WHAT REALLY SQUISHES MY TITS?"

The first-floor sitting room was quiet for a moment, and then Maxim began coughing. Uncontrollably.

I narrowed my eyes at him. "Not knowing who to trust," I supplied without invitation.

When Maxim was finally able to breathe again, he straightened and pinched the bridge of his nose. "In the name of all that is sane and logical, I know I will regret these next words, but what, Violet, do you mean by that?"

"You're trying to kill me," I said simply.

The dark slash of his brows intensified. "You are a lunatic. Are you aware of that? So much so that you belong in an institution where proper care can be administered to you."

"You're deflecting, Maxim. And it only makes you look guilty."

"You. Are. Insufferable."

"So insufferable that you want me dead?"

Maxim looked up at the ceiling. "Dear gods, please grant me the fortitude to endure the preposterous ignorance of this woman."

"I am a good fighter. I'm skilled. And competent. I've learned from the best. And none of my training has ever involved beating me to a bloody pulp." I crossed my arms and pursed my lips.

"So, if you're not trying to kill me, why are you leaving me closer and closer to death every night? What's your end goal here? And . . ." I huffed. "My god, Maxim. The insults. You have made this viciously personal."

I glanced down at the floor. "You're hurting my fucking feelings."

Maxim let out an irritated breath and I darted my gaze back to his. "Don't even try telling me how that makes me such a child," I warned.

"Besides," I continued, crossing to the doorway and lowering my voice, "you're driving him over the edge. You know that, right?"

I glanced out into the main hall before closing the door. "Hasn't he been through enough? You can't keep doing this to him. Every night, without fail, he comes to collect me in a psychotic rage."

I wrapped my arms around myself at the thought of Zagan, feeling incredibly guilty about what we were doing to him. Because the only way Maxim and I were able to spend our nights alone in the stables, was with the implementation of a spell.

The Crone had warded the old structure against Zagan. He was only able to enter once Maxim had left. And I knew it was a certain kind of torture for him.

With my arms crossed I leaned against the door at my back. "I really don't see the point of all this, Maxim. Is there a point? You told me you were going to help me. *Train me* . . . All you're doing is beating me senseless."

After staring at me for a moment, Maxim finally spoke. "Are you quite finished?"

I shrugged.

With an exaggerated exhale, Maxim removed his suit jacket and tossed it over the back of the sofa. The outline of his shoulders and chest against his crisp white shirt made me uneasy. I fought not to sink deeper into the door behind me.

I knew how strong he was. How powerful. And how brutal.

He unbuttoned the cuffs of his shirt before rolling the sleeves up his forearms. The muscles there flexed with his movement, and I closed my eyes for a moment, composing myself. I also knew what it was like to have those forearms pressed against my neck while I fought to breathe.

Straightening his jacket to ensure it was free of creases, he took a seat. He was the only fool I had ever sparred with who wore a suit.

Not that it ever got dirty.

"Violet," he began, leaning his forearms on his knees, "you possess technique. I am not here to try and teach you the same skills you have already mastered. What I am trying to do is help you understand how to control the power you possess."

29

I pushed myself off the door. "But I've gotten so good! I'm able to keep all that—" I waved my hands around my torso, "—stuff locked away. I don't lose control!"

Maxim shook his head. "That is not the point. It does you no good to possess an incredible power and lack the ability to use it. Are you truly that dense?"

"So you want me to let go of the—" I didn't know how to talk about this with Maxim. It was silly, but I somehow suddenly felt embarrassed.

I had a certain power, an energy, that I had always known. It was something I had been born with. And it was bright, and hot, and strong. It was Light.

Every time I fought with Maxim, I reached for it. Using it. But it never seemed to be enough.

There was something else, though. Something that I had not been born with. Something I had only recently been . . . I didn't know . . . *Infected with? Possessed by?*

It ran deep and cold and it, too, was strong. It was Darkness. And the power it offered was intoxicating. I had been fighting it ever since it had seeped into my bones. I had been defenseless, lost, forsaken, and it had slipped right in.

After the last time it flooded my veins, I promised myself I would not free it again. If Zagan had not stopped me, I would have done something truly awful. I just knew it.

I had to give myself a shake and readjust my eyesight to focus on Maxim. "You want me to let go of it?" I asked, hesitant to hear his answer.

He looked at me in all seriousness and nodded.

I threw my hands up in the air. "Well why didn't you just say so?! What am I? A mind reader?!"

Maxim pinched the bridge of his nose. Again. "There is merit in discovering some things for yourself. There is power in that. In learning where your limits lie. In how far you will allow yourself to be pushed until you push back.

"The reason I have been pushing you harder and harder is to find where that limit lies. In the hopes that you will acknowledge what you are capable of, what you possess, and use those gifts— while properly exercising control—without exploding in a heap of violence and fury."

I shook my head. "That's just stupid. You should have told me."

Maxim stood. "I weary of this."

"You're not the only one," I pointed out. "I've grown sick of this . . . this . . . *routine* we're all in. We're not making any progress. And we've wasted weeks. This whole time if you had just told me . . ."

I could feel my anger ignite. "I've been beaten bloody, my bones broken. I've been torn down all for nothing!"

The Darkness began to stir. I clamped down on it.

Maxim raised his brows. "Release it, then. Let it out."

My anger was immediately replaced by fear. Without realizing what I was doing, I wrapped my arms around my waist.

I had to keep it locked away. I couldn't let go of it. I was terrified of what I would do. Of what I would become. It was too powerful. And the longer it sat buried deep down inside, the more it grew.

31

He didn't understand. If I lost control over it, it would consume me. Completely.

Maxim looked as if his point was made. He held out his hand. "This is why I've been pushing you. Additionally, you are making no progress fighting the commands I use against you."

"You haven't taught me how!" I exclaimed in frustration.

"I tell you nightly," Maxim boomed. "Your will must be greater than my own!"

"That's impossible! I don't know what sort of deal with the devil you've made, but you are clearly more powerful than I am. My *will* will never be stronger than yours!"

"Then why do I bother?" Maxim countered, throwing his hands up. "This is a waste of my time. You will be of no help against The Contessa, her people, or the Umbra.

"Everything hangs in the balance. The time draws nigh for my people to take back our government, and we must prepare. The revolution is at hand, I am needed to aid and train those who believe in themselves while also protecting them from the Umbra.

"I had thought you and your *prince,*" Maxim scoffed at the word, "could be an ally. Powerful in your own right. Yet all the two of you do is fap about. One of you, too afraid to use your power. The other, too obsessed with the former.

"And," Maxim glanced to the door as if he could see through it. His hand curled into a fist and there was a certain desperation in his eyes. His voice dropped. "Still, I have not found the stone."

But Maxim was too stringent to lose his composure. He closed his eyes, his big chest expanding, and he released a steady breath—immediately calming himself. I could see him visibly relax. After a pause, he sank onto the sofa once more.

And I couldn't help but sigh. Because for the first time, I could see the weight of everything he carried on his shoulders. He was exhausted.

His deep voice turned quiet—the precise notes of his formal accent softening, and he looked at the floor as he spoke. "If I do not succeed in this . . . I will fail them all."

Then he looked up at me with thinly veiled hope. "Has there been any word from your mother? Perhaps she can somehow be of aid with the Umbra."

I shivered at the thought of those tall, gaunt, ghastly figures. Then I let my head roll to the side as I considered Maxim. I decided to be honest with him. "No. And, I mean, you did chain her up and parade her around as your prisoner. Even if she could, I don't know that she would want to help."

Maxim's eyes narrowed. "It was the only way to get her to listen. I tried numerous times to begin a dialogue with her. My requests were never answered."

I gave a reluctant huff. "Yeah, I know. I don't know what to tell you, big guy." I reached up to rub the back of my neck. "I haven't heard from her. I'm worried. With how ill she seemed to be . . . and everything going on with the Council and my . . . I don't know."

Too tired to stand any longer, I took a seat in the armchair opposite Maxim.

I stared at the fire in the hearth. It was the first night, in a long time, that I did not spend in the stables. I wore leggings and a sweatshirt, so I was able to pick my feet up and curl my legs onto

33

the chair. I had left my hair down, and I knew the long waves were obstructing Maxim's view of my face. I was glad for it.

Because I had a secret. Something I had not shared with Maxim. And I honestly wasn't sure if I should.

I had the stone Maxim wanted. I just didn't know if I should tell him. I wanted to help him. I did. I wanted to see The Contessa overthrown, to see the Umbra locked away, for the Radiants and Shadows to be at peace.

I just didn't know about Maxim.

I trusted him. Mostly. But not completely.

And then there was the whole ordeal with the Council wanting me dead. I knew if I set foot outside of the surrounding Shadow village that the Archangels would be after me. And somehow The Oracle was supposed to be able to fix it all. I had no idea what had happened to Elijah. Everything was just a mess. And whatever Maxim was trying to teach me was not sinking in.

So Maxim and I sat in the room together, without speaking, both staring at the fire, for some time. Eventually, my eyes began to feel heavy.

When they somehow shut altogether, I snapped them open and darted a glance at Maxim. I found him watching me. Feeling too vulnerable, I ran my hand through my hair, and I sat up.

"You should get some rest," he said simply.

I was about to argue the point, but instead, I nodded. The training sessions with him left me feeling continually exhausted.

"I do want to help," I told him.

"I know," he replied.

"I'll meet you in the stables tomorrow after sunset."

"I am afraid not," he said, standing.

I rose as well, and we stood face to face in the center of the room. "Maxim, I'll keep trying."

He placed a hand on my shoulder and looked down at me. "We are out of time."

"One more night," I insisted.

Maxim drew in a breath and his shirt stretched across his chest and shoulders. Then he turned to retrieve his suit jacket from the couch. "Violet, I must meet with the members of the Shadow Court tomorrow night. I am still acting as their Master-at-Arms, and although The Contessa has yet to return, her . . . *assistant* as it were . . . Marax, has called a meeting."

"Ugh," I shivered. "That asshole?'"

Maxim cocked his head and looked surprised at my comment.

I had shared everything with Maxim, filling him in on my encounters with The Contessa and my time away from the Dark Manor. But I had forgotten the exchange with Marax.

"It was after I left the manor," I explained. "We crossed paths outside of that club—The Den of Iniquity. He used commands in the Dark Tongue against me, but a friend and I were able to escape. I had thought he was working for the Shadow Prince at the time. But I realize it was The Contessa now."

I adjusted my stance, planting my feet farther apart. I wanted nothing more than for all the secrets and lies to be over with. I raised my chin as I looked at Maxim. "What does she want with me anyway?"

Maxim's eyes roamed over me, as if he could find the answer somewhere in my hair or skin. Then his jaw tightened and the shadows in the room shifted.

"I don't know," he admitted. He seemed to snap out of whatever tension had momentarily overcome him. "You said she wished to possess your Light. Does there need to be more of a reason than that? You have been molded to become the most powerful of your kind. Why would she not come for you?"

"What do you know about her?" I asked. "How long has she had control over the Shadow Court?"

"She served as an adjunct to the Shadow King. There is record of her. The king was the one to bestow the title of Contessa upon her," Maxim explained.

"You will recall that the Shadow king ruled the Umbra," he continued, "and as a result, those beings served as a royal guard. The Contessa spent many years alongside the king which, in turn, meant she spent many years alongside the Umbra—learning about them and learning the ways in which the king controlled them.

"And while the king did lock away the Umbra before departing this world, he did not leave an immediate heir. It was not until much later that he returned one fateful night."

"So, he left The Contessa in charge?" I asked.

Maxim shook his head. "No. The Shadow people were to rule themselves. Those in parliament were meant to govern. But as we know, The Contessa had other plans. She freed the Umbra and took control of the Court—"

"And she got to the king's heir when he was just a child," I finished.

Maxim seemed to contemplate something. His mouth opened as though he were about to speak, but then he closed it and gave a reluctant nod.

I had been carrying something in the waistband of my leggings—at my back—wanting to talk to Maxim about a suspicion I had. I had been waiting for the right moment.

Pulling free the book, I held it out to Maxim. "This journal," I began, "It's the only one I could find in this place. The only one written by the Shadow King. You said that you also have some of his writings. Have you read this one?"

Maxim shook his head. "When I inherited my position with the Court, one of the first things I did was visit this manor. I cited security purposes for the visit. But while here, I collected any pieces I could find which were penned by the king and hid them in my possession. It seems one book escaped me," he said nodding at the journal.

"There's only one entry in it," I said. "All the other pages are blank." I pushed the small book closer to Maxim. "You should read it."

Maxim eyed the journal for a moment before taking it from my hand. He flipped open the cover and scanned the contents. Then he shut the book and handed it back to me.

"While I have not read this particular entry, I am familiar with the story. The king wrote of it several times." Maxim gave me a leveled stare. "Am I to assume you have drawn a conclusion from this?"

I nodded. I had to clear my throat, afraid my voice would not work.

Because I knew something important. I knew something terrifying.

I knew who The Contessa was.

I looked up at Maxim, worried he would laugh or scoff, but all I found were those cold gray eyes.

"Seraphina." I said the name quietly, fearful of it.

Maxim did not laugh or scoff. He did not pinch the bridge of his nose in frustration. And he was not taken aback. He simply held my eye and nodded. "I believe so."

I couldn't stop the breathiness in my voice. "So, The Contessa is one of the Originals? From the Dark half? The one the king mentions in that entry—Seraphina." I repeated the name, giving Maxim a second chance to dispute my suspicion.

I knew from the entry that she had been helping the king. He had tasked her with trying to find the other members of the Dark half.

Maxim said nothing. Unaffected, he refuted none of it.

My eyes grew wide. "Have you known this the whole time?"

Rolling his shoulders, Maxim said simply, "It was not difficult to deduce such from the king's writings. Just as you have."

"What else is there? What are you not sharing? Is she a spurned lover? Was she jealous of the Shadow king? Of his child? Is she carrying out some orders he left with her? Does she want revenge on the Light half of the Originals? What else did the king write about her?!"

"Nothing absolute!" Maxim snapped. The shadows in the room flickered at his outburst.

"Maxim! Even if you are able to lock away the Umbra, how are you going to stop her?" I knew I sounded frantic. I knew I needed to take a minute.

Maxim's nostrils flared as he took a calming breath. "I do not know, but I will have a better understanding of the *how* once the Umbra no longer stand in the way."

I shook my head in disbelief. In disappointment. Feeling as though it was all a lost cause.

I had a crucial decision to make. Now more than ever. I bit my lip before I spoke next, wanting to tread carefully, wanting to ensure I did not give anything away. I knew how perceptive Maxim was.

"What about the stone, Maxim? Why do you need it? How will it help with the Umbra?"

Maxim's eyes narrowed by just a fraction. If I hadn't been looking for the reaction, I wouldn't have noticed in the slightest. It took all I had not to let guilt wash over me. I knew if I did, my cheeks would begin to burn.

Just to prove how innocent my question had been, I began to run my fingers through my hair. But Maxim's hand immediately clamped down over my own.

He held me there for a moment, both our hands next to my face, and the sides of his fingers brushed my cheek. I fought not to let my breathing deepen, not to wilt under his intense stare.

"What do you know of it, Violet?" His question was soft, easy. But I knew by the way he looked at me that he was a predator stalking his prey.

I rolled my eyes and huffed, wiggling my hand out of his. "My god, Maxim, lighten up. Didn't you once tell me that not everything is a conspiracy theory? You're aware that I came across the stone before." I shrugged. "Maybe I can help in finding it again."

I wanted to look anywhere but at Maxim. Instead I forced myself to look up at him.

His jaw was tight and the muscles on the sides of his face ticked, but he nodded. He leaned back on his heels, his shoulders straightening. He looked at me, probably trying to decide how much, or how little, of the information he wanted to divulge. Then he spoke.

"It is incredibly powerful. Although relatively small in size, the amount of energy—*of Darkness*—it can hold is unlimited. In theory, the stone could contain the essence of the Umbra. It is a means by which they could be imprisoned."

"Is that what the Shadow King did?"

Maxim's lips thinned and he looked agitated. "No, he did not require the use of any tools. He was powerful enough to cage the Umbra by his will alone."

"So, then, couldn't his son do it? Is it really so important to have the stone? You have the king's heir." I knew Zagan didn't believe in himself. But I also knew the depths of his power were unfathomable.

Maxim's nostrils flared, and his jaw tightened. "It is not as easy as that." His hand gestured to the floor. "Tragically, similar to you, he has no belief in himself."

"Is there a way to bring back the Shadow King? To have him imprison the Umbra and stop The Contessa? Where is he? Why has he not returned?"

A tremor ran through Maxim's body. I could feel his anger through the space between us. My questions were infuriating him.

"The king is gone," he growled. "I have had to pick and scrap clues and details about him through ancient texts. How do you expect me to speak on his behalf?"

I didn't bother trying to argue with Maxim or push him any further on the matter. I could see how irritated he was becoming. "Okay, gotcha," I said. "You're right. You're right, and I'm sorry."

I looked up at him and raised my brows, not sure what to do other than accept the facts. "So, you're done with me, huh?"

Maxim's jaw tightened even more, his cheeks flexing, but after a moment he gave a begrudging shake of his head. "We will continue to train for one week more. I will attend the Dark Court summons tomorrow night, but I will return to meet with you the following evening. However, you must be willing to let go. Completely. If not, there is no point."

What he was asking was a mistake. I knew it was. But what choice did I have?

"What is it, Maxim? This power, this Darkness? It's not the same as that which the Shadow people carry. I didn't feel it in any of them the times we've gone into the village. Not at this magnitude. But I feel it in Zagan, The Contessa, Marax . . . *you*." And Zagan, Maxim, and The Contessa could all wisp . . .

Maxim leaned forward, his expression grave. "It is the same Darkness found in the Umbra."

I opened my mouth, about to ask him how he had become possessed by it. But he replied before any words left my lips.

"If you look into the face of Darkness long enough, it begins to look back at you." He gave me a pointed look. "And if you do not learn to control it. It will swallow you from the inside out."

41

There was a long moment of silence between us as the weight of his words settled at my feet. But finally, I spoke.

"Alright, Maxim," I told him, my voice dropping. "I . . . I will."

He gave a tight nod before brushing past me. Then he opened the door to the sitting room and disappeared into the dark hall beyond.

"But, Maxim!" I called after him, twisting where I stood.

I peered into the dark hallway, unable to see him. Still, I called out my question. "Does that mean we're all evil?"

I followed after him, leaving the light from the fire behind. I found myself engulfed by the shadows that stretched and coiled out in the foyer. I stood there for a moment, realizing that I would not receive an answer that night.

Because Maxim was already gone.

CHAPTER 3

I STOOD ALONE AT THE BASE OF THE STAIRS. It was dark, and the shadows of the space seemed to tower all along the surrounding hall—the way they did whenever Maxim was present.

I was about to send a pulse of energy to the chandelier overhead, when I heard something. It was low and dark and slow. It was hollow. And it had become achingly familiar.

The notes seeped up from below. Ghostly. It was difficult to tell if they truly floated in the air around me or if they were a memory, refusing to leave, trapped in this place.

The one thing I did know was that they called to me.

I couldn't help but follow the desolate sound. Whether or not the notes would linger within the manor for all eternity, I knew they would always live in my memory. Haunting me there.

I swept through the hall, down the cold stone stairs, into the Darkness. Into *his* wing. I went to the room with the piano. The door sat ajar, and I pushed it open.

I walked up to him, standing just behind him.

Red embers smoldered in the fireplace. Their glow, their heat, did not dare bleed beyond the crumbling hearth. And so, the entire space was filled with the hollow music from the piano and nothing more.

I noticed then just how well he fit there, how he didn't have to fold himself into the piano. It had been made for someone tall. Someone just like him.

And I couldn't stop myself. My hand hovered above his back. I tried not to touch him. I wanted to let him have this moment. To exorcise whatever demons he could and let the bleak notes carry away what they may.

But as I watched the muscles under his skin flex and release with the movement of his hands, I couldn't stop my finger from skimming the line of his shoulders. And it wasn't enough. Touching him wasn't enough.

I didn't know if anything ever would be.

Without warning, the music came to an abrupt stop. He twisted away from the piano to grab my waist. Then with a shout of incongruous notes, he sat me on the keys in front of him.

He placed both hands next to my thighs, and he rose from the bench. The piano gave another bellow at the motion, but it quieted by the time he was towering over me.

Leaning into me, standing between my thighs, he swept a hand through my hair, clutching it at the base of my neck.

He looked at me with those ice blue eyes, and they sparked in the dark, dreary room. "You smell like him," he said.

I shifted where I sat, and the piano chimed. I stared up at him for a moment before responding. "I told you to meet with us."

The muscle under his eye ticked, and he didn't have to voice his reply.

He knew I was going to speak with Maxim. I had told him he should come. And he had refused the invitation.

Instead of debating the issue with him, I ran my hands up the sides of his torso. He leaned into me. Then he placed his lips on my throat, before sweeping them up over my chin and hovering just above my mouth.

"I need to take you to your room," he insisted.

"No," I told him.

"No?" he repeated, his other hand grabbing my waist.

I wrapped my legs around his hips from my perch on the low end of the piano and more deep notes rumbled. The sound reminded me of thunder . . . a brewing storm.

I grabbed his forearms and looked up at him, barely able to keep my eyes open. "Now. It has to be now." My voice dipped to a whisper. "Please. Don't make me wait."

His jaw ticked and his nostrils flared. He looked at me with a mixture of anger and confusion. I had come to know the look well. I learned he had a very difficult time saying no to me.

Especially if I begged.

And I was not too proud to beg.

I couldn't understand how he was still caught off guard by the hold I had on him—the connection between us. How had he not accepted it by now?

I couldn't help but let out a quiet, dark laugh.

His chest expanded with the next breath he took. And I knew the sound had shot straight down his spine.

He released his grasp on my hair to run his hand down my neck, down the center of my sweatshirt, down to the hem at my waist. I arched my back at his touch and the slight movement caused a single low note to sound from the piano.

He ran his hand up over my skin, and I hitched in a breath. The feel of his hand did things to me. A flare of power and energy made my heart beat faster, and my breathing turned hectic. I could feel a slow steady pulsing between my thighs.

I pressed my hands down at my sides and lifted my hips. The piano gave another shout at the movement, an ominous underscore of the lowest notes.

The simple motion was all the invitation he needed. With a deft tug, he slid the waistband of my leggings down my thighs. As my weight settled back onto the keys, he covered me with his free hand, sliding his palm over the spot where he wanted to be, unable to hold back a deep groan.

"Tell me," he demanded, his voice blending with the low notes vibrating through the room.

"I want you," I breathed as I reached forward to free him from his trousers. This time, I didn't hold back. This time, I didn't dare make him wait.

He wedged himself into me—drenched and swollen—forcing me to accommodate him, to accept him, without a word. Without any more need of reassurance. My lips parted on a silent cry, and I could feel the tendons in my neck straining as I let my head fall back.

Somewhere in the recess of my mind, I realized this was progress. Maybe it had something to do with where we were. With what this space meant to him. With how the notes somehow carried away who he was, and what he was, and all that had been.

But that was something I would reflect upon later. Because just then, I couldn't focus on anything other than him and the swell that was building.

With each subtle rock of my hips, the same low note sounded through the room. Steady and slow. Then growing. What began as a quiet rumble in the dark, began to build, louder and louder until the entire dark, decrepit wing was filled with the hollow vibration.

The note, the tone of it, was just the right timbre to cause my bones to rattle. It filled the room, spilling out of it. Too big and deep to be contained. The sound swelled so greatly, I was certain it must be climbing, floor by floor through the entire manor. Stretching and spreading across the walls. I could imagine the chandeliers high above, swaying with a slow rattle.

As the low note hit a deep steady rhythm, over and over again, I let out a strangled moan. He covered my mouth with his own and swallowed my cry.

I could feel how wet and slippery my thighs had become. How I had drenched him. And I bit his bottom lip, darkly elated in the way I could wring every last bit of pleasure from him.

This big, cold, dangerous man was suddenly weak before me. *I* was his weakness. And still, even in weakness, he found the strength to pick me up. To stare at me in wonder. To kiss my lips. To take me to my bed.

Where he felt I belonged.

I smiled to myself with my face pressed against his shoulder. He didn't understand that I belonged down in that cold, dark space with him. He didn't realize. But he would. Eventually.

I would see to it.

Looking back, I can see how stupid I was in that moment. I thought I had time. I thought I could give him time. I had been so foolish. With everything that was pressing down upon us, we had anything but time.

We should have stayed buried down in the Darkness forever, where nothing could reach us. Where we would have been together.

But instead we spent our time in the light of day. The muted rays of the sun filtered through my room, filling the space. I was wrapped around him. He covered me. I gave him my affection.

I appreciated every solid plane and angle, each dip and ridge— the way he touched me, the feel of his hands, the way he looked at me as though I were an incredible secret he couldn't quite believe he had discovered.

He wouldn't laugh, wouldn't smile. But I would. And I learned how his eyes changed. How the tension eased. How his breath slowed. The tight line of his mouth would relax causing his bottom lip to part for a moment.

I don't know why I said what I did. Why I set us upon the course I did. If I could somehow go back in time, I would sew my lips shut. I would stay there in that bed with him. And I would let the world burn down around us.

But I believed in him. I saw what he was capable of. I saw a glimpse of all he was—of the power he possessed—of what he held inside.

So, I came to a decision. Resting against him, feeling his skin under my palm, tracing the three intertwined crescents on his chest, I made my choice.

"I want to return the stone," I told him.

Knowing who The Contessa was had made the decision clear for me. She was more powerful than I could have imagined. The stone would be better put to use in stopping her.

I knew . . . I just knew the Umbra could be contained by the king's heir. It was The Contessa we had to worry about.

Zagan nodded. He did not question me. He did not care to offer an opinion or ensure that I had pondered my options carefully enough. He simply accepted my decision.

A short time later, I would wish with all that I was . . . that he hadn't.

CHAPTER 4

"**I** NEED A BODY."

"A. Body." Zagan repeated with stilted words.

He sat, propped in the bed, with his arms crossed over his chest. There was still a hint of sleep across his face. His eyes still drowsy. His dark hair tousled.

And that big, dark man tracked my every movement, my every breath, with incredible precision.

I stopped and turned back to face him. I wobbled a little where I stood. And I set my hands on my hips to right myself.

Seeing him sitting there as he was actually made my heart ache.

I cleared my throat, trying my best to respond. "Yeah, you know, a body. But I can't remember now if it was supposed to be . . .?" I trailed off, my eyes searching the vaulted ceiling high above trying to recall Adriel's instructions. I shook my head, giving an unconcerned shrug before sauntering away.

With a hint of fascination in his voice, Zagan murmured, "You are a peculiar woman."

I couldn't help but smile. I shrugged again and threw him a glance over my shoulder before leaving the room.

After a moment, I heard his low voice float through the air. "Are you obtaining one now from your closet?" he asked.

I stepped back into the bedroom glancing down at the bra and undies I had put on. "I'm getting dressed, wise guy."

He gave a quiet growl from deep in his chest, and his lips thinned. Although it was barely a reaction, I knew it was a disappointed one.

And it was too adorable. To see someone so big, so cut with muscles, so strong, so powerful . . . and to know he objected to my getting dressed . . . well, it was nothing less than endearing.

It was no use. It was impossible to stay away from him. I ambled back to the bed and leaned down to plant a solid smack on his lips. "I think we should go tonight," I said.

There were too many people who wanted the stone. Too many people who knew I had been last associated with it.

"I want to return the stone, and I'm going to need a body to do it," I clarified.

With Maxim away for the evening, it was the perfect chance to slip out. I needed to return it before anything else could get in the way, before anything else could go wrong, and before Maxim figured out that I had it.

More than anything, I wanted to get my answer; I wanted to know how to defeat The Contessa.

"Uh," I added as I backed away from Zagan to finish dressing, "I need a body and, um, a few other things."

53

"Other *peculiar* things?" he asked.

"Kind of," I answered. "You could say that."

"Violet . . ." he growled my name, and I knew it was a warning.

"It's no big deal," I promised, keeping my voice light, continuing to back away from the bed. "Just a quick little stop in the city and then off to visit the god of death. No biggie."

"Violet." He rumbled again, louder this time.

"Zagan," I countered. His name was soft and quiet on my lips.

He tensed, and his arms tightened across his chest. Then after a moment, after a small battle of wills, he released a grumbling breath from deep in his throat.

I turned to make my way back into the closet, knowing the matter had been settled. As I left the room, I heard him muttering something about making him do things he didn't want to do.

And I smiled as I got ready to return the Heart of Darkness with Zagan.

***

Having prepared, having briefed Zagan on as much as I could, we found ourselves outside of a seedy looking *adult* shop in a seedy part of London. There was no signage for the place, just three X's in big red letters above the door.

And while I was slightly embarrassed about going in, having never visited such a shop before, I figured the best thing to do would be to get it the hell over with.

So we walked inside.

A little bell jingled as we opened the door, and I stopped short, uncertain if we were in the right place.

"Well hello dears. Come in, come in. Don't just stand there in the doorway. You'll be sure to catch your death."

The little old lady behind the register put down her knitting and pushed her large rimmed glasses up her nose.

"Come in, come in. Would you like a cup of tea and a biscuit?" she asked, gesturing to a tray laid out on the counter.

I looked around the shop, incredibly confused. There was a little sitting area in the middle of the store with old looking armchairs that were covered in doilies. But surrounding the sitting area were shelves and racks filled with adult items.

And the old lady just flat-out threw me.

She was rather plump with gray hair and rosy cheeks. There was a chain around her neck that connected to her eyeglasses. And as if that weren't enough, she wore a kitchen apron.

I was already uncomfortable about visiting the shop, but this was too much. I was not about to ask this sweet old lady if she carried a particular subscription of magazine.

"I'm sorry, ma'am," I told her. "I think we have the wrong place."

I wanted to tuck tail and scurry the hell out, but there was a big dark wall right behind me. "Back-up, back-up," I hissed out of the side of my mouth, trying to keep the words from traveling through the shop.

"Nonsense," the little old lady countered. "I keep my shop well stocked. I'm sure whatever it is your looking for, old Mrs. Plumbum's got it.

Mrs. Plumbum?

"Now look, I'm already off my chair," she announced as she waddled over to the tray on the counter. "And I've got two nice hot cups of tea ready to go." She filled two dainty teacups from her matching teapot and held them out.

I paused for a moment, wracking my brain for some excuse. But when the teacups began to wobble in her outstretched hands, I was guilted into crossing through the store to take them from her.

"Uh, thank you," I said.

Zagan had been my second shadow, passing through the shop with me. I handed him the other teacup.

He looked down at the delicate lavender china in his hand as if it were a foreign object. He didn't bother taking a sip from it.

"Now, drink up, drink up," she insisted, waving her hands at us.

I eyed Zagan while he eyed his teacup. His upper lip curled. Not wanting us to both insult Mrs. Plumbum, I took a sip from mine.

"Isn't that better?" she asked. "Yes, of course it is. Nothing better for a chilly evening, if you ask me. Well, except for a fine scarf, perhaps. Or a warm pudding. But that's neither here nor there. Now is it?

"So. Tell me dears. What is it—"

A middle-aged man in a trench coat carrying a folded-up newspaper walked in the door then. He took one look at the little grandma behind the counter, one look at us with teacups in hand, and he turned bright red. Walking himself in a tight little circle, he dashed straight out the door without saying a word.

"Happens all the time," Mrs. Plumbum said with a sigh. "No one wants to purchase their romps and fromps from their mum-mum." She sighed, dejectedly shaking her head.

"Mum-mum?" I asked.

"Their nan, dear," she explained. "Grandmother."

She picked up her gray little head, and her fluffy chin-length hair bobbed around her rosy cheeks. As she stared at me, her eyes were magnified behind her thick lenses. "And yet I've the most knowledge to share, I do. Been at it for years. It's how I ensure the mister maintains his cardiovascular health; it is. Suggested by Mr Bunson; it was."

"Mr. Bunson?" I repeated.

"The doctor," she replied, as if I should have known. "Well the cardiovascular exercise," she clarified, "not the hanky-panky. But, you know, it's as good as a brisk walk, I'd say.

"And, I say, if you're not getting a good seeing to now and again, then what's the point of keeping the ticker ticking?

"I try the items out; I do. I've written reviews for them all.

"Bah," she concluded, waving her hands dismissively at the front door where the man had just been. "Who needs 'em. Probably doesn't know how to wiggle it properly anyway."

She looked around the shop. "It's more of a passion than a business at this point." Then she lifted the teapot. "Now, who needs another spot of tea? And after you've finished your biscuits, you can tell me what you're looking for."

I choked on my sip of tea, embarrassed at the idea of asking her for anything.

"Goodness!" Mrs. Plumbum cried. "Small sips, dear. Small sips." She leaned across the counter to take the teacup from me. "Arms up if you must."

"I'm fine," I managed between coughs. And while, she seemed like a nice old lady who could use a little company and some patrons, I didn't want to stay any longer than necessary.

I decided to act like a grown-up and flat out ask for what I wanted.

"Do you carry a magazine called *Buttman* by any chance?" I asked.

"Buttman!" she cried, clutching her generous bosom. "What in blazes do you want with that filth?!"

I was instantly mortified. "Oh, no. It's not for me!" I tried to explain, fumbling for words. "I'm sorry! I thought—"

Mrs. Plumbum began tittering, waving her hands in front of her body as if gesturing for someone to get away. "I'm too much," she snickered. "Such a hoot! The devil's mistress, I am!"

"Oh," I mumbled, raising my brows, realizing she might have been pulling my leg. "Oh, yes. Ha. Ha."

"Those will be over in the classics," she amended, giving her nose a good wipe with her handkerchief. "Now, is that all you're looking for? What about something for your gentleman here? Hmm?" Her magnified eyes traveled all the way up Zagan.

"Or perhaps something for when he's away?" She pulled her glasses down to peer over them at me, raising her brows.

"Just the magazines," I replied, my voice a bit higher than necessary.

Mrs. Plumbum shoved her glasses back up her nose. "Very well, then. Follow me."

I was terrified that she was going to try and keep us in there all night. And although we had to agree to taking some biscuits with

58

us and promising to stay warm, we were eventually able to make our purchase and be on our way.

Once we stepped out of the shop and back into the seedy alley, Zagan eyed me.

"What?" I asked, my tone a bit too defensive.

"Nothing," he replied in that low silky way of his. "I am simply learning new things about you all the time."

"I told you, they're not for me."

"Violet," he chastised, tilting his chin down.

"They're not!"

"You're right," he said, his voice even and level. "It makes much more sense that *a rat* has requested them."

I huffed, doing my very best not to laugh. "Whatever. Look. This is only half of it. Let's just get this over with."

"Whatever you say, buttman."

For the second time that night, I choked on the next breath I took.

***

I needed a body.

And not surprisingly, finding one was an easy thing. There is a simple reason why:

Monsters are everywhere.

They walk among us. Some wearing a disguise, others not bothering to try and hide what they are. Some terrible souls from the start, others molded over time.

But they exist. More than you know. And while not everyone is bad, while there is more good than not, evil does take shape in human form.

After our stop at Mrs. Plumbum's establishment we collected our weapons.

Then all we needed to do was slink through the shadows of the city. To listen. To wait.

It didn't take long to find someone.

I did not pity him. His death was quick and painless—a gift he clearly did not deserve. I would like to think the world would be better off without him. But the world is a large place, and he was one roach amid an infestation.

With our newly acquired stack of magazines in one arm, Zagan hefted the mortal over his shoulder, scooping the body up with his free hand. The man's head lolled on his broken neck.

"I can take those," I said, reaching for the pile of magazines.

"Keep your hands free," he countered. "You might need to draw your weapons . . . considering the ever-growing list of beings that are after you."

I cocked my head, evaluating him. I had no idea if he was merely being considerate, or if he was actually heckling me.

He stared back at me, his face giving nothing away. Then he looked at all he held. "Is there more you need?"

"No," I told him, letting his little comment drop. But I made a note to be on the lookout for any future quips. I had a growing suspicion the Dark Prince found himself to be hilarious.

Then I eyed the body and the magazines. "This should do it."

Stepping up to me, he asked, "Where now?"

I could feel my jaw tighten as I recalled the Realm of Lost Souls, and I shivered. I reminded myself that I was better prepared this time. I would not become lost this time.

And this time, I was not alone.

"Are you able to take us directly to the realm?" I asked.

"It depends." He narrowed his eyes, focusing on me. "Are you thinking of it now?"

I nodded.

"No," he concluded after a moment. "I cannot connect to this place."

"Then we'll have to . . ." I realized what our option was as the words were leaving my mouth. And I couldn't say it. I couldn't ask him to take me there. I didn't want to face what I had left behind there.

But I knew I was being cowardly. I needed to acknowledge what happened. I had to own what I'd done.

I took a breath and forced myself to continue. "There is a cabin in the woods behind the Radiant Court." I stopped. I met his eye. "I think we've both been there before."

While I fled to Aleece with Elijah, I thought, picturing the memory so clearly.

I had run from Zagan. I had seen him as the beast he believed himself to be. No wonder he found it difficult to believe that I *wanted* to be with him.

We hadn't talked about it. Hadn't discussed it. I looked at him then, and I wanted nothing more than to take it all back.

"I'm so sorry," I whispered. "I didn't know."

Yet, before I could say another word, we were swept away in a swirl of shadows and I found myself before the very cabin.

I blinked. Surprised it had been so simple. I thought we would have to enter from outside the Court boundaries and make our way through. But apparently Zagan was more powerful than whatever defenses Adriel had in place.

After surveying the surrounding woods, I settled my gaze on the small structure, haunted by the memory of it.

Zagan started straight away for the front steps. He was going to completely disregard what I had said.

I, however, stood where I was, my boots planted in the dirt.

I had run from him. When he needed me, I had run from him. To this place. With another. I had done that to him. I had *hurt* him. I felt sick at the memory of sinking my knives into his abdomen.

With a snarl, Zagan dumped the items in his hands onto the ground. Then he spun and stormed back to me. Those black veins were branching through the ice blue of his eyes.

He took my chin in his hand, holding me still. He gave one slow shake of his head. I swallowed. But I did not take my eyes off his.

He didn't want my apology. And he had nothing to say on the matter. It was all clear in the wordless tick of his jaw.

Despite his desire to shove it all away, I looked up at him feeling as though I needed to serve a penance of sorts.

He leaned into me, and something lethal slipped around my shoulders. Tightening. His eyes were fully black then, and an icy blast of air stabbed at us. His dark hair was swept off his face. And the shadows of the forest became dense and thick, pressing down upon us.

His voice was measured as he grappled for control. "You do not understand. You cannot begin to fathom . . . You should have stayed away. I gave you several chances to leave. Time and time again, I demanded it of you."

He shook his head, as if addressing someone who'd made a grave mistake. "You did not. That time has passed. Nothing that came before matters now. Because now you will not be free of me."

When he was done speaking my lips parted, but I did not reply. Instead, I gave a slow nod knowing there was nothing for me to say. I understood the meaning and truth of his words, the gravity of them.

Zagan released the hold he had on my chin and backed away.

I stood there, feeling a bone numbing chill crawl over my skin at the frigid tone that now saturated the night.

But something happened as I stood there in the forest before the cabin, as I stood in the center of the dark of night amid the pressing shadows. Something happened as I watched him back away. Something *sparked*.

My skin began to thaw. And then warm. Degree by degree my chest grew hotter and hotter until finally, it burned.

Zagan turned to collect the mess of items on the ground, and I had a realization. "You know what?" I snapped. "Screw you!" Then I charged past him, towards the cabin.

I turned to point my finger at him while I continued walking backwards. "YOU are the one who doesn't understand, buddy. What happened before doesn't matter? Good. Fine. I agree with you. I don't care about any of it. What I care about is now. And here's what you do not get—

"I want to be with you. Now. I choose to be with you. What do you think? That I'm some weak, sniveling, little child? That what I want wouldn't matter? I am not here against my will. I make my own goddamn choices. And you don't see me going anywhere, do you?

"Just FYI, it's pretty insulting to insinuate that I have no say in any of this. Stop treating me like I'm a victim. Do you want to know who I am? Do you know who the hell I am? I'm the mother fucking hero.

"If I wanted to . . . If I really wanted to, I could lay you out in three seconds flat. I just haven't had the heart to. Not truly. So here is your one warning: Don't make me want to."

With what I'm certain was an awe-inspiring flourish, I reached behind my shoulders to draw my short swords. I spun them in a blur of deadly skill and grace before seamlessly sheathing them—all in one continuous motion.

Admittedly, the display might have been a bit . . . *much*. But he had pushed me too far. I was so tired of trying to prove myself.

I gave Zagan a hard stare, driving home my point. I expected to come face to face with the wrath of his anger. I tried to brace myself for it.

I cared that he had his hang-ups. I did. But sometimes someone needs a good slap in the face.

Sure enough, his lips thinned in a tight, straight line. His eye twitched and his hands fisted at his sides. Then his irises began to change. Only, they weren't darkening. Instead, streaks of blue began to break through the black.

Something was off. He didn't actually look angry. He looked like he was . . . *trying not to laugh?*

He didn't smile. He never smiled. But just then, he looked like he wanted to.

"Are you . . .? Are you *laughing* at me?" I asked, on the verge of being enraged.

He swallowed and gave his head a shake. "No," he managed. And while the single word was convincing, the tension in his face implied otherwise.

I bit my lip and I could feel my nostrils flare. I held out a finger, pointing at him. Again. Waiting. He stood there, still as a statue. I didn't think he was even breathing.

His eyes had become electric blue in the night, piercing the dark. And for that reason alone, I let my hand drop. I turned and charged up the small steps to the cabin door, flinging the thing open. As I did, I could have sworn I heard coughing.

I pivoted at the sound, but he was already bending down to collect the mess of items on the ground, his face hidden from view.

I crossed my arms and leaned against the door jamb. Once he had everything collected, he walked up to the small entry, stopping just before me. I eyed the little items balanced on the stack of magazines.

Finally, after clearing my throat, I said, "I don't understand why you took the key chain and bumper stickers." I knew my tone was flippant. And I knew I sounded childish. I just couldn't get past the need I felt to repair my dignity. Somehow, giving him a hard time seemed like one way to get back on level ground.

"Mrs. Plumbum said they came with the purchase," he replied. There was something about the timbre of his voice, something low and silky, that made me feel like a hand was running down my back. I fought not to react.

"Right. Right. So you said." I gestured at the emptiness of the black room before us. "I really don't know what Filbert is going to do with a *Buttman* bumper sticker. I'm pretty sure he's not a car owner."

He leaned his face down to mine and his words were hushed. "Are you mocking me, Violet?"

I searched his eyes before finally biting my bottom lip, and I nodded.

"I will punish you for it," he promised. Then without waiting for a response, he pushed past me to enter the cabin. He walked right over to the trap door and flipped it up with his foot.

"Now, take me to this *Buttman*. I'm tired of carrying his reading material."

***

Making our way to the Vestibule proved easy enough. We slipped down through the trap door into the long underground tunnel without incident.

This time as I walked down the dirt path, I was not afraid of the Darkness. This time as I walked down the dirt path, I was a part of the Darkness. And the lord of it walked by my side.

We did not have to push through the shadows. They parted for us, flowing around our shoulders before knitting together again at our backs.

And when we approached the Veil of Light, we were able to pass through with ease. I understood now how Zagan had been

66

getting through the Veils when he was chasing me. When I had run from him, I hadn't known he was a Prism, and I hadn't known I passed my Light on to him.

I was able to manipulate my energy so that my Light surrounded me, allowing me passage, while the Darkness sat buried deep inside. I prepared myself, aware that we might have the Archangels after us in just a moment.

But when we entered the Vestibule, we were alone. And it didn't take long to locate the door with the ankh. Before we crossed through the Threshold, Zagan adjusted the bundle in his arms.

I looked over at him. "Are you sure you don't want me to carry any of that?" I asked glancing at the body he had draped over one shoulder and the adult magazines he held in his opposite hand.

He gave a single shake of his head, repeating his suggestion from earlier. "Keep your hands free for your weapons."

It wasn't a bad suggestion.

"Alright," I agreed. "Let's go."

I placed my hand on the door. A small glow of Light flared at my palm, and then the door swung open.

We stepped out onto the simple geological shelf. There was sheer rockface to our left, and nothing but an infinite drop of gray, misty sky on the right.

It was exactly the same as before.

And for some reason, I was surprised to find the old man and the rat sitting on the bench in front of us. I couldn't help but believe they had taken a seat there, one day long ago, and never left.

They, too, appeared the same. The old man was wearing his sweater vest and flat cap. He had his large wire rimmed glasses perched on his nose. And his hands were resting on a cane propped in front of him.

He seemed to be unaware of our sudden presence. His eyes were gazing off at some distant point, and every once in a while, he would mutter or nod.

The child sized rat sat in the same spot next to the old man. His spine was slouched against the back of the bench, and his front paws rested on his bloated, balding belly. He picked his head up the instant we arrived.

Rubbing his tongue over those long yellow-brown incisors, he gave a "thwack." The nasty vermin looked straight at me with his beady little eyes, and his matted, tangled whiskers twitched. And that foul waste of space had the gall to stroke a paw between his legs.

I glanced up at Zagan, wondering if he was about to turn Filbert into roadkill. The seedy gesture had been undeniable.

I was going to have to reel him in.

However, when I looked over, I was confused. And I couldn't understand what was happening. I wondered if there was some invisible force at work on him. I wondered if he needed help in some way.

Because when I looked over at Zagan, I saw him visibly recoil.

I had never before and never since seen the same look on his face as he had in that moment. He appeared completely horrified and disgusted . . . *by Filbert.*

Figuring we had better get the whole thing over with as soon as possible, I threw my finger in the rat's direction. "He's the one who gets the magazines."

Before I could even register what was happening, though, Zagan shoved the stack into my hands and pushed me forward. The bumper stickers and keychains, which were balanced on top, went flying.

I turned around to stare at him. "What are you doing?"

"Seeing as you know one another, you should be the one to present *the thing* with its gift." He nodded in Filbert's direction and frowned as if fighting off a bad taste in his mouth.

While I smiled between clenched teeth I spoke in a forced sing-song voice. "I think it's better if you do it, honey. Remember the plan?"

I couldn't understand what was going on. Had Zagan not seen the way Filbert looked at me? What about the lascivious gesture? He was the one who suggested I keep my hands free in case any weapons were needed. And he was right to have suggested so.

I had only one encounter with the old man and the rat. It was not enough to go by. I had no clue how volatile they might be. And Zagan still had a body draped over his shoulder.

But at my suggestion, Zagan's eyes rounded and he looked shocked. "You want me to go up to *the thing*?"

"It's a big disgusting rat, and its name is Filbert. You don't have to call it '*the thing*,'" I said, trying to reassure him there was nothing to be fearful of.

"Yeah, fuck you!" Filbert called in his deep, raspy smoker's voice.

I withdrew one of my short swords, while balancing the magazines, and pointed the weapon in Filbert's direction. "You be quiet or so help the Light, I will gut you like the filthy pig you are."

"I thought you said it was a rat," Zagan protested.

"Oh. My. God." I didn't bother turning around to Zagan. If it was that big of a deal, I'd hand over the magazines myself. I began to take a step forward. But just as I did, Zagan drew next to me and took the stack from my hand.

"I'll do it," he hissed, clearly unhappy about the situation. I didn't actually know if he was talking to me or trying to psych himself up.

Zagan took a step towards Filbert and then he . . . *hesitated.*

Filbert was revolting. There was no question about that. But this was a man who had dissected the Umbra—creatures far ghastlier than Filbert. A man who had been splattered in their sticky tar-like blood from head to toe after eviscerating and dismembering them. A man who was currently carrying a corpse over his shoulder. A man who would have slayed a dragon had I not intervened.

And yet he was genuinely perturbed by an overgrown rat.

To his credit, though, Zagan did finally take a few more reluctant steps towards Filbert. However, he grumbled the whole time under his breath about how I continued to make him do things he didn't want to do.

While still a good distance away from the bench, Zagan extended his arm, drawing the rest of his body as far back as possible. Then he shook the magazines as if Filbert were a dog he could entice with a treat.

In response, Filbert gave a long low belch before saying, "Nah. I want it from the girl."

"Oh, for fuck's sake!" I stomped up to Zagan, snapped the magazines out of his hand, and threw them in Filbert's face.

Done with the disgusting little rodent, I stepped up to the old man. "We have something for you too."

"What . . .? Who . . .?"

I remembered my mother had referred to the old man as Horace. He spluttered for a minute while looking all around before finally spying me. I had no idea how he could have been so oblivious to our presence.

"Oh! Why hello there, pretty lady." He patted the bench next to him. "Come join me, won't you? Make an old man happy with a moment of your company."

At that, Zagan drew close, towering next to me. Clearly, he was quicker to sense the sinister air to the old man than I had been.

Horace's eyes widened behind his glasses as he craned his neck back to take in Zagan. "Oh, my. You're a big one, aren't you?" There was a certain excitement in the old man's voice—a gleam in his eye—that made me want to shiver.

"He's not for you," I said. "But this is." And Zagan dumped the body at his feet.

Although I cringed at the offering we provided, I felt no sympathy for the mortal. I'd seen a glimpse of the things he'd done with his life. I wanted nothing more than to forget them.

The thought was interrupted, though, by a low raspy moan. "Aw, yeah. Ohh, baby."

I couldn't contain my revulsion and an audible "ick" left my lips. I tried my hardest not to look in Filbert's direction. I knew he was flipping through his magazines.

But keeping my gaze on the old man was no better. His neck and arms began to bend in unsettling ways as he leered at the body before him. And one long, stringy line of drool dribbled from his bottom lip.

Convinced the pair were enthralled with their gifts, I grabbed Zagan's hand and tried to step around the sitting bench as discreetly as possible. Neither Filbert nor Horace seemed to notice us any longer.

While keeping my eye on the pair, I did see Zagan glance over his shoulder several times, and I was fairly certain he was checking to make sure Filbert didn't follow us.

I squeezed his hand in reassurance, feeling bad for earlier. I had been completely caught off guard. I mean, of all the things to make his skin crawl, who would have thought it would be a big talking rat?

I smiled a little to myself, realizing something; I had uncovered the one thing that could scare the Prince of Darkness.

My skin felt warm as I grasped the importance of that. The intimacy of it.

And I knew I would never tell a soul.

After another squeeze of his hand. I turned my attention to the space behind the bench. There was nothing, just a few more feet of the geological shelf before it tapered off into the cliff face. That, and the drop of gray sky all around us.

But as I walked along the rockface, I saw an opening in the wall where mist was funneling out. It was impossible to see from the other side of the bench because of the way the opening was engineered. One side of the rock wall overlapped with the other side. However, there was enough of an opening to step into the divide and walk around it.

We slipped through and found ourselves in a sloped tunnel with that thick rolling fog covering our feet.

"I guess this is it," I said.

Zagan glanced over his shoulder before pulling free the torch that was strapped to his back. "I don't understand why we had to bring *that thing* a gift. We should have just killed it."

I did my absolute best not to laugh. Instead, I focused on lighting the torch with a small flare of energy.

Clearly the old man had not bothered Zagan the way the rat had. He hadn't suggested they both be killed. Just Filbert.

"It was what Adriel suggested. But maybe next time," I offered, giving him a pat on the shoulder. "We can come back for your birthday."

I gave him a little nudge forward and we began walking single file down the narrow path.

"You're mocking me again," Zagan accused.

"It's my way of flirting," I countered.

"Then by all means, continue."

I gave a laugh. "I like you."

He stopped abruptly, and I almost ran into him. He didn't turn to face me. And I became worried that something was blocking the path. But after a long, long pause, he spoke seven words that broke my heart.

"I cannot say the same to you."

It was quiet in the tunnel for a moment, but then I regained my composure. "Alright." I spoke the word slowly. "I guess that's fair enough. You're not obligated to——"

"Violet——"

"No, it's okay. Really. You don't have to say anything."

But I was thrown. And it stung. I had thought there was something between us. And I knew there were big things between us. Things beyond our control. Incredible forces.

But I thought, somehow, somewhere, in the middle of it all . . . it's embarrassing to admit . . . and it sounds so juvenile . . . *but I thought we had become something.*

"Violet."

The way he said my name . . . He might as well have taken his fingertip and swept it down my spine. And when he spoke this time, I didn't dare interrupt.

"I do not know what it is to 'like' something. I do not have things in my life that I 'like.'

"Nothing has mattered to me. Do you understand? In my life, there has been nothing of value. Nothing of worth."

He paused, and I realized I was holding my breath. I waited, unsure if he would continue.

"And then you walked in the door."

His voice became achingly quiet and low. "And the nothing has been replaced with everything."

When his words sank in. When they penetrated the last of my bones. I pressed my hand over my mouth. Certain not to say anything in reply. I wanted to let his words be. I did not want to disrupt them.

And I was grateful for the pressing walls of the tunnel, because I sagged against one and closed my eyes.

I knew then, he was my greatest weakness.

After a long moment, he started forward again.

And I peeled myself off the wall to follow that man all the way to death's doorstep.

CHAPTER 5

I BRACED MYSELF FOR HOURS OR POSSIBLY DAYS of hiking through the tunnel. However, unlike the other path I had taken, this one did not go on indefinitely. While it was a long walk, we eventually found that the rock at our sides began to smooth and the dirt beneath our feet became stone. Then the path widened. And just like that, the tunnel transformed into one of the channels within the Gwarlock's temple. The mist at our feet thickened.

Within what felt like an hour, we found ourselves stepping into the cavernous room located in the base of the pyramid.

This time when I stepped into the spacious hall, all was quiet. It was dark, aside from the dim lights which lit the depictions along the walls. And the Gwarlock's throne sat empty.

Zagan looked around, crossing to the middle of the chamber. As he did, the flame he carried extinguished in a fast clap of smoke. At the same time, there was a clanging which disrupted the silence of the hall. The two statues guarding the back exit stood at attention. Their spears which had been crossed, were pulled to the sides.

Zagan glanced at me, and I nodded. I had a feeling we were being directed to the back of the pyramid. I remembered the tree which stood out there. The enclosure. The Gwarlock's wife.

I remembered Entropy.

We left the temple and stepped out into the barren, dark valley of mist. The pyramid soared at our backs. And the ankh, high above at the very top of the temple, faintly glowed—the only source of light in the fog covered wasteland.

In the distance to our left, up a steep slope, I could just make out the faint line of the dark forest. And I immediately turned my back to it. As I did, I spied the lone weeping willow.

Something was off.

The leaves and branches of the tree were still thick. They still served as an enclosure. But they were no longer green and lush. Most of the leaves were now gray and shriveled. And the fog which sat at the base of the tree was climbing and stretching up around the branches, consuming it.

More disturbing still was what was happening within the enclosure. Every few seconds the entire tree would shake. And the wild commotion was accompanied by piercing shrieks that made me want to cover my ears. Then there was a scream.

I cringed, remembering the last time I had heard wailing down in this place. I looked up at Zagan. "I should warn you, they're into group stuff down here."

He narrowed his eyes. "Group? Stuff?"

I opened my mouth to reply, but when no explanation came, I shrugged and continued trudging through the thigh deep fog. I reasoned we could wait just outside until they were . . . finished . . . in there.

I cleared my throat at the excessive vigor; it seemed things were much rougher this time around.

But when we reached the entrance to the willow, the sweeping branches were already parted. And I let out a gasp at what I saw.

I could see Entropy inside along the quaint stream bank. She appeared the same as before—her opal, iridescent skin shimmering in an array of faint pastel hues. And her excessive amounts of lavender hair tumbled down, framing her body. Covering her.

The Gwarlock was there with her. It didn't matter that I had seen him before, I was still awed at the sight of him. Nine feet tall. Smooth, onyx skin like that of a statue. Head of a jackal. Body of a man. Crackling light from within his eye sockets.

And they were entangled with three small women.

Only they weren't engaged in the pursuits of pleasure. They were fighting. Viciously.

One of the women had her hand shoved over Entropy's mouth while thrusting a pin-like sword at her neck. A thin trail of blood was trickling from the shallow puncture. The other two women were battling the Gwarlock.

The second one leapt upon his back and wrapped her slender arms around his throat, while the third jabbed her sword into his abdomen. Then the two wrestled him to the ground.

The sunlight, which dappled through the canopy of the shriveled tree, had a harsh red hue. And it continuously flickered, creating long glowing moments with a sinister, dim crimson light.

In the air above, three huge cranes circled. Gliding. They occasionally flapped their wings, appearing sanguine in the light.

The petite women wore delicate scale armor that molded to their torsos. It wrapped up and around their shoulders, fanning out across their upper arms. The individual scales were thin, ethereal mirrors. As a result, the three glinted whenever they moved.

Their skirts were made from overlapping strips of leather which hung from a large belt. And while the bottoms of their sandals were simple, the leather laces were intricately fastened all the way up their thighs.

With their matching wardrobes and identical sizes, the three were impossible to tell apart. They all looked exactly the same, each with long spirals of dark burgundy hair.

They were calling to each other. "Sisters, I have the wife!"

"Sisters, I have his neck!"

"Sisters, I have impaled the God of Death!"

There was a shrill piercing sound to their voices, and I had a sense that it served as a type of echolocation. Because when we appeared at the entrance, each one of the three women froze. And at precisely the same time, each one cocked her head before turning in our direction.

But there were no gazes to meet our own. Because none of the women had eyes. Where their eyes should have been were large white wings which extended off the sides of their faces.

The Fates.

It had to be. Entropy had spoken of them; she had taken their eyes.

And I knew. Somehow, I just knew it was them.

"It is the one we named, sisters."

"Indeed, it is, sister," the other two replied.

"But why is the one here?"

Their heads tilted and swiveled as they spoke.

Their winged faces all turned in Entropy's direction. The Fate who was holding her, tightened her grip over Entropy's mouth. "This one meddles in our affairs."

There was a moment of stillness, a moment of quiet, then without warning, the third Fate withdrew her sword from the Gwarlock's abdomen and cut open his chest. With her diminutive hands, she grabbed a hold of his ribcage and wrenched each side up. Then she thrust her fist into his chest cavity. Yet she let out an ear-splitting screech when her hand came back bloody but empty.

It was all happening so fast. I was horrified by the unexpected gruesomeness of torn flesh and muscle and bone. I didn't know what we were supposed to do. I wasn't prepared for this.

I had come to return the stone. That was it.

Zagan's hand immediately slipped around my arm. He was about to pull me back. But I gave my head a quick shake, refusing to leave without the answer I'd come for.

Perhaps there was still a chance.

Because even though she was held fast in her captor's grip, I could see Entropy staring at me, her eyes wide. I could have sworn she looked right at my pocket, and then her gaze darted to the side, towards the Gwarlock.

81

It seemed as though she knew I carried the stone. And she desperately wanted me to give it to him.

She started nodding vigorously, until the Fate holding her mouth stilled her. The delicate woman began to swiftly tick her head this way and that, trying to understand the reason behind Entropy's movement.

I felt the need to make a snap decision. I had come to return the stone. I wanted the answer owed to me. I needed to know how to stop The Contessa. Now more than ever. Especially after learning who she was.

Without hesitating—somehow certain of what Entropy wanted of me—I removed the gem from my pocket, and I launched it into the air.

All three of the Fates froze, cocking their heads in that unnerving manner before letting out a screech. The one at the Gwarlock's neck threw her hand out, trying to catch the stone. But the moment she released her grip from him, he wrenched his body free, sitting upright. Leaning forward, he extended his snout just past the Fate's hand. With a snap of his jaws, the Gwarlock swallowed the stone whole.

In that fraction of time, all was still. And silent.

With his chest cut open as it was and his rib cage wrenched apart, I could see the ruby fall into place. The deadened arteries, which hung black and rotted there, sprang to life as they suctioned onto the stone. And the stone—the Gwarlock's heart—began to morph, growing larger and softer and wetter until finally it gave a single pump.

There was no physical change to our surroundings. Everything looked the same. But the power, the energy, shifted.

Yet shifted is too delicate a word. The change of energy in the space was more like a dam bursting. The pressure of it was crushing. I had to fight not to stagger to my knees. Even Zagan was thrown off balance by it, widening his stance as he grabbed both my arms to keep me from falling back.

The Fates all swiveled their heads in Entropy's direction, battling to remain upright. And their perfectly synced voices were an ominous, prophetic cry.

"She will be the death of us."

At their keening words, the three cranes dove down towards each of the Fates. One by one the small women leapt onto the backs of the birds, and one by one they took flight, climbing higher and higher until they pierced the canopy of the tree above, disappearing from sight.

I had expected the Gwarlock to rise in some terrible and vengeful fashion. To witness his wrath and ire. Instead, though, he slumped to his back while the crackling light within his eye sockets dimmed.

Entropy ran over, kneeling at his side, her copious amounts of lavender hair tumbling over them both. Leaning down, she began to whisper to him while stroking his head. Butterflies flew from her lips, covering The Gwarlock, flitting across his face and chest. They even landed on his beating heart and settled on his bones still jutting up in the air.

And he seemed to ease.

Feeling that the turmoil had ended, I stepped into the tree enclosure. Zagan tried to hold me in place, preventing me from entering, but I shook myself free uttering, "It's safe."

He stood next to me and looked down. "Is this what you call 'group stuff?'" he murmured, confused.

I gave my chin a sharp slice to the right, silently urging him to hush.

With each passing moment, the light within the tree enclosure brightened. The stream began to trickle. The birds chirped. And the rabbits hopped along, nibbling on the grass.

All the while, Entropy stroked the Gwarlock's snout and whispered to him, covering him with butterflies.

I began to feel awkward. So I cleared my throat. Entropy looked up and she smiled, the butterflies on her eyelashes fluttered as she blinked, fanning her cheeks.

She looked at me as if I had been let in on some wondrous secret. "You see?" she asked. And as she spoke, a plume of butterflies flew our way, twirling around us.

"Oh, what fun," she continued, her eyes sparkling. Then she turned to the Gwarlock. "What fun!" she repeated. "Do you see, husband? The gift I have given to you? Has it not been fun? It has been an experience!"

Entropy turned back to me, her iridescent skin shimmering with pastel hues. "And you have returned the heart!" She clapped her hands and her cheeks flushed. "Do you see the significance? Balance is restored. It is the only way."

Her tone turned serious. "Balance cannot be forced. You must respect the tides of entropy. You must throw the pebbles up and let them scatter where they may."

I shifted from one foot to the other. I could see how much this topic meant to Entropy. And I knew she detested the

84

Fates—detested the idea of interrupting the balance and chaos of life. But I honestly just wanted what I had come for:

My fucking answer.

"I'm glad we were able to help." I took a small step forward. "And I hope the Gwarlock is satisfied with the offering. I would like to leave you both in peace. If I can just have the information which we agreed upon, we will make our exit."

I took another step forward and straightened my shoulders. "Please, Gwarlock. How do we bring an end to The Contessa?"

The Gwarlock began to sit up and Entropy took a hold of his elbow, helping him. Once he was upright, he nuzzled Entropy's neck, burying his snout in her lavender hair. And I was oddly . . . *touched*.

When he looked at me, some of the crackling light had returned inside his hollow eye sockets, and the space within the tree enclosure seamlessly turned to night. His rib cage was still wrenched open, his massive heart beating within his exposed chest.

His otherworldly voice seemed to reverberate from the very ground. And we did not need to wait any longer. The Gwarlock finally revealed how we could stop The Contessa.

"She must find that which was lost long ago."

At his words Entropy's eyes rounded, and her lips made a perfect O. She placed a delicate hand over her mouth. It was as if the Gwarlock's answer had been the most exciting thing she'd ever heard—as if it had made perfect sense—and we should be elated and exhilarated as well.

I had heard him clearly enough, yet I still tilted my chin to the side, trying to direct my ear towards him. "And what is that? What, exactly, did she lose long ago?"

The mist from outside the tree began to funnel into the enclosure, surrounding our feet. The Gwarlock did not reply. Instead, he rose, as if he had not heard me. Taking a hold of his jutting ribs, he shoved them back into place with a loud crack.

Then he looked down at Entropy. The night air surrounding us turned peaceful, and the tree canopy above filled with millions of glittering stars. "You will come to our bed," he told her.

Still the mist rose higher, stretching to my waist.

Entropy's opal cheeks grew fevered. Her eyes glinted in the starlight. The butterflies upon her lashes fluttered wildly. And she nodded.

The Gwarlock turned without waiting for her and began to walk away from us, into the rising fog.

"Wait!" I called. "That isn't an answer! I need to know what must be found!"

I attempted to follow after the Gwarlock, but Zagan grabbed my elbow, pulling me back. I tried to yank my arm free, tried to stretch onto my toes to keep my eyes on the god of death. But he disappeared.

"No. Wait! That's not an answer! Come back! Come back here! I bring you your goddamn heart and this is how you repay me?!" I snapped my gaze in his wife's direction. "Entropy," I cried. "Please! I returned his heart."

With my words, the mist climbed higher. It rose to my chest and crept towards my neck with clutching fingers. I struggled to keep my head above it, knowing it would suffocate me.

Entropy tilted her head, her lavender hair tumbling over her arm. Somehow the mist did not cover her. She was allowed a small radius of space. And the starlight from above made her opal skin shimmer.

Her face was alight with a mischievous grin. This time when she spoke, the stream of butterflies that filled the space between us twinkled. With each beat of their wings, the starlight sparkled.

The excitement and envy in her words were undeniable. "You have something to find! How . . . uncertain!"

The butterflies landed on my own cheeks and eyelashes, fluttering their glittering wings—blinding me. Then they flitted away.

As they cleared, I heard Entropy's excited giggling, but I could no longer see her. I tried to go after her, angered by these games. But there was no passing through the mist.

It climbed higher and higher, and I knew I was going to drown in it.

I felt Zagan's grip tighten on me. I tried to pull my arm free, determined to make my way to the Gwarlock and demand an explanation. But Zagan had had enough. He picked me up, ensuring my head was above the fog, and he pushed against the tide of thick gray haze.

Powering his way through, we exited the tree enclosure, passing beneath the parted branches. Out in the grim, barren valley the fog was still at thigh level. Zagan set me down on my feet, but the moment he did, a gale force wind funneled through the valley. The blast was so strong, I slammed into him. He wrapped his arms around me. Steadying me.

I looked up at him, knowing what he was about to do. I had felt the way his energy had wrapped around me in the tree enclosure—had felt the way he tried to wisp me out of there. And I had known he couldn't.

But out here, out in the valley behind the Gwarlock's temple, I could feel that same energy wrap around me. And I could feel how I was becoming a shadow of myself.

I tried to take a step back from him, and he shook his head.

"No!" I cried. "We can't leave! They haven't—" My last words were lost, becoming nothing more than smoke, carried away on another bluster of icy wind.

***

The instant that we slammed back into the Dark Manor, I kicked the beautiful, oversized wingback chair that sat in my sitting room. It flipped several times and went crashing into the wall.

Two fires sprang to life, chasing away the chill and darkness of the room. And although I was not the one to ignite the flames, they popped with a loud bang at my outburst.

I clenched my fists at my sides, staring at the cracked piece of furniture and the dent in the wall. I didn't cry about things. I didn't. But if I were someone who did, I would have fought hot tears in that moment.

I had been double crossed.

I had been a fool.

And I had lost the stone.

With my chest heaving, I took a step towards the chair, determined to smash it into tiny pieces of wood.

But a dark, silky voice floated through the air behind me. "I like that chair, and you're ruining it."

It took a millisecond for the statement to sink in. For my brain to recall it. Then I whipped my head in his direction. "Is that supposed to be funny?" My voice was a hiss.

I had used those very words on him, regarding that very chair, not all that long ago.

"Just a suggestion that you might want to . . . '*chill*.'"

As an aside, he tried to recollect the exact phrase. "What was it you called me? Ah, yes. 'Bonehead.'"

"This is different," I snarled. "Do you have any idea what this means?"

"You returned the stone which Maxim desired. And you are unsatisfied with the answer you were provided."

I opened my mouth, about to shout at him. He had oversimplified everything.

But . . . *he was right.*

Oh, god. He was right.

I closed my mouth, the rush of anger and frustration draining from me. And my head fell forward as my shoulders sagged.

I had made a costly mistake. I had ruined our chances. I had forsaken us all.

My chest heaved on a strangled breath.

I was about to collapse in on myself.

I covered my face with my hands.

He was somehow before me in the blink of an eye, looming above me in the firelight, inundating me with his presence.

I couldn't help but feel startled as I looked up at him. I became even more confused when I saw the anger tightening his features.

He grabbed my arms in a bruising grip. His jaw clenched and his shoulders rose. He looked at his hands. He struggled at the sight of them. He struggled at the sight of them *on me*.

The muscle under his eye twitched as he said, "Stop this now!"

"What?" I cried, not understanding.

He stared down at me. "This . . . this . . ." His eyes darted all across my face and his hands squeezed me tighter. "Do not do this. I cannot take it."

His eyes flew to the chair, and he stepped back from me, pointing to the elegant piece of furniture lying on the floor. "Kick it."

I was so confused, so thrown. My gaze shifted back and forth between Zagan and the chair. Finally, I concluded, "I don't want to."

"You have to," he growled.

"No!" I insisted.

"I don't like this. Be angry," he insisted. "I don't know how to do this," he seethed, grabbing me again and giving me a shake.

I looked up at him, searching his eyes, seeing his pained expression.

And a rush of air left my lungs at the comprehension. I closed my eyes, and I let my forehead drop against his chest. I understood fragile emotions were difficult for him. I understood *this* was difficult for him.

"Just hold me," I whispered.

His chest expanded with several heavy breaths. He simply stood there unmoving for a time with his hands clenched on my arms and my head against his chest.

But finally, at some point, ever so slowly—inch by excruciating inch—he wrapped his arms around me.

And I became lost in him. So small next to him.

He cupped the back of my head, and he leaned his face against my hair.

He held me.

I was upset. And Zagan held me.

After a time, with deadly seriousness, he murmured, "If you like, I will go back to that place and remove the beast's heart." He made the offer sound so effortless, as if it were as simple as running out to the market for a carton of milk.

And I realized something then. I realized why it was so easy for him to say that. I pulled back to look up at him.

"You aren't afraid of death," I said.

Zagan's shoulders rose slightly and he looked like he was considering my words. Finally, he said, "You cannot fear losing something you never had."

It took me a moment—searching his eyes for a moment—to realize what he meant. But then it dawned on me.

Life.

I knew then, he felt like he had never really had a life.

I vowed that I would do whatever I could to change that. If Entropy could cut out her husband's heart just so he could have an experience, I was certain I could find something to do for Zagan.

91

Hell, I would go back and slay Filbert myself. I'd lay his bloody carcass at Zagan's feet, if it meant something to him.

He pinched my chin and forced me to look up at him. "I will do whatever you wish. If you would like to banish the Umbra, help Maxim's people, return to your Court of Light . . ."

He searched my eyes, his own narrowing. "I am unable to let you go now. And I am sorry for that. But I will do whatever I can to make up for it. To . . . to . . . make you happy." He spoke the word as if he didn't understand the meaning of it.

He still saw me as a victim. Someone who was forced to be there against her will. He acknowledged that he wanted me. Needed to be with me. He knew he could not let me go.

But he didn't realize that I needed him just the same.

"I wish I could make you understand that I choose to be here. With you," I whispered.

He looked at me, searching my eyes, as if making an honest effort to try and see something there.

And it was a start.

Perhaps we were useless. Perhaps we could do no good. And maybe that was okay. There were better people than us. People like Maxim, who could stand up and fight. Maybe we should just remain locked in the Dark Manor forever. As long as we had each other, the world could burn down around us. We could roam these empty halls.

Together.

But the next night, any hopes I had of locking myself away with Zagan were lost. And my world did burn to ash while I stood in the center of it all.

Unable to do anything but watch.

CHAPTER 6

BANGING. Incessant banging. On the door to my suite.

I knew who was on the other side the moment I approached. The Dark power had already permeated the anteroom.

Cinching the belt of my robe, I yanked the door open. "What is your problem?!"

"Where have you been?" Maxim demanded.

I shook my head in confusion.

"Three nights!" Maxim bellowed. "The two of you go off and disappear for three nights, without a word, without a trace, and now you feign ignorance?!"

"I . . ." I began searching for words, for something to tell him. I knew time moved differently. But on my last visit to the Realm of Lost Souls, *less* time had passed here. I was expecting the same.

According to Maxim, though, apparently more time had passed than I anticipated.

But I realized something, and I stopped struggling to find some commentary; I didn't owe Maxim an explanation.

"We're here now," I told him.

His lips thinned and the dark slash of his brow intensified, but he didn't reply.

I was accustomed to the cold gray glint in Maxim's eyes. His icy stare was not what made me shiver just then. It was the three words he spoke as he barreled past me. "She has returned."

"Who?" I demanded.

Maxim stopped in his tracks, turning to glare at me. He didn't even bother to answer.

I knew. I did. But I wanted to hear it.

After he had thoroughly lashed me with his stare, he pivoted. Before he could go any deeper into the suite, though, Zagan appeared, and the two stood eye to eye.

It was the first time I had seen them together for weeks. And I could tell something had developed between the two. A certain kinship. A respect. Neither seemed to care that one wore a crisp suit while the other was clad in nothing but dark trousers; the balance of power was equal.

"It's time," Zagan said.

"We are not ready," Maxim countered.

"I will take her head," Zagan promised. "We do not need anything more than that."

Maxim threw his shoulders back. "If it were that simple, I would have done it years ago!" His voice boomed through the room. Then he threw his hand, gesturing to the night outside beyond the suite walls. "She has the power of the Umbra. You will not be able to reach her. We need the stone. The Umbra must be imprisoned once more. The Council must be stabilized. Then, and only then, will we *possibly* be able to take her."

Maxim turned from Zagan to cross the room, standing before the fireplace. He bowed his head as if picturing what he was saying—as if he had played it out in his mind a thousand times. "The Umbra must be locked away. The Dark Court, captured. The Contessa, beheaded. Each step must be executed with precise timing. Otherwise our risk of defeat increases exponentially. We cannot attempt one without the others."

I felt sick where I stood—my stomach on the verge of heaving. I had surrendered the stone. And for what? At what cost?

I had doomed us all.

I should have given the Heart of Darkness to Maxim. I had to fight to stay standing. I wanted to drop to my knees in repentance.

The only thing that kept me upright was my faith in Zagan. I still believed he could lock away the Umbra. He was the king's heir. If his father had done it all those years ago, then so, too, could he.

He had to be the one named in the prophecy. He was the one who was whole. He was born with both the Light and the Dark. He was the one who could defeat the Umbra. Even the Fates had acknowledged him under the willow tree.

"How do you know she has returned?" Zagan asked.

Maxim looked at us from the fireplace. "Her adjunct, Marax, held council three nights ago, announcing her return. He spoke of the uprising. He has gathered the Court's guard. And he warned us to be prepared. According to him, The Contessa has decided it is time to sweep through and destroy those who would stand against her."

"He could have been lying," I offered.

"Perhaps," Maxim allowed. "But you cannot tell me you do not feel the litany of powers saturating the skies. Something is approaching. And it is almost upon us."

Maxim was right. I was surprised that the pressure of it all hadn't shattered the windows of the manor. There was incredible Darkness brewing in the skies.

But that wasn't all.

There was something else, other forces which whorled and clashed with the Darkness. Light and heat. Jagged electricity. Scattered voltage. A collection of warring power and energy threatened to rip apart the fabric of the heavens.

I knew Maxim was right. And just as he spoke those words, as if the very gods above had heard his proclamation, I felt the power in the air around us begin to expand with an incredible pressure. As the fire gave an unexpected lick from the hearth, the three of us stood where we were, assessing the rapid approach of something . . . *great*.

A soft tinkling noise filled the silence. We looked up to the chandelier. A single crystal swayed, clinking against its brethren. Then another. And another. In just a moment's time, the entire chandelier was shaking.

I looked at Maxim, clearly infuriated with him. He just had to open his big mouth. As if his words had conjured some power out of thin air, something was happening.

You fucking asshole.

I didn't speak the words, but I hoped he could read them in my eyes. I didn't stick around for a response.

I began to run for my bedroom. Straight in the direction of the approaching force. Straight to the towering windows which overlooked the east lawn. I gazed out across the manor grounds, out to the wrought iron gate which stood before the tree tunnel. Inky clouds churned and collided in the predawn.

Then the sky began to glow along the horizon. In a blistering display of light, the sun was rising.

Only it couldn't be. It was much too early.

But the light grew, glowing brighter and brighter, illuminating the sky with blinding rays. The power of it—the force of it—made me raise my arm to shield my eyes.

Maxim and Zagan stood at my sides, one at each shoulder.

Then the bottom of the window cracked, and a small fracture formed at the base. As the pressure outside bore down upon us, the hairline split crawled up the glass straight through the center.

I could feel the Dark power from both Zagan and Maxim at exactly the same time as it swept around me.

Maxim's deep voice was level and quiet as he spoke. "They've come for you."

Before I could ask what he meant, the imposing black gate at the bottom of the drive burst open in an explosion of Light. And when my pupils recovered, when the sky settled back into darkness, I was able to focus once more.

Standing at the floor-to-ceiling window in my room on the fifth floor of the manor, I looked down to see the lawn filled with a small army, each member aglow with wings of Light and swords of fire.

The Archangels.

And standing before them all, staring up at me with blazing sparks in his eyes, was Elijah.

For a moment, I was paralyzed with shock. But it was for a moment only.

I met Elijah's burning gaze. Without taking my eyes off him, I asked, "Can they enter?"

"No," came Maxim's confident response.

Then I turned from the window.

Zagan's voice shot through the room. "Where are you going?"

"To my closet," I replied without looking back.

"I'm getting dressed."

***

I stood mere feet from Elijah.

Dark power was coiled so tightly around me, I wasn't sure if I could be seen by the angels filling our lawn. Maxim and Zagan stood at my sides, looming over me, somehow seeming larger than they were.

I knew Zagan was on the verge of wisping me away. It had taken incredible convincing to stop him from doing so while we were still in my quarters. But when I explained why I had to speak with the Archangels, Maxim had agreed with me. And he successfully persuaded Zagan to stay.

It wasn't going to be an easy situation, though. Standing mere feet from him, I could see Elijah's rage and sense of possession as it boiled over. It would have burned my skin as it erupted and filled the space between us had I not been so possessively wrapped in Dark energy.

I stared at him. Waiting. His voice was gritty and guttural as he spoke. "I am taking you home, Violet."

I raised my voice as I responded, craning my neck, trying to stare down each and every one of the Archangels spread across the sloping lawn. I particularly narrowed my eyes at Giddeon. "So the Council can have me executed?" I snapped.

"No," Elijah countered. He looked like he was about to take a step forward, but before he could, before it could become anything more than an impulse, I felt the shadows at my shoulder stretch and rise with silent wails. My skin became ice cold and I could feel a frigid blast sweep through my hair. Elijah's eye twitched, and he stopped himself from coming towards me.

"You don't understand," he said. "I have been freed in order to collect you. The Council has instructed that I bring you home. Safely. You have been cleared of any wrongdoing."

I scoffed. "And you believe that?"

I took a moment to stare at Elijah, to open myself up to him, to allow him to see the truth.

"Elijah," I tried to cradle his name while keeping a firm grasp on it, knowing he would have difficulty believing anything I said. "The Council wants us dead. The only reason they haven't killed you is to use you. It's obvious you are meant to find me and bring me back. Then they will kill us both."

He looked like he was about to throw out some harsh, grinding reply, in that way of his. But instead of snapping, he sucked in a deep breath. He stared right back at me and he kept his next words level—the way one might when talking to a lunatic—the way one might when attempting to stop someone from doing something stupid.

"I won't let that happen," he promised. Then he eyed the dark, towering men behind me. "But you need to leave this place. You are not staying here." His voice softened just a fraction and his eyes blazed. "Come on, princess."

He was trying to coax me. He wanted me to make a break for him. I could see it all in his eyes. If I would just pull away from Zagan and Maxim, if I would just lean in Elijah's direction, he would snatch me in his arms and take me away. He just needed me to give him that one inch.

Yet, all I could do was shake my head. And I felt sorry for him. Because I could see how it looked to him. I could see it all from his point of view. And I could see how he believed he was doing the right thing.

I flung my hand out, sweeping across the expanse of the lawn. "Why send an entire army, Elijah? Why would the Council do that? If I have been pardoned, why not send a message and let me decide for myself? Why bother with trying to collect me? Don't you see? The Council wants to ensure that they get a hold of me. And you. This is not a rescue party. This is insurance that we don't slip away."

Elijah raked a hand through his hair, clearly frustrated. "This is not some bounty hunt." He jerked his head to the side, indicating the group of angels behind him. "This is insurance that you make it home alive."

"You don't understand," I told him. I lifted my chin and raised my voice, addressing the crowd assembled before me. "None of you do."

I didn't know how the Archangels would react, but now was not the time for hesitation. I didn't know how long I would have. Taking a step forward, I raised my voice, letting it carry through the frigid night air.

"The Council is lying to you! They learned of a prophecy, long ago. One that foretold their downfall. They were told that a Prism made whole would bring an end to them. The Oracle shared this prophecy with the Elders. And in response, the Council has employed the Shadow people to assassinate those you've lost! To prevent any of you from bonding with your other half. They have ensured that none of you could connect with another, none of you could enact the Vinculum, and as a result, none of you could be the one who brings their doom. They have secured their fate at the expense of yours!"

The gathered angels began to glance around at one another. I repeated the point, stressing the truth to them.

"They are the ones who have kept you isolated and alone. They are the ones who have seen to it that you cannot connect with another. The Shadows have been hired assassins—employed by the Council!"

Elijah's face contorted. "You have been brainwashed!" he countered. "Of course these monsters would tell you this. What else would you expect? Don't be so gullible, Violet! Think about what you're saying! They've turned you into one of them."

I kept my voice strong and certain. "There is documented proof. And the Lady of Light will verify this all."

A slight hum vibrated through the air as the Archangels began to murmur to one another.

Then Giddeon stepped forward from just behind Elijah. "Hey, baby doll. Look . . ." His tone was completely inappropriate for the situation. You would have thought we were friends bumping into each other at a bar, instead of facing a *fate of the world* type showdown.

He rubbed the back of his neck, causing the muscles in his arm and chest to strain against the fitted tee he wore. And he was unbelievable. The shirt was bright yellow with a picture of four elderly women, and it read: SQUAD GOALS.

"I know you're pretty sore about the whole 'trying to kill you' thing." The bastard used air quotes when referencing his attempts on my life. "I know how much it pisses you off when people do that. But come on, whatta you say? Truce?"

When I simply stared at him, he continued. "You gotta know, I feel terrible for what happened. I mean really. I didn't want to come after you like that, baby doll. You gotta believe me!

"You just, you don't understand. I had no choice. I had to follow Council orders. And when you and Eli skipped town after your Council ruling . . . I knew it was bad news.

"But making up a bunch of shit about the Council," Giddeon shook his head, "it's not gonna help any. I mean for fuck's sake, look at who you're standing with. I know you're sore about the whole death sentence thing. Hell, I'd be too. But it's over. You've been pardoned."

His eyes roamed over the facade of the Dark Manor and he gave a slight shiver. "You don't need to stay in this freaky place anymore."

I almost felt bad about pressing the matter because the look of relief on Giddeon's face was undeniable. He truly believed the conflict with the Council was over. And it had lifted a huge weight from his shoulders.

But I couldn't make this easy for anyone. They had to know what was happening. I widened my stance and stood my ground. "I'm telling you the truth, G."

Giddeon gave the most exaggerated sigh, his massive shoulders heaving dramatically before offering, "What proof do you have?"

"The Shadow King's journals. He wrote about the Council, about what they have done. He had evidence that the attacks on the very first Prisms were directed by the Council."

"Oh come on, Violet," Giddeon cried. "Are you serious? Are you actually serious with this shit?"

"Look, Giddeon, I can see how you and everyone here can't accept this information . . ." What could I say? What could I do that would convince everyone? It was pointless.

"You don't belong here," G repeated, softly this time, as if he pitied me.

"No, Giddeon," I countered, the softness in my tone matching his own. "This is exactly where I belong."

I glanced above my shoulder to look at Zagan. His gaze was intent on Elijah. I knew it was requiring immense self-control for him to remain. I knew, more than anything, he wanted to take me far away from here. Far away from Elijah. Zagan did not trust him.

Turning back to address the crowd I said, "This is Zagan. He is the other Prism."

Audible gasps and additional murmurs filled the front lawn.

Giddeon held his fists up to his forehead as if discovering the worst. "Aw. Sweetie, hunny, no. That Dark dude next to you is the *Shadow Prince*." He spoke the words as if I had trouble hearing. "See? All that Dark nastiness floating around him? See how it's creeping all up you too? Aww, baby doll, you're talking all kinds of crazy."

"Giddeon, don't talk to me like I'm a child."

"No, of course not. You're a big girl."

I ignored G, focusing my indignation on Elijah. "You didn't tell him?"

Elijah just stared at me, unapologetic.

"Ask, Elijah. He can tell you who this is," I said gesturing to Zagan, "because Elijah is the one who took him when he was a small child from within the walls of the Radiant Court and handed him over to Shadows."

Elijah crossed his arms over his chest. "I did you and everyone here a favor. I knew what he'd become."

"Fuuuucck me!" Giddeon mumbled, his eyes going wide. "Are you serious with this?" he asked, turning to Elijah.

Elijah's jaw was set as he nodded once.

"Okay, this is some crazy shit," G said, stabbing a hand through his hair. "I'll give you that. But still, it doesn't prove anything about the Council."

Cord stepped forward then. Slightly taller and broader than Elijah and Giddeon. Although his brown hair was neatly combed and his formal white robe crisp, there was a sickly gray tinge to his skin. And while my actions had been in self-defense, I felt an incredible guilt at what I had done to him back in my mother's study.

At least—I reasoned—I hadn't killed him.

Cord always stood so still and erect. So emotionless. But when he spoke, there was something in his deep voice. It was barely noticeable, but something had rattled him.

"She speaks the truth."

Giddeon looked worried. It wasn't hard to guess that he was concerned Cord was coming undone, succumbing to whatever illness I had inflicted upon him.

"Come on, buddy," he said, clapping Cord on the shoulder. "You know this is nonsense."

Cord stared ahead as if somewhere else, not actually addressing anyone in particular. "The Council has ordered I kill them both upon their return."

There were more gasps and murmurs from the crowd of Archangels.

Cord's words were enough to turn Elijah's head. He wasn't sure whether to believe him or not.

Giddeon opened his mouth, about to say something in response, but we never heard his words. Because just then, we were all deafened by ear-splitting shrieks from high above.

The air became hazy with heat. And in the middle of the dark frigid night, a hot wind blew across the manor grounds.

We all raised our faces to the skies.

CHAPTER 7

DRAGONS.

They circled in the black sky above before swooping down to land on the manor grounds. Surrounding us.

And the earth shook at our feet.

The massive beasts crouched on their haunches; their great wings outstretched. And here and there, streams of fire licked the ground before them as they snorted and chuffed.

The largest of them, the one who was midnight blue, landed next to us. I could instantly feel the weight of his reptilian stare.

It seemed Hellion had come to collect the Heart of Darkness.

Before I could tell him he was wasting his time, a pack of leather clad women strutted through the mangled, broken gate at the end of the drive, their hips and shoulders rolling with each step. Somehow, every last one of them oozed sex appeal and violence.

Leading them all was a set of platinum blonde pigtails.

Apparently, the dragons and the Fatales had decided to band together. The enemy of my enemy . . . and whatnot.

I gave a snort at the alliance. There was no way they weren't both planning on screwing the other over.

But they could not have picked a worse time. I had to get rid of them. Too much was on the line.

At the same moment, I could feel myself become wispy—a shadow of myself. Inky tendrils had engulfed me. I knew I was no longer visible to the others.

I spun around and grabbed Zagan. I could feel the way his muscles swelled under my hands. It was taking all his strength not to snap. "Please, wait," I begged. "I need to stay here. I need you to do this for me. Don't pull me away."

I reached my hands up to place them on the sides of his face. Going up on my toes, I forced Zagan to look at me. "I'm not going anywhere," I promised. "I'm staying right here with you."

His features were tense. Pained. And his eyes black. "You ask too much," he countered between clenched teeth.

"I know," I told him. "You're right. I do. I know it. But I want to be here. We need to face this. I don't want to run from it. Please don't pull me away."

He shuddered again, but he did not wisp us. I looked up at his rigid jaw, where I held him, and I felt my hands freeze. I could see those inky marks begin to form on his neck.

Yet, I pressed my lips over his. I opened myself up to him, offering my reassurance with more than mere words.

When I pulled back from him, his eyes roamed my face for a moment before he closed them. Taking a deep breath, his chest expanding, he released me from the shadows.

I turned to stare at Lilly and gestured to the small army of angels on the lawn. "I'm a little busy here," I told her, none too gently.

"I want the stone." She planted her feet shoulder width apart and placed her hands on her hips, making it clear she was not planning on leaving without it.

I didn't turn to look at Maxim, but I could feel his eyes on me.

"I don't have it," I told her.

"Honestly, Violet, that's really pathetic. We all know you have it. Don't be a pathetic hoe. No one likes a pathetic hoe. You're better than that."

With a deep inhale, I threw my shoulders back. "I returned it to the god of death. I don't have it."

I could feel the shadows grow at my side where Maxim stood.

I was on the verge of having every single being wanting my head.

"You lie," Lilly accused. "No one likes a pathetic liar either," she warned.

"I. Don't. Have. It." I repeated. "The Gwarlock sent me to retrieve it. I took it from you. And I gave it back to him."

Lilly looked at me for a moment. Her cheeks puffed. Her fists balled at her sides. Then she wailed on a dramatic exhale.

"Ugh! You are the worst," she cried, stomping her foot. "Like really, the fucking worst." She shook her head and walked in a little circle with her hands on her hips before stopping in front of me again. "And I hate how much I like it."

"Lilly!" one of the Fatales chastised.

"Okay, but really. Like, of all the things in the world that she could have done with the stone, would you have ever guessed she'd return it?"

Lilly looked around, shrugging. "And, like, what the hell is even going on right now. I mean, did any of you think we'd finally get our break with this gate because a battalion of angels would blow it open?

"And fuck me! Who is that?!" she asked, eyeing Maxim. "My god, I think my panties are going to explode." Then her eyes wandered over Zagan and she immediately closed her mouth and drew a step back, fighting off a shiver.

Shaking the moment off, she turned her attention back to me, nonplussed. "You are one crazy bitch."

I couldn't let Lilly go on any longer. She and the other Fatales needed to leave. "Look," I said, addressing the life-like barbie dolls and the dragon pack. "If you want the Heart of Darkness, you're going to have to go and cut it out of the Gwarlock's chest. I don't have it. And I can't help you. You're wasting your time here."

When no one moved, I began to make a shooing motion with my hands. "Okay. Time to go now. Take your dragons with you. Bye-bye. Nice to see you. Maybe we can catch up another—"

Something was slithering around my ankle. Something cold. Something Dark. Something vaporous.

I didn't want to look down. I didn't want to see it. I didn't want to confirm what I *knew* it was. But my eyes darted across the manor grounds.

Dark shadows were beginning to creep from the earth. Rising from the ground to slink and snake their way around all who had assembled on the front lawn. And they held the caustic stench of burning rubber.

A blanket of silence spread across the manor grounds for the briefest of instances as the night lost its breath.

They should have left: the Fatales, the dragons—the Archangels, too. They all should have left when they had the chance.

Because it had become too late.

A cold wind blew from the cliff that buffered the manor grounds. I felt it. And I knew. Before I turned my eyes skyward . . . I knew.

She had come for me.

The time had come. There would be no more waiting, no more preparing or training. I had run out of time.

But it was all for naught.

Zagan would have me out of there before she could do anything. I was surprised, really, that we were still standing there. That I remained long enough to lay my eyes upon her. To see the black, flowing dress that seemed to absorb all light, to see her paper white skin, her black lips and shining hair piled atop her head.

Those gray crystalline eyes.

And the Umbra who stepped out of the dark to surround us all in the night.

A thick gurgling noise—low and great—broke the silence which had settled over the grounds. The earth shook at our feet, chugging and churning, and an incredible crack began to form along the ground at the base of the cliff. The dirt and rock began to split and separate, and all who had gathered fought to remain upright.

Lightning arced through the sky. Thunder crashed above us all. And the rain began to pour.

A chasm opened up in the earth at the base of the cliff, between us and The Contessa. Acrid smoke billowed from the abyss, and the caustic fumes burned our eyes. The underworld had been brought to our doorstep.

The Umbra advanced.

And all hell broke loose.

I cried out for the others. For what would happen to them. I couldn't save them from this. I prayed Maxim would be able to do something, because I was about to be pulled away from it all.

Zagan would sweep me away at any moment.

Yet, still, I lingered. I couldn't fathom why.

I turned to look at him. And I wished I hadn't. I wanted to squeeze my eyes shut at what I saw. Because in that moment I understood all too clearly why I still stood where I did . . .

We would not be wisping anywhere.

Something came over me then. A certainty. Somehow, in some way, I knew it was the end.

Maybe life is an endless loop. Maybe I had lived this moment before. Maybe that was how I knew.

Maybe Entropy was wrong. Maybe the Fates had a carefully composed script that was written for all of us, and we'd looked it over during rehearsal before the play of life began.

Maybe it's only because of fate, that life marches forward. Perhaps it is the sole driving force.

Whatever the reason . . . I turned. And I begged.

If I had just let him wisp us, only a moment ago . . .

"Take me away from here. Please. Now. Right now. I want to leave," I shouted at him.

The rain was punishing, throwing a scattered veil between us. I tried to grab his face, tried to force him to look at me.

My words were nothing, though. The moment they left my lips they drifted away into the air. Never to be heard. Never to have existed.

Because he did not hear me. He did not look at me. He was too far gone.

"Stay here with me. Don't leave me!" I begged.

He was right. It was too much. I had asked for too much. There is a price for everything. And we all must pay our due.

He didn't even look at me. "Take her." The two words Zagan spoke were a knife to my heart. The low murmur was barely audible. But Maxim heard him clearly enough. And that traitorous son of a bitch grabbed my arm.

Before Zagan could leave us, Maxim beseeched, "You cannot do this. Now is not the time. Do not be shortsighted. You will throw away all we have worked towards."

Zagan turned his head to meet Maxim square in the eye. Shadows twisted and swept over his skin. And his voice began to take on layers, as silent shrieks and wails consumed him.

"The Contessa will not have her."

I saw Maxim's other hand reach for Zagan—knew he was about to wisp all three of us away. But so, too, did Zagan. In a flicker, he had slipped from Maxim's reach. And he was running.

Straight for The Contessa.

There was no doubt, no hesitation; I could not let him go alone. I had to help him.

But Maxim had taken a hold of both my arms from behind my back. He was going to wisp. He was going to force me to leave.

And I refused.

"Ah, bloody hell! Now you find your will?!" His bellow filled my ears in spite of the rain and thunder, the shouts and screams, the clang and hiss of swords, the beastly roars of the night. "You are the most infuriating woman!"

I tried to step back, to wrap my leg behind Maxim's and kick it out from under him. But he anticipated the move and stepped back with me.

He was the only person I'd fought who was faster than me, better than me. I twisted my arm to the point of breaking, and it was released. I spun around with my one arm freed. I looked up at Maxim and I screamed at him to let me go.

An Umbra came for us then. Maxim drew his sword and sliced its neck in one swift motion, while aiming a kick at the thing's torso. It flew to the ground. Not for an instant did Maxim loosen his grip on my arm.

"He cannot defeat her! Not while she controls the Umbra. If you go with him, you will only be a distraction."

"Then we have to stop him!" I countered.

"He will not be stopped."

Two more Umbra came for us. I drew one of my short swords with my free hand. The blade landed at the precise spot on the thing's neck to take its head. And while I was skilled with a sword, I lacked Maxim's honed precision. A spray of black sludge spattered across us before the Umbra thudded to the ground.

116

"Duck!" Commanded Maxim as he slayed the other at my back.

And still that stubborn son of a bitch gripped my arm. I kicked at his ankle, attempting to sweep his leg out from under him again. He blocked my boot with the flat side of his sword.

He looked at me with that controlled anger he possessed and squeezed my arm tighter.

Then someone cried out next to us. A Fatale. She was doing her best to fight two Umbra, but they had the advantage over her.

I knew it was my out. I knew Maxim would be compelled to help her.

I raised my sword and I swung for him with all my might. Because I had to. Because he would not let me go any other way. I could not pull my advance. I could not pretend. If I did, if there was any hesitation, any lack of commitment, I knew he would hang on to me. So I swung my sword at Maxim with every intent on landing a deadly blow.

With a roar of outrage, he shoved me away and spun through the air to fight the advancing Umbra, heading straight for the Fatale. I didn't stay to help him. I didn't stay to see what would happen next. I turned. And I ran.

I could see Zagan up ahead. But he was too fast; he moved in a blur of shadows. Despite the fighting which warred around him, the gash in the earth, the fumes and the rain—despite it all, he headed directly for The Contessa.

And she was descending the sloped path from the side of the cliff. The excessive folds of her gown billowed behind her before trailing off into inky strands of smoke, unaffected by the deluge. Her full black lips were parted in the vilest of smiles.

And between the two of them lay the raw split, open up to the very bowels of the earth—a smoldering cleft of slag and sulfur.

They were both approaching the chasm.

And again, my arm was captured in someone's grip. I was going to cut the fucking thing off. I couldn't afford to stop. I had to catch up to Zagan.

I pivoted into the hold, using the momentum to power my other fist, swinging my sword handle straight into the face of whomever dared to grab me. However, my wrist was captured in a large palm, the blow effectively blocked. And I gazed into Elijah's blazing eyes for a fraction of a second before his lips came slamming down over my own.

I immediately tried to break free, pulling back from him. But he jerked my soaked body into his. And when I began to shake my head, he only kissed me harder—dominating me, demanding from me. Bright and hot. Sparking and crackling with intense determination amid the melee. He was too strong, too confident to care about the chaos rupturing around us.

My heart gave a desperate, bruising pump, knowing full well that I was losing Zagan.

I thrashed again, finally breaking free. Elijah stared at me with the rain running down his face, expecting some flaring response, some pull, some sudden connection or desire. But the only thing my eyes held were a cold fury. I yanked my arm free and slapped him across the face, gravely insulted by his liberties with my body and my time.

He did not try to grab me again. He did not try to hold me, or shake me, or kiss me. With a look of crushing disbelief, he let me go.

I turned. And again—and faster still—I ran.

It didn't matter what came for me, nothing was going to stop me.

And beings came at me on all sides as I ran. Whether to aid or attack, I didn't know. I didn't care. I barely noticed them.

My arms flew, slicing, pushing, and dodging where needed. Archangels, dragons, and Fatales fought the Umbra all around me. But it mattered not. I kept my eyes forward, locked onto Zagan, determined to reach him.

There would be no more obstacles. I would not permit it. I would reach him. I had to.

But he was approaching the chasm without slowing. In fact, he seemed to be speeding up.

It didn't make sense. I couldn't understand why. He was heading straight for the abyss at full speed. My face contorted as I ran after him. He was just a few steps away from the edge . . .

And then he was airborne, having leapt at the foot of the split. He was a streak of shadows. A massive black harbinger of ill omen, silently rising through the dark sky. He was flying through the rain and lightning straight for the other side.

But just a moment after he surged into the air so, too, did The Contessa.

She was a graceful nightmare. Her black gown floating around her. Her dark, glinting hair shining despite the lightless night. And I could swear I could see every gleam, every facet, of her crystalline eyes. Although she was set on a collision course with Zagan . . . I could have sworn she stared at me.

She was coming for me. The Dark Prince was an insignificant impediment in her path. For whatever reason, I was the key to what drove her. And she was not going to leave without me.

Zagan and The Contessa arced across the sky in perfect balance—bound for one another.

With a clap of thunder, the two immovable forces collided in the night. Zagan's arms instantly wrapped around her. She became wispy for a moment, the edges of her becoming smoky and blurry as if she were about to disappear. But Zagan's hold tightened, and she solidified. I could see her eyes over his shoulder. I could see the shock, the realization, as the two of them began to plummet. She had thought she'd wisp away. Zagan was somehow preventing her.

And he wasn't going to wisp away, himself. He was falling.

He was taking her with him.

"No!" I cried out my objection, but the word was smothered by the night—a small bird crushed before it could take flight.

I was almost at the edge of the chasm. I could make it. If I leapt for them, I could grab a hold of him. I sheathed my sword while I ran.

He would have no choice. He would have to let her go and wisp away somewhere with me. If I forced him to save me, I would be forcing him to save himself.

I was just about to leap for him. I needed only a few more yards. And while I kept my eyes on the two of them, while I watched them plummet inch by inch into the abyss, I noticed a figure in my periphery standing at the edge of the drop. A hooded figure in a brown tattered robe. One gnarled finger held out in the air before her.

The Crone.

I didn't know why she was there or what she was doing. And I didn't care. All that I could focus on was calculating the precise trajectory I would need to crash into Zagan. I neared the edge, gaining speed. Two more steps were all I needed.

One. Two.

I threw myself into the chasm. I became airborne.

But with the most horrifying realization, I slowly became aware of the fact that I was not streaming forward.

With the most horrifying realization, I slowly became aware of the fact that I had hit an invisible wall. I was flung back, flying through the air as if someone had punched me. And as I went hurtling away from the chasm, my eyes were wide open as I watched . . .

I watched . . .

Zagan and The Contessa . . .

Fall into the depths of the abyss.

The moment I crashed to the ground, I scrambled, tripping and stumbling over the soggy earth, back onto my feet. I frantically clambered to the edge of the rift pushing on the solid air in front of me, desperately running my hands over it, trying to find an opening—a way through.

The Crone. It was because of the Crone. She had committed this heinous act.

"Let me pass!" I screamed at her. But when I hit the wall, the waves from the impact had knocked the Crone to the ground. She lay in a crumpled heap. Unmoving.

I clawed at the wall. I shouted commands. I made symbols with my own hands. And all the while, intense power poured from my palms.

Massive arcs of Light scattered through the thick plane of solid air, illuminating the millions of drops of rain behind it. And when that didn't work, when the Light did nothing, the Darkness came.

Inky black swaths stretched and swirled in front of me, coiling around the crackling Light, drowning out the noise of the chaos with silent wails and screams.

They came for me then. I could feel them begin to swarm around me, feel them at my back and sides. The Umbra.

I did not care. All that mattered was getting through the wall. I could not stop to turn and fight them.

But the gruesome figures in their black robes did nothing. They did not try to fight me or capture me. They did not go for my neck with their claw-like fingers, nor did they suffocate me with the caustic brume from their lips.

I could see them in my peripheral vision. They simply stood at my back and my sides. Each one of their lifeless, reflective eyes, staring at me.

I don't know why I did it. I often wonder if it was the moment of my undoing—the tipping point. But just then, I turned to the Umbra. And I roared at them.

I demanded they help me.

Instantly, the wall of air in front of me began to fill with that acrid black smoke which billowed from the mouths of the Umbra. Drifting, expanding, devouring the wall of air, becoming denser and denser, until it began to seep out through the other side.

I was choking on the fumes, my eyes watering, my throat and nose burning, but still I managed to find my voice.

"Yes! More!" I shouted to them. Then I heard the sound of a sword—that unmistakable ring of cold steel.

I glanced over my shoulder. I could see Umbra beginning to fall.

"Faster! Hurry!" I shouted.

I tried to redouble my effort, leaning my entire body into the wall, pouring all I had into it. Every second that passed was a chance that I might not find them.

But Maxim had cut a path to me. He was just behind me. I had to turn and fight him. I could not let him grab a hold of me.

I spun, drawing my swords, and then I swung for him. He blocked. But instead of advancing, the way I anticipated he would, he took a step back. He stared at me. He had a look of disbelief and *horror* on his face.

I stood in front of the smoky wall of roiling air. I could feel my hair flying around my face and shoulders, feel the Darkness crystalizing my veins. I could feel how it rushed through my arteries to collect beneath my ribs, hardening.

Instead of shaking himself into action, as I suspected he'd do, Maxim threw his sword to the side and fell to his knees before me, in the punishing rain.

"He's gone, Violet! Kill me, if you want. Throw yourself from this world. But it won't bring him back. He has made his choice. I do not know what will become of him, but if we have any chance to help him now, we must work together. You must stop this. This is not the way. I can help you."

Maxim stared at me with his gray eyes, with such . . . *purity*.

"Is this what he would want of you?"

At Maxim's words, I closed my eyes. I wanted to hide. I didn't want anyone to see me. If Zagan had been there in that moment—the thought of him, seeing me as I was . . .

But I couldn't just let him go. I couldn't just let him fall.

The weight of what was happening was too great. I could not bear it. I was only one person. And it was too much. I, too, sank to my knees. My swords falling at my sides.

"Maxim!" I cried.

He nodded. "Dismiss them!"

My voice cracked as I spoke, raw and gritty from the acrid fumes. "Leave us," I said, not taking my eyes off Maxim's.

Just like that, in a muted clap of smoke, the Umbra vanished from the manor grounds.

Behind me, the wall of black fog churned. Before me, the Archangels, the dragons, and the Fatales all pivoted, their eyes somehow turning to me as the foe they battled disappeared.

It was too much.

"Maxim," I pleaded, barely keeping myself up on my knees, opening myself up to him.

With a cold glint in his eyes, Maxim spoke a few harsh, unintelligible words.

And that powerful, Dark man saved me.

From myself.

CHAPTER 8

~Violet's Playlist: The Night We Met, Lord Huron~

*I*T WAS DARK, *save for the faintest of light that glimmered around us. And we were floating somewhere, water lilies drifting at our sides. I could feel my hair and the skirt of my dress as they ebbed weightlessly around me.*

Beyond us, beyond our spot of existence, was infinite darkness. We were *the existence. We were all there was.*

My head on his shoulder. His arm around my waist. That was all. That was all there needed to be.

I heard something. A song. Faint and fair. Something I had known once. Whether it actually played somewhere, or in my memory only—I did not know.

The Night We Met. Lord Huron.

There was no need to speak. To move.

But at some point—a small eternity later—from somewhere far below, a question floated to the surface. It bobbed in a fragile bubble. And when it

126

silently popped with a delicate burst, the words tumbled from my mouth as if formed there.

"What is this?"

Another small eternity later, he answered. "Peace . . . Rest . . . The end.*"*

Silence.

A sound. A quiet, steady drumming. And although it was faint, I found it jarring. It had not existed before. And now it did.

Little by little the steady rhythm grew louder. And thump after thump, I realized the sound was coming from beneath my ribs.

"What do you mean?" I asked.

"This, love, is the end."

Had I been anywhere else, those words would have made me cry. They would have broken me.

But a thought took hold.

It did not matter if this was the end. It did not matter what it was. We were together.

Yet, still and even so, the sound of drumming grew.

"You cannot stay," he said simply.

"But I am here," I stated just as simply.

"You will leave."

For a reason that was not clear, those three words caused the pounding to pick up speed.

"Tomorrow?" I asked, not knowing why.

He did not answer. And he did not need to. The barest hint of water had seeped up between us.

I knew there was no point in playing the fool. I knew what it meant.

My voice began to diminish as the void around us devoured it. And I made a promise. A vow. One I knew I would keep. "If you let me go, Zagan Black, if you don't come back for me . . . I will haunt you for eternity."

The truest words I had ever spoken.

His lips pressed against my forehead, and his hand brushed my cheek. "Ah, Violet, love . . . you already are."

The water surged between us. I did not try to fight it. I did not try to cling to him. I knew better. And my arms hung suspended in front of me, open and empty, as I was swept away.

***

Talking. There was talking. A conversation nearby. Not an argument, but an urgent discussion. The voices were vaguely familiar as they came in and out of focus.

"Not well . . . speaks of dreams . . ."

"The stone . . ."

"Now is the time . . ."

"Not our problem . . ."

"A matter of time . . ."

But there was one voice that rang out, snapping my attention into focus.

"I'd rather my vag fell off than face those things again. There's no fucking way we're sticking around for more of that."

The voice. I knew that voice.

"Yeah," someone agreed. "I'd rather go home with the dragon pack than face those things again."

A pause.

"Well, is that really the best comparison?" A feminine voice countered. "I mean, that would actually be kind of fun, wouldn't it? The dragon pack? There are worse ways to spend a Friday night. Amiright?"

Another voice joined in. "Ooh . . . just think of it." The voice turned breathy, "One of those big males . . . just . . . just . . . coming after you . . . wanting you . . . the heat coming off his body . . . putting his hands on you . . ."

"Like I said!" the first voice insisted. "I'd like to go home with someone from the dragon pack. Tonight. I thought I was making that pretty clear. With my first choice being—"

"Ladies! Please!" Maxim's voice boomed. "This is," he cleared his throat, "neither the time nor place."

"Hey!" A deep gravelly voice. "Don't be rude. Let the females continue. Go ahead, darlin'. What were you in the middle of saying? What, ah, exactly, do you want one of us to do to you?"

"Knock it off!" someone commanded.

Hellion. I knew that was Hellion.

After the objections and grumbling settled down, Maxim began speaking again. "I believe their fealty is to her now. I do not know what, exactly, the fissure was. But whatever it was, when The Contessa fell into it they no longer answered to her. The moment their mistress was lost, they found a new one, as it were."

"Dude, she looked freaky. Those eyes seriously freaked me the fuck out." Lilly.

"Why her?" Hellion.

A deep sigh. A pause. "I do not know." Another pause. "She is . . . *special.*"

129

Hellion cut straight to the point. "What are you asking of us?"

"She is young and inexperienced," Maxim began. "This is not a responsibility she can manage. Very few could. There are two possible outcomes. Either she maintains command over the ancient evil—which will in turn destroy her—and she becomes our worst nightmare. Or she is unable to control them for long, and they become freed to the night. And neither you, nor your people, will be safe from them. Either way, we must find the stone. We must have it to imprison the Umbra."

"You heard what she said," Lilly countered. "She gave it to the god of death. The stone is gone."

"We have to take it back," Maxim replied.

"That's impossible." Hellion sounded like his opinion of Maxim had rapidly plummeted.

"It is our only option," Maxim insisted. "You had it in your possession before, did you not? It is clearly not impossible. Those things will consume her mind, body, and soul. And once she has become one of them, they will answer to no one."

I lay in my bed, hearing every word through the open door. As I tried to clear the cobwebs in my mind, I began to blink my eyes. I noticed that they were gritty, and my throat burned. On a sharp inhale of painful air, I couldn't stop myself from coughing violently. And everyone assembled out in my suite suddenly fell silent.

"She rouses," Maxim finally said.

There was a pause, and I just knew they were having a silent conversation about me.

"Ladies," Maxim pressed. But the minute the word left his mouth, there were a slew of various feminine objections.

However, one Fatale's voice cut through the others. "Come on, Lils. You know it's your turn."

"Ugh," Lilly grumbled. "But her room still smells like a burning tire! Why can't sugar tits do it?"

There was a burst of sound, like palms slamming down on a table. Then Maxim's voice thundered through the suite. "You have been warned about calling her that!"

"Omg! But calling her a *crone* is okay?! Sugar tits is way nicer. It's a compliment. I'll bet you anything she's got a rockin bod under that gross robe."

A pause. A battle of wills.

Then a stomp of a foot. "Ugh! Fine! Whatever! I can't wait to get away from you losers." The angry click of Lilly's stilettoed boots pinged across the floor.

But there was an abrupt halt to her steps before the sound grew fainter, as if she was walking back to the group.

"And although you're clearly a loser and I hate you . . . I still wanna smush. But you're on thin ice, Maxim!"

Then the angry clicks started up again.

The instant she walked through the bedroom doorway she began talking to me while throwing her hands up.

"I don't even know why he's sending me in here," she complained. "Obviously, you're awake. You can take care of yourself now. You don't need us babying you anymore."

I didn't bother to sit up. Because I knew. I already knew the answer to the question I asked. Even so, I turned my head towards her and whispered, "Is he back? Did you find him?"

She cringed and glanced at the door behind her, clearly dismayed that she was the one who had to answer me. Then she looked at me and her lips became pinched at one side of her mouth. Finally, she shook her head, her low pigtails bouncing with the motion.

I turned away from her, staring at the wall. The instant I had come to, I had known my bones were hollow and my heart black. I wanted to return to oblivion. I wanted to return to nothingness and be with him again.

So, I stared at the wall, ignoring Lilly, wanting to close my eyes and drift out of consciousness.

After a long moment, I could feel the mattress give by my legs as the Fatale took a seat on the bed.

"At least you've stopped screaming," she said. "Honestly, if I had to listen to you scream that guy's name one more time, I was going to shove daggers in my ears."

I showed no reaction to her comment, but she continued with her unwelcome rambling.

"And hey, look at you! You're not all crazed and rabid, so that's cool, right? Oh, and hello virility gods, you've got that four-course meal of a man babysitting you out there. I'm honestly planning on going full psycho in the hopes that he'll want to stay with me night and day too."

While I wasn't really listening to Lilly, the fact that she'd said "night and day" hadn't escaped my notice. I guessed I'd been out for a while. And I vaguely wondered why she was still here.

"Why did you not tell me about him sooner, you little vixen? It should be a crime to be that good looking. It's impossible to focus around that man. He speaks and all I can think about is him being all bossy and commanding and rigid while I'm tied to his bed," she said with a thrilled little sigh.

"Luckily, whatever sugar tits has been doing has helped us all after being exposed to those things out there. Because I would be sorely disappointed if I had to die without giving that stallion a ride."

I heard the sound of Lilly's words—the aimless, lighthearted chatter—but they meant nothing to me. I had no use for them. So when she stopped talking, I had nothing to say to her. Nothing to give.

I just wanted her to leave.

But Lilly didn't leave. Instead, she sat there in silence. Simply offering her presence. Finally, though, she gave another little sigh. One born from sincerity. "I wouldn't know what that feels like—to care that much about someone."

I could feel her shift, drawing her legs onto the bed. "You know, our hearts turn to stone. When you're a Fatale, your heart no longer beats once you come into your powers. It just . . . stops one day. I don't know the explanation behind it. I guess it's self-preservation, really.

"I mean, how else could you seduce a man, get close to him, share yourself with him, share your life with him, become a part of his life . . . do it over and over again with male after male . . . all the while lying to him. And then kill him. Each and every time."

For just a moment, Lilly's voice was softer than I would have thought possible. "How could someone with a heart do that?"

"Sure, it's the bad guys we go after," she qualified. "But the longer I live, the more I realize it's not that simple. Everyone's a villain if you look at them from a certain angle. Everyone's a victim. And everyone's a hero. It's not the person that changes. It's the point from which they're viewed.

133

"And some . . . Some of them—when you get to know them—when you start to see things the way they do, well . . . eventually you start to wonder if maybe you're the bad guy."

She paused for a moment, contemplating her own words. Then she released a heavy breath, and I could feel her sink deeper into the mattress.

I thought she was done speaking. I lay there, in the flickering firelight with the deep murmur of low voices drifting down the hall, waiting for her to leave.

But Lilly surprised me. And after another long pause she seemed to come to a conclusion.

"I guess I'm lucky, though," she murmured. I'll never scream someone's name over and over again. I'll never know what it feels like to care that much about someone."

Lilly's voice dropped. And I couldn't help but turn my head to look at her. She stared out the window, and although she spoke in a whisper, her words were clear.

"Pretty fucking lucky."

She sat there, on the bed with me for a while longer. And I couldn't help but stare at her profile. I thought I could see something then, something that I hadn't noticed before, something that the wild partying and danger chasing had hidden.

She was lonely. Empty. She was hollow, too.

I wanted to tell her that she *was* lucky. That it was better to be hollow, than hollow and broken.

But I was only a shell of a person. I could not speak of such things. I lacked any ability to. All that existed inside of me was Darkness. A vast nothing.

I was too hollow and too broken to say anything.

So Lilly sat—with her empty heart—staring into the black night. Then at some point her weight lifted from the mattress, and without a word she left the room.

But the minute she stepped into the dining room, where I could hear the others, Lilly made an announcement. And the confidence in her voice was undeniable.

"Alright, look. I've been thinking about it, and I've come up with a solution for this whole mess we're in. Hear me out."

I could imagine Lilly with her fingertips on the dining table while she leaned in Maxim's direction—black leather molded to her curves—her feathery lashes fringing her smoldering brown eyes.

And then she shared her idea. "I won't call your old lady sugar tits anymore—as long as that's what you start calling me. Whatta ya say, lover? We got a deal?"

Silence.

Finally, a dragon spoke up. "You got it sugar tits."

I couldn't be sure, but I thought I heard something that sounded a lot like the heavy split of an axe lodged in the dining table.

"What the fuck?!" the dragon yelled.

There was a chilling quality to Lilly's tone when she replied, "I wasn't talking to you."

I sent a pulse of energy towards the door, slamming it shut. Blocking the others out. Not interested in the commotion.

But Lilly had proven my point. She solidified the belief I held.

Yes . . . Definitely better to be hollow, than hollow and broken.

CHAPTER 9

I GOT OUT OF THE BED, furious that I'd stayed in it for so long.

The moment I awoke, I should have jumped out of it. I wasn't thinking clearly. My mind was too scrambled. Too hazy. It was difficult to concentrate.

I didn't know what had happened to Zagan. I didn't know if he was alive. *Or dead?* I didn't know if he was somewhere deep in the earth outside or . . . or if he and The Contessa had eventually wisped somewhere.

And the more my mind cleared, the more that I moved away from a sleepy dream-like state to consciousness, the angrier I got.

What was Maxim thinking? How could he sit out there and hold a meeting? He should be out looking for Zagan.

Why wasn't he?

I got out of the bed with a single purpose. I was going to find Zagan. I was going to charge out of the room.

But looking down as I pushed the blankets aside and stood from the bed, I saw myself in a nightgown. And I was unsettled.

Someone had put me in it. Someone had touched me. I was sickened. I didn't want anyone to touch me. To be near me. To look at me. I didn't want anyone to think about me.

My hands squeezed into fists at my sides.

I had to calm down. I had to slow my breathing. Find my center.

I closed my eyes. I breathed in and out several times, focusing on the movement of air, trying to ignore the burning in my throat and lungs. I had to be logical. I had to strip everything away into simple steps.

Step one: Get dressed.

Step two: Clear my suite of anyone who was not going to help me in my search.

Step three: Find Zagan.

Okay. Step one. I would tackle step one. I would turn ninety degrees to the left. Walk along the length of the bed. Turn another ninety degrees to the left. Walk into the bathroom. And with a final turn, I would be in the closet.

Now. I would start the process for step one now.

I would turn away. I would stop facing the windows.

I did not need to walk to the windows. I did not need to look outside. That was not part of step one.

I told my body to move. I told my body to follow the necessary path to accomplish step one.

138

But I couldn't move. I couldn't look away from the wall of windows.

I did not want to look at them. I did not want to cross to them.

There was a sick bubble in the pit of my stomach.

I knew I wouldn't see him out there. Logically, I knew I wouldn't. But for some painful reason, I had to check.

In long, slow steps, my feet carried me to the towering glass. My hands pressed against the pane—the thin crack running between them. My eyes lifted to the last place I'd seen him. Perhaps there would be some sign, some clue.

I saw the dark hole of the tree tunnel. The mangled wrought iron gate. The buffering cliff. The scorched front lawn.

I looked to the split in the earth. My eyes darted to the last place I'd seen him. But the fissure was gone. In its place was a raw seam of blackened rubble.

And while the seam devastated me, while it made me feel like he had been buried out there, it was not what made my skin crawl. The seam in the earth was not what made me hate the skin I was in. The finality of Zagan's disappearance was not what made me want to vomit.

Out there, in the dark, spanning the front lawn and the buffering cliffside—dozens of lifeless, reflective eyes stared back at me. Standing still as statues.

Waiting.

For me.

I pushed myself from the window. I ran into the bathroom. I heaved at the toilet over and over again.

When I vomited black sludge, I realized why I had tried to follow Zagan into that abyss. I hadn't known at the time. But it became clear as I retched.

I had gone after him to save him. Even if it was an unlikely outcome, that had been the purest truth of it.

But there was a second reason—an underlying factor—which had just come into focus.

I had also gone after him because I knew without him I would turn into something . . . I did not want to be.

**

The chattering, the conversations, the arguing, it all died down the moment I stepped into the dining room.

The first thing I did was take in everyone present. It seemed a few members from each faction had stuck around to discuss matters with Maxim: Hellion, another member of the dragon pack, Lilly, three Fatales, Elijah, Giddeon, Cord, and—

"Mom?"

Adriel stood from her seat at the table. The way she looked at me, at my eyes and skin—I could see the hopelessness in her face, the sense of loss. Failure.

I knew what I looked like. I had glimpsed my reflection in the mirror. But seeing the way my mother looked at me . . .

My skin was pale white, my eyelashes and lips incredibly dark, my hair shiny. And the gray crystalline flecks in my eyes made them glitter in the firelight. It did not matter that I was dressed in leather pants, a jacket, and boots. Or that my hair was in a braid.

No amount of discreet clothing was going to hide the way I looked.

And I couldn't stand to be seen. I pretended the others weren't there.

"Mom, what are you doing here?"

"I came to see if I could be of assistance," she replied. "Maxim arrived at Court and explained what happened."

All I could think, standing in front of her, was that she didn't look well. Adriel wasn't getting better. And I believed I understood why.

She had opened herself up, she had expended a massive amount of power. For just a moment, she had turned the night to day. She had chased away the Umbra. And in doing so, an infection had found its way in. The Darkness.

She was sick.

She was slowly dying.

I saw it clearly. It was exactly what Killian had said was happening to our people. The Darkness—the disease—was spreading.

"How bad is it?" I asked. "How many people are sick?"

My mother shook her head. "Do not concern yourself with it now. We are working to save people. We will find a solution."

"Killian?" I asked. If people were in trouble, I had no doubt that he was leading the charge to help.

Adriel glanced at her hands folded in front of her. "He is missing," she said.

I laughed with a note of hysteria. "Of course he is! How stupid of me for asking!"

My mother took a step forward, and she took my hand in hers, giving it a squeeze. "I will find him," she promised.

"Dad?" I asked, not knowing how to place my thoughts about him into words.

Her lips thinned. "The Council has been sequestered. I have not spoken with him."

Before I could ask any more questions, she continued, "Everything will be sorted. It will just take some time."

Then she looked at our joined hands for a moment before turning to Maxim. "There may be something I can do, but I will need to reference certain texts. I will need to return to my study. I should leave right away."

I knew she was talking about me. It was obvious Maxim had collected her in the hopes she could . . . What? Fix me?

Maxim nodded at my mother.

My mother's grip was firm when she turned back to me. "Do not lose hope. It is not yet the end. I will return."

It was wonderful that she was so self-assured and valiant. I hoped it helped in lifting up her and those around her. It was how a leader should be.

But I found it sickeningly trite. I gave an unconvinced nod and pulled my hand back from hers. Then I vaguely glanced in Maxim's direction as I turned to leave the room. "Before you take her back, get everyone out of here," I said. "Then we're going to find him."

I didn't care if they were all banding together to form some rag-tag team that would steal back the stone. I didn't care if Maxim had forged some kind of impossible truce with the

Archangels. They could hold their clubhouse meetings somewhere else.

I needed to prepare. I started straight for my room. I would gather weapons and make a list of items we might need.

But Maxim's voice sounded at my back and his words stopped me in my tracks. "They are waiting for you to allow them passage."

I didn't understand at first. But then I stiffened. When I realized what he meant, I felt as though I'd been punched in the gut. I wanted to vomit again.

Maxim could wisp Adriel back to the Radiant Court, but I hadn't considered the fact that the Angela could not pulse in the Shadow territory. They had to leave on foot. As did the Fatales. Even the dragons would need to venture onto the manor grounds to shift.

And the Umbra waited outside.

Still, I did not spin around at his words. I did not show any reaction. And after the brief halt in my steps, I found my footing once more and continued on to my room, choosing not to address Maxim's comment.

Once I passed the towering windows, I growled a single word into the night.

"Leave!"

The haunting figures, with their black robes fluttering in the cold air, dissipated across the manor grounds becoming nothing more than lingering funnels of inky smoke.

I yanked the curtains shut, nearly ripping them. Then I began to rummage aimlessly through the room, trying to decide what I would need and where I would start.

I knew Maxim was my best hope. He could wisp, and he was incredibly knowledgeable. He seemed to know everything.

He mentioned once that his mother was a scribe for the Shadow Court. I knew he was well versed on their legends and history. He would probably have some ideas as to how we should begin.

Then I glanced at the draped windows. And I had a thought that frightened me, a thought that made my skin cold. But all options would need to be exhausted. There was nothing I wasn't willing to do.

Perhaps the Umbra would know—

I felt the hot energy, the connection, the pull. In spite of the immense Darkness I held, in spite of how incredibly powerful it had become, there was still Light. And it flared to life the instant Elijah walked into the room.

I turned around to see him standing there.

I wanted him to get the hell out.

His very presence was a violation. The impudence of it . . .

I barely stopped myself from ripping free the dagger strapped to my thigh and hurling it at him. But, somehow, I managed to hang on to my self-control.

I did not send a dagger into his heart. Instead, I crossed my arms, silently waiting for whatever derisive comment he was about to throw at me.

The gold flecks in his eyes sparked as he looked at me. Yet his voice was not harsh and demanding when he spoke. And I was caught off guard at his quiet, easy tone.

"It doesn't have to be like this, Violet."

I didn't say anything in reply, I kept my lips pressed together while I looked at him.

He took a step towards me, and he rubbed his hand over his broad chest. "You don't have to do all this," he continued. "Come with me."

He took another affable step, drawing closer. "This isn't you. This, all of this, is for someone else. Not you."

My eyes darted over my shoulder. I glanced at the shuttered windows for just a moment, imagining the raw seam of rubble.

I met Elijah's burning gaze. "This is exactly where I need to be," I told him, my voice steeled with conviction.

Elijah looked sickened. "You think he's coming back, don't you?" He shook his head then, as if he felt sorry for me. "Come on, princess. He made his choice. And it wasn't you." He began to look disgusted. "And now you're going to pay for it."

I hated how his words immediately destroyed me. Flayed me. Shredded me. Eviscerated me. My breath was punched from my lungs.

"Get out," I told him, gasping for air.

Elijah closed the distance between us and grabbed my arms. His voice turned guttural. "I had the same fucking choice. Do you realize that? I had the choice between revenge and you. And I chose you! I'm here! I'm standing right in front of you. Where the fuck is he?"

He gave me a shake. "Over and over again, I have chosen you—above all else. Don't you see? There is nothing I wouldn't do to have you. And to keep you."

He took my hands and placed them on his chest, holding them there. "I'm right here."

145

Then he searched my eyes—my crystalline eyes. I could see the pain on his face as he murmured, "And, Violet, you need me."

I . . . my chest . . . my breath . . . my lungs . . . I just couldn't. His words were so big, so weighted, so consuming. They held such a searing implication.

They crushed me. My bones were not strong enough to hold me up under the pressure of them. I was going to sink to the floor.

But there are many times in life when we believe we will do something. Yet we do not.

I *believed* I would collapse.

But I did not.

I didn't find myself pooling at his feet nor did I find myself falling into his arms. I was not defeated. Not entirely. Not yet.

And although it took a minute, although I had to find some fortitude, some sheer grit, I silently shook my head.

It wasn't Elijah. It could never be Elijah.

I looked up at him. He stood there, without pity, staring down at me. There was no mercy, he would not grant me reprieve. Even still. Even now. He was going to fight for me.

So I did what I had to do. Because I was strong. Because I was the hero of my story.

I said goodbye to Elijah.

"I am not the one for you," I told him. "And nothing will ever change that. No matter what you do, no matter how many times you choose me . . . I am not yours."

He inhaled sharply, about to object, but I cut him off. "This is goodbye, Elijah. It has to be."

His muscles tensed, and I could feel his intention. He was about to pick me up—kicking and screaming—and drag me out of this place. He would fight anyone that came after us, and as soon as he was able, he would pulse away with me.

"Wait," I told him. "There is something I want to give you. Something you need to know."

I looked back and forth between his eyes, desperately trying to find the right words. "The girl—when you were a child—the other Prism . . ."

I twisted free of Elijah, taking a small step back. "It was my mother, who came and drove the Shadows away, wasn't it? And she was too late. Although she arrived in time to save you, it was too late for your family."

I could see Elijah was caught off guard by my words, and the muscle in his jaw ticked as he looked at me in confusion. "It was a long time ago," he said. "So what?"

"Elijah, do you know why she didn't get to you in time? To help your family?"

He gave his head a slow shake.

"It was because of the girl—the other Prism. Adriel took her and hid her somewhere safe. Somewhere from which it is difficult to return. She's out there somewhere. Adriel will be able to tell you where. She has been trying to protect Prisms, from the very start. She's been hiding them from the Shadows and staging their deaths."

Elijah's eyes narrowed and he searched my face, uncertain what he should do with this information. Then he parted his lips. Wary. About to question what I was telling him.

147

I held my hand out. "There is someone you should be pursuing to the ends of the earth. But it's not me, Elijah . . . it was never me."

He looked at me and squinted, as if he couldn't quite focus on me. But I knew he could feel the veracity of my words. We still shared a connection. And he could not deny the truth that settled between us.

"Talk to Adriel," I told him. "Ask her. She will tell you what happened that night. Please, just talk to her before you make any more decisions."

Elijah stared at me. Considering it all. After a long moment, he swallowed and asked, "You're really staying here?"

I nodded.

And he did as well. The golden flecks in his irises were still bright. But they no longer blazed. A single revelation—at least the possibility of one—had changed everything.

I pressed on. I did not want to dwell on all that had happened. It was too suffocating.

"You can't return with the Archangels," I told him. "It's not safe."

He gave another slow nod—not entirely convinced of my allegations against the Council of Elders, but no longer quick to dismiss them.

Then Elijah glanced at the bedroom door, and finally, he spoke. "You and Cord have Giddeon worried. He's considering the things you both said."

"He should be," I replied in all seriousness. "What is he going to do?"

Elijah shrugged his big shoulders. "He's trying to figure out the next steps. But . . . we were in Aleece. Together. If the Council wanted us dead, they had a perfect opportunity. Why didn't they take it?"

"They wanted to keep our deaths a secret from the Archangels," I replied. "Sentencing me to return to the Dark Court was the perfect excuse. Maybe you would have come with me, and we would have been killed here at the hands of a Shadow contracted by them. Our deaths would be blamed on the Dark Court. And when we defied the order, they had a second chance. They sentenced me to death as a penalty."

I shook my head, staring up at him. "I'm telling you, Elijah, the only reason you were not killed was because you were useful. They probably believed that you could find me, and you could lure me out. You were bait."

Elijah reached up to rub the back of his neck, and I knew my words were sinking in. I knew I was convincing him. I hoped he would decide to believe me fully.

I glanced at the door, knowing we had come to the end.

Elijah tracked the movement of my eyes. His jaw clenched as he began to shake his head, and he let out a heavy breath as he rubbed his chest once more.

"Violet." He growled my name.

I shook my head, and my voice was quiet. "There's nothing left to say, Elijah."

He released another aggravated breath.

He gave me one last, long look. Then with undeniable determination, he ripped his eyes from mine, and he turned to leave.

But before Elijah left, before he walked away from me, he rumbled one final parting.

"Good luck, princess."

And as he exited the room, as he took all that hot burning energy with him, the fire in the hearth sizzled . . . before extinguishing all together.

CHAPTER 10

I KNEW EVERYONE LEFT. I could feel how the emptiness flowed back into my quarters, filling the space. With the reassurance that I would not have to face another soul, I ventured to the dining room, and I took a seat.

The fire burned in the hearth—black edges with a red center.

I didn't care. It didn't matter. It was not my concern.

I sat in the empty, dark room, and I ran my fingers over the split in the table where Lilly's axe had been.

I didn't have to wait long.

I felt the shadows shift and sway. Felt the power of him. Maxim stepped out of the Darkness along the periphery of the room, into the dim red glow of the firelight. He stood across from me on the other side of the table, and his rich voice rumbled through the space between us.

"Everything now hangs in your hands, Violet."

I met Maxim's gaze with nothing to give. I shook my head. "I don't know what that means, and I don't care. The only thing I want to hear from you right now is an explanation of what happened to Zagan and where I can find him."

"You need to understand the severity of the situation at hand," Maxim pressed.

I was unable to work my jaw at that. I had to speak through clenched teeth. "You think I don't understand the severity of what has happened? I was out there. I watched what happened. Right before my eyes. Unable to stop it."

I leaned in my chair until my torso was pressed against the dining table, my arms outstretched in front of me. I was just short of climbing over the furniture to get to Maxim in my desperation when I said, "What was that, Maxim? What happened to him? Is he alive somewhere? Did they go somewhere? Are they literally buried in the earth out there?"

My breathing was short and fast. "Where is he?!"

Maxim shook his head. "I do not know."

"Is he alive?!" I demanded.

"I do not know," Maxim repeated.

"I have to find him," I said. "I need to find out. You have to help me."

"I do want to find him." Maxim assured, his voice soothing and strong. "I vow to you; I will do whatever I can."

My hands shook as I placed my head in them, trying to think, grateful and surprised by Maxim's immediate willingness. "Alright, what do we do first? What will I need—"

"Before we are able to begin," Maxim continued, his voice rising above my own, "there are a few imperative details which we must address."

My hands dropped to the table and my head snapped up. "What? No! We need to go now!"

"Violet!" The urgency in the way he spoke my name made me feel as though I were hysterical, and my shoulders drew back.

He took me in, eyeing my fingernails. My face. My eyes. My hair. "You cannot ignore what has happened to you," he insisted.

I stood, and my chair went tumbling behind me. "I wouldn't be like this if it weren't for you! Why did you hold me back? You should have let me go! You should have gone after him with me. You should have helped!"

Maxim shook his head. "It would not have done any good for both of us to go down with her. Someone around here needs to think of others before himself. If that leaves me, so be it. I told him repeatedly that his crazed obsession with you would be his downfall."

"And that old bat!" I continued over Maxim, unimpressed with his excuse. "What was she doing out there?! Why did she put up that wall? Was she trying to keep The Contessa out? Keep Zagan from leaving? Was she trying to stop me? What was the point of that?!"

Maxim turned silent. He offered no elucidation. No emotion.

And I stood there staring at him. Desperately wanting answers. Wanting Zagan back. Wanting to feel better. Wanting to feel anything but what I was feeling.

I needed a plan. I needed something to work towards. My chest was heaving uncontrollably at the lack of immediate action.

Yet Maxim stood there quiet and blank.

I could see it then. In an instant, I could see what he was doing. He was shutting down. He was going to let me rant and rave. And he would wait as long as he had to, until I no longer had anything to say.

My control was slipping. I could see that. I turned my focus inward. I forced myself to take deep, slow breaths. And I quickly assessed my situation.

I needed to find Zagan. I needed Maxim's help to do so. He wanted to address "imperative details" before we acted. So I needed to make him feel his checklist was met.

I opened my eyes. I picked up my chair. I sat at the dining table. And I folded my hands in front of me.

"What do we need to do?" I asked Maxim.

Maxim took the seat across from me.

"With The Contessa's disappearance, it seems the Umbra have turned their allegiance to you. Her absence paired with the Umbra's loyalty is a temporary advantage. We must act swiftly. You must appear before the Shadow Court and solidify your place as the new ruler."

I couldn't focus on him. I couldn't really listen to his words. Not in their entirety. All I could think about was whether we would need to begin digging at the craggy seam out front. He said something about going to the Shadow Court.

"Okay, fine. Let's go," I said, desperate to get the bogus conditions out of the way.

Maxim held up a hand. "It is not as simple as that. I will call a meeting for tomorrow evening."

I tried not to scream. I couldn't wait until tomorrow evening. Too much time was passing.

"It will not be simple," Maxim repeated. "But we must act swiftly before the Court carries out their plan of attack against the Shadow people. And we will need to navigate this precisely.

"I will announce the death of The Contessa. I will provide the Umbra's allegiance to you as evidence. I will also announce the loss of the Shadow Prince. I will specify that by law, you are the new ruler of the Shadow Court."

Wait. What? What was he saying? He couldn't mean . . .

I started to actually listen to Maxim. And I began to realize just how frigid it was in the room.

Maxim's eyes ticked around the table as if he were assessing a chessboard, predicting every move left in the game. "This appointment will be met with backlash. There are members of the Court who will question your legitimacy. Worse, those who are rabid for power will make their move for dominance.

"Most notably, Marax will not accept you. He has served The Contessa well. And she has rewarded him throughout the years. He will undoubtedly covet your new role.

"During his time beneath The Contessa, he has come to hold some sway, some influence, over the Umbra. He very well may try to turn them against you.

"Therefore, your safety will be in question. There will be some who have the thought to immediately see to your demise, then and there. There will be others who argue you cannot act upon this position alone and insist you wed a Court member. They will most likely vote to make it law."

Maxim paused for a moment then, and his shoulders heaved as if struggling with a large weight. He leaned forward in his chair and his lips were thinned when he spoke next. His voice slowed, dropping in volume. And as he stared at me, he made sure to cushion each of his words.

"You will need to announce your engagement to me. It is the best way to ensure both your safety and legitimacy. Those who would defy you, those who would make an attempt to either destroy you or force your hand to wed, will be dissuaded.

"If you have me—along with the Umbra—at your side, you will have your best chance at successfully taking the Court."

Maxim drew back, seeming confident in the outcome. "With The Contessa gone and the Court captured, the Shadow people will be safe. The only obstacle left will be the imprisonment of the Umbra."

And with his last words, Maxim let out a breath, some of the burden easing from his shoulders. For a moment, the room was silent. Not even the slithering, dark fire made a sound.

I leaned back in my chair and folded my arms across my chest. I tilted my head. I stared at Maxim.

And there he sat. In the Dark Manor. The original seat of the Shadow Court. The ancient, forgotten home of the king.

Maxim was framed by the large hearth behind him. And as I stared at him, at his broad build and dark, handsome features, that silent fire undulated behind him—black, inky flames with crimson centers.

And there I sat across from him. With my shining hair and crystalline eyes. I, who now controlled the Umbra—the ancient evil.

Maxim continued to meet my gaze, waiting for me to speak. I didn't rush. I took my time, taking in all we had become.

Finally, I said, "Funny how this has all worked out for you, Maxim."

He held my eye, not responding.

I glanced at his chest. "You've even got the brand, all ready to go. It wasn't enough by itself, was it? They could have cut it off or burned it. That's what you told me once, remember? You couldn't become king with the mark, alone. But now you have me. Zagan is gone. The Contessa is gone. All the obstacles are falling away. You just need to get past the Court. And once you do, you'll finally have what you want."

I leaned forward and rasped two words.

"The crown."

Maxim's lips thinned and his nostrils flared. His chest expanded, the muscles there straining against his crisp shirt. He rose from his seat then, pressing his hands on the table, leaning across the dark wood towards me. His deep voice was low and the shadows in the room climbed the walls.

His eyes narrowed on me. "I could say the same for you. Why not look at yourself? Here you sit, the *Shadow Princess*. There is no prince, no Contessa, to stand in your way. And you now rule the Umbra.

"Convenient that you gave back the stone, is it not? I could theorize the worst of you. I could assume that you are somehow working with Marax. Perhaps that night you spoke of, when you encountered him, perhaps that was when he got to you. Perhaps the two of you have set a plan in motion.

"Then again, perhaps not. Perhaps this is your doing and yours alone. A brilliant work of seduction and deception. One you formed the moment you arrived at the Dark Manor.

"Yes, I could think the worst of you, Violet. I do not know your true heart. No one does. But I choose not to. I choose to believe that you want what you think is best. Not only for yourself, but for others. I choose to believe that you speak out of ignorance. Out of pain and anger.

"Tell me, why did you give the stone to the god of death? Was it in the hopes of ruling the Umbra?"

"No!" I cried, horrified by the accusation. "How could you suggest such a thing?"

"Then why?" Maxim demanded, his voice growing in volume with each word. "That was where the two of you were. When you went missing those nights. Wasn't it? You knew how vital the stone was. How much I needed it."

Maxim's voice rose to a crescendo, his words thundering through the room. "I have done everything for you! Why would you betray me so?"

I stood then, square with Maxim across the table. "I did what I thought was best. The god of death himself told me I would learn how to defeat The Contessa if I returned the stone. When I realized who she was—that she was an Original—of the Dark Half no less—I knew I had no choice. We needed that information. And I believed that Zagan would be able to imprison the Umbra. I made what I thought was the right call."

Maxim's eyes narrowed. "As have I. Repeatedly, I have made the best choice with what was available to me. What must I do to prove myself to you, Violet?"

I stared back at him, my jaw clenched so tightly I thought I would break my teeth. The rage I felt towards him at that moment . . . because I didn't know.

The disappointment in Maxim's eyes was obvious. "Perhaps you cannot trust me. Perhaps you never can. But these are our circumstances. Your very council is after you. Your people are ill. My people have been forgotten—on the verge of decimation. The Umbra walk the night. We have no stone. And without a present leader, the Shadow Court will fall to Marax in a matter of days."

"I care enough to set these wrongs right." He paused and looked at me with genuine uncertainty. "Do you?"

After a long moment, I spoke my truth. It was difficult to admit, but it was honest. "I don't care about any of it. All I care about is finding him."

Maxim gave a solemn nod. "I vow to aid you in that endeavor as soon as we have established stability. But, Violet . . . he made his choice. He knew what he was doing. I cannot sacrifice the many for one."

After a pause, the hard line of Maxim's mouth softened as he spoke his next words. "I have no doubt he will make his way back to you. You are something a man would cling to life for."

He searched my face then, looking for something. "In the meantime, do what you know is right."

There are different skins to sorrow and pain. Different dimensions to it. When everything inside is black and hollow, you do not need to wallow and pray. Those are the actions of someone who is raw and wounded and bleeding.

When you are empty, when you are a shell of the person you once were, you can walk around and do as commanded, do what is expected of you, because none of it really matters.

I stood up. And I left.

But just before I took my leave, I looked at Maxim. I felt the reprehension as it bubbled in my chest and filled my mouth. And that reprehension, that rancor, slithered through the quiet, dark room on a breath of air. "Whatever you say . . . *darling*."

CHAPTER 11

I WALKED DOWN THE ABANDONED WING—*the dark, decrepit corridor. Rotting floor at my feet, crumbling walls to my sides. The despair. The desolation. The frigid, dank air.*

And haunting notes, low and slow, drifted past me.

I walked down the hall, and I saw a beautiful girl. She was lovely. An innocent vision.

There was no Darkness in her, only Light. Even in the shadows of the hall, her skin had a certain glow to it. She could have been an angel.

And as she stood there, she could not understand the depths of the solitary notes that floated through the air around her—chilling her bones. Because she had never known misery. She had never been lost and forgotten. She had only truly known Light and warmth.

But she did not need to understand the ghostly notes to become awash in their dolor. So there she stood. Frozen. A lovely statue.

It was a difficult scene to witness. And my eyes drifted from the fragile girl, no longer able to watch her. It was too much to know what lay on the other side of the door.

As my gaze shifted, I saw him there—just beyond her—another shadow in the hall.

The way he looked at her—with such awe and longing—made my chest ache. He began to lift his hand. Yet, he did not reach out to her. Instead, when he raised his hand, he reached for the door that was ajar just in front of the lovely girl.

And he began to close it.

On a sharp inhale, I realized what he was doing. I realized he was going to shut her out. He was going to prevent her from entering the room. He was going to stop any of it from ever happening.

He wanted to make it as though we had never been.

"No!" I cried.

He looked at me with those electric blue eyes. "It's better this way," he said, his voice drifting through the shadows.

I stumbled forward. I knew I had to reach the door before it shut. I knew I could not let the door close. She had to go in. She had to find him.

I stretched my hand out, and just before he could seal the entry to the room, I forced my palm against the old rotted wood, preventing the door from shutting.

At the clap of my palm against the wood, a single tear fell from the girl's eye, slipping down her cheek. And she seemed to take a breath for the first time. She was no longer a statue. She pushed the door open, and she entered the room.

We stood in the hall looking at each other.

"You never should have gone in," he said.

"You never should have left," I countered.

I reached my hand out. He looked at it and paused. Then he lifted his own. He stared down at his hand as if it were not good enough to extend. I tried to reach for him anyway. And I clasped my small, delicate hand around his. I felt it for a moment. I swear I felt it for a moment. It was so large around my own. So strong, and somehow, at the same time, so graceful.

But there was nothing in my hand. Not truly. I looked down at my palm, and all I found were shadows.

He was gone.

***

It was not a dream. It could not be a dream. Because I did not sleep.

I drifted where I sat, but I did not sleep. And I continued to sit, unmoving, at the foot of my bed just as I had throughout the entire day.

The room was dark. The heavy curtains drawn, blocking out the sunlight. I did not lie down.

I didn't move from my spot. The entire day, I sat in the dark room and waited. As each second of time ticked by, I sat and waited.

I was numb. I had to be. Otherwise, I would drive myself to the brink of insanity. I would peer over the edge, peeking at the abyss, and I would throw myself into that infinite black pit. Never to return.

I knew I could not find him on my own. I knew I needed Maxim.

So I sat very still. And I waited. And I drifted.

But after peering into my hand, after opening my eyes, I was no longer with him, no longer able to reach him.

So I sat at the foot of the bed. My hands folded in my lap. The curtains drawn. And I waited for nightfall.

Then the waiting turned into doing. Because at some point, I sensed a presence. At a certain point, I was no longer alone.

In response, my body stood and carried me out of the room. I walked down the hall and through the suite. I walked to the dining room. And I found a large box surrounded by several smaller ones sitting on the table. Without emotion, I gathered them in my arms and took them to my room.

I knew what was expected of me. I placed the items on my body without an opinion of them. And in a short matter of time, I was done.

***

The dress I wore was black.

The velvet bodice had a slim, deep plunge directly down the center that stretched to the high waisted skirt. The sleeves were lace with embroidered rose applique, and a row of delicate buttons traveled from my wrists to my elbows.

The fabric at the skirt was the same lace. It wrapped around my hips and thighs, flaring at my knees with layers of sheer black chiffon. And all that material pooled at my feet and trailed behind me in an excess of gossamer darkness.

Around my neck was an elaborate jewelry piece which covered the entire length of my throat. Filaments of gold stretched from my clavicle to just under my chin in a structured collar. And beaded throughout the gold strands were rare black pearls. The dark gems also lined the base and top of the collar. From the back of the piece, threads hung down my shoulders and across the open back of my dress, beaded with even more dark pearls.

I cared neither for the dramatic dress nor the detailed neck piece. Instead, I looked down at my hand. At the black luminescent diamond on my finger. The one I never took off.

I closed my fist around it. I could feel my nails dig into my palm. I welcomed the sting of pain, knowing I deserved it.

I looked into the mirror. I saw the cold reflection staring back at me. The dress. The jewels.

I was Dark. Exquisite. A haunting vision.

My hair was pinned atop my head. The strands shining in the firelight. I did not bother with makeup. My lashes were too black. My lips, too plum. My skin, too pale.

And my eyes . . . well, there was nothing to be done about the way they glittered and refracted the light.

I knew Maxim had left the items. And I knew I was to wear them.

I would do as instructed. I would put on whatever little show Maxim required of me. And I would expect my payment in return.

I walked through the bedroom straight for the window. I threw back the curtain, knowing night had fallen. I stood next to the towering glass and gazed out at the tall gaunt figures littering the grounds—robes flitting in the wind.

Waiting.

I would give Maxim one chance. I would play my part in our exchange. And if he failed me, if he did not follow through with

167

his end of the bargain, if he crossed me—if somehow his people or his morals or his sense of nobility hindered him from helping me find Zagan—I knew who I would turn to.

And I knew very well, the moment I did, there would be no going back.

I looked at them out there. Waiting. Just for me.

I would turn away this time. But I would be back if I needed them.

I let go of the curtain, and it fell into place blocking out the night. I turned and walked down the dark hallway. I let my fingertips brush along the cold wall as little tendrils of inky smoke curled at the contact. And step by step, I made my way to the sitting room, where I knew Maxim waited.

I found him pacing. He stopped when I entered and turned to look at me. I could see he approved.

He held out a black velvet cape that had been draped over his arm. I walked up to him and gave him my back, allowing him to place the garment over my shoulders.

In another life, I would have noticed how regal Maxim looked. I would have appreciated his dark suit. How it fit him perfectly. How impeccable he was. I would have admired the sturdy wool cloak he donned.

In another life.

Dashing, tall, strong, and powerful, Maxim held his arm out. And in what I knew was a traitorous act . . .

I took it.

In a wisp of shadow and smoke, we left the Dark Manor. And the next breath I took was one of crisp, cold air.

I blinked. A wintery scene lay before us.

Snow blanketed the hill where we stood, drifting in plump flakes from the night sky. And I stared at castle ruins, crowned with a silvery moon. All that remained, of what was surely a once grand fortress, were crumbling walls.

My breath hitched at what I saw through the thick veil of falling snow. I had been to this place once before. The Contessa had brought me. Trussing me up against one of the walls.

And *he* had come for me.

We stood at the stone arch—the entry to the bailey—the very one Zagan had passed beneath. I was reliving it all. The way he had looked at me. How he defied The Contessa. How he held me and wisped me back to the manor.

I had fought him that night. And in doing so I had torn down some walls. That was the night I began to see him for who he truly was.

I remembered it all. *Feeling* it all.

It was enough to drive a woman mad.

Although I kept my chin from wavering, I knew my eyes became wet.

Maxim looked down at me. "Don't," he warned. "This is neither the time nor the place for emotion."

I turned my head from him, suddenly not willing to help with any of it. Suddenly wanting to return to the manor.

Maxim's voice was low as he leaned into me, and I could see his warm breath on the frigid air. "You think this is a betrayal." He was not asking; he was stating a fact.

"You think this is cowardly and weak. Yet the true betrayal, the true weakness, lies in putting yourself first. This is for the good of the many not the few. If you possess even a hint of the

169

strength I believe you are capable of, you will do this now. You will do this to make things right. To fight for what is right."

Maxim grabbed my chin, turning my head, forcing me to look at him. And he began to search my eyes. "You will lock this away. Now. Or you will be the death of us all."

He pinched my chin harder, staring at me, daring me to turn from him, to push back.

I closed my eyes. I drew in a breath. I took a hold of anything I cared for, and I tucked it all away—somewhere deep, where no one else could ever reach any of it. I left it all there. And when I opened my eyes again, I met Maxim's cold hard stare with a frozen lifelessness of my own.

With the firm set of his lips and the dark slash of his brow, Maxim appeared as callous as I'd ever seen him. He gave a single nod and released my chin. Then he threaded my arm through his, and we turned away from the ruins.

Below us, surrounding the hill we occupied, was a forest. The trees were bare, the white bark of their slender trunks and branches stark. And each and every one was coated with a sheen of ice which caught and reflected winks of moonlight.

I stood with Maxim at the onset of a path. It had been cleared through the snow, winding from the castle down to the forest below, disappearing into its depths.

Without a word, Maxim began pulling me forward. And once we traversed down the hill and reached the tree line, Maxim did not stop. Without pause, without hesitation, with the snow falling down upon us and the white, bare trees shimmering, Maxim pulled me into the dark forest.

All was still and quiet.

Yet, as we walked, weaving our way through the birch trees, I began to sense a cold presence at my back. I stopped. I knew that feeling. I had come to know it well. And I felt a strong connection. A deep, Dark power.

I turned to find the Umbra trailing behind us, two by two.

Maxim tugged on my arm, dragging me forward. "Let them follow," he uttered. "And say nothing before the Council. I speak for you."

While traipsing obediently alongside Maxim, I couldn't shake the chill that crept from behind. I glanced over my shoulder again, questioning if the ancient evil truly served me now.

The impact of what that might mean began to hit me.

And if, in fact, they did respond to my wishes, then why go through all this? Why bother with it? If I controlled the Umbra, no one could stop me. Not Marax. Not Maxim. Not the entire Shadow Court. Why try and win the Court members over? It was a waste of time.

But I had slipped. My thoughts had grown and consumed me. And I knew Maxim had picked up on the aggressive air because he began to shake his head.

"You are too quick to violence. That has always been your problem. You do not understand that it should be avoided at all costs. You do not understand the scars it leaves, the scars you carry from it. Matters can be solved without such damage to one's soul."

Maxim's voice dropped and I could hear the foreboding in his tone. "And if you use the Umbra against others to bend them to your will, you are no better than The Contessa herself."

At Maxim's words, I felt an uncomfortable heat over the skin on my chest, something akin to shame. And I was angered at him for making me feel such discomfort. For making me feel emotion when I believed I was numb.

I tried to pull away from him, but he held on to my arm, securing it in his grip. "We are almost there," he murmured. "Be certain not to speak."

I could see the path widening ahead. And just then, an animal crossed in front of us. One unlike any I'd ever seen before.

It was a black stag with incredibly tall ivory antlers. And nestled throughout the branching ivory—crowning the buck— were a multitude of burning candles. The slithering black flames glowed with a red center that flickered across its sleek, sable hide.

The stag stopped and turned its fantastically adorned head to look at us. When it spied the Umbra at our backs, the beast dashed away.

Maxim did not pause or slow at the sight of the animal. He continued forward with an incredible determination, with confidence. And finally, we reached the end of the path.

We emerged through the trees to a clearing in the woods. While the snow did not fall in the glade, there was a blanket of pristine powder at our feet.

The space was open to the sky above, and a soft glow of moonlight glinted across the frozen ground. Here too, the leafless trees were coated with a fringe of ice.

I couldn't stop my gaze from darting up. Dotted throughout the barren, glass-like branches sat crows. Their sharp beady eyes seemed to study all the beings gathered. And more dark candles were scattered throughout the tree limbs causing their jet-black feathers to shine.

A long, jagged table made from stone was set in the middle of the clearing. And a lavish winter's feast had been spread over every inch of the dining surface with polished silver and sparkling crystal. Beyond the clearing, bears and deer paced throughout the forest. All with black fur. And the antlers of each stag were embellished with more dark candles.

As I stepped into the space with Maxim, the Umbra filed in behind us. At that, the gathered animals scattered. Bits of ice rained from the surrounding trees as the crows took flight.

And the men—all men—who were seated and feasting at the grand table, turned at the interruption. There were a dozen of them. They wore finely tailored suits and dark woolen cloaks. Expensive watches and cufflinks flashed at their wrists. They were neat, refined men. Attractive and tidily groomed.

Instantly, every eye fell to me, and then to the Umbra at my back. Finally, the men took in Maxim.

I could see an array of envy, admiration, and animosity directed at him. But regardless of the opinions any held, all clearly sensed the magnitude of his power.

The conversations were abandoned as the Court members dabbed their hands and mouths with the linen from their laps and immediately rose to their feet.

The member closest to us stepped forward. "Master Steele," he greeted in surprise. "When you did not arrive at dusk or thereafter, we believed you were no longer attending this evening." His eyes drifted to me and the Umbra at my back. "Our apologies," he offered.

But Maxim did not seem to care for any sort of formal greeting or polite introduction. And he did not allow time for speculation and conjecture. He took command of the space. And his words rang out causing the very air to vibrate around us.

"The Contessa and the prince are dead."

There was no deafening shatter from beneath my ribs. I did not become lightheaded. And I was not doubled over. Maxim's words did not affect me. Because I had locked away all that I cared about. I was not full of sensitive tissues and organs. All of that had been cut out. I was merely an empty shell. There was nothing within to break.

"The Shadow Princess is our new leader," Maxim announced.

There was a brief moment of silence. Confusion. Then the Court members began to glance at each other, clearly confounded over the abruptness of Maxim's announcement. Finally, several members began speaking at once.

However, the same member who had greeted us, Barrister Corbett, took another step forward, his voice rising above the others.

I knew his name because I had recognized him. He was the one who had visited the Radiant Court. He was the one who had presented The Contessa's proposal. He was the one who had started it all.

Everything that had happened—he had been the one to lay it all at my feet.

"Master Steele," he tried, "perhaps you would like to sit down for a moment." He gestured to the table. "We are honored that you have finally brought the princess for an introduction. I do believe it would be courteous for us to focus on welcoming her."

174

Then he lowered his chin, looking up at Maxim from beneath his brows. "And we can speak of any private matters which need attending, at a more appropriate time, back at our offices."

It was obvious the Barrister was attempting to diffuse the situation.

"There is no need," Maxim countered.

I felt something crawling across my skin then—the weight of an insidious gaze. And from the corner of my vision, I spotted Marax. There was no denying the immediate calculation in his eyes.

He stepped forward. "What is this?" he demanded. The contempt he held for Maxim was clear across his face. "You cannot simply walk into a Court gathering and make such claims." And although he was speaking to Maxim, he did not tear his gaze from me.

Yet Maxim continued as if he had not heard Marax. "She inherits this role from her matrimony with the Shadow Prince. Furthermore, she wields the power of the Umbra. Their loyalty now lies with her."

Then Maxim took a moment to look around the clearing, meeting each member of the Court solidly in the eye. "And I speak on her behalf."

Barrister Corbet tried again to politely shut Maxim up, but Maxim raised his voice, unimpeded. "The Shadow Court, as you know it, is no more. This parliament was never meant to take the place of the monarchy. The king's heir was found. He was wed. He has died. The Contessa was never a legitimate leader. Regardless, she is gone. Before you now stands the true queen of the Shadows. You will pledge your fealty to her or face treason."

"This is a coup," Marax accused, his gaze swinging wildly from me to the Umbra to Maxim. "We don't know who this girl is. And there is no proof as to the demise of The Contessa. You should be held in contempt and stripped of your title for such a crime."

Marax glanced around at the group of Court members. "Convenient that we do not have a Master-at-Arms to take you into custody, seeing that he is you!"

Maxim threw the cloak from my shoulders, snaking his arm around my back and along my rib cage. He shoved his hand against my breast, groping me over my dress. His fingers dug into the velvet where it met my skin, pushing the fabric just a few inches to the side. The mound of flesh swelled at my chest.

"She is the consummated bride of the Shadow Prince."

All eyes landed on the silvery outline of the three crescent moons. The faint symbol, the one that had formed above my heart, came to life, glimmering in the moonlight.

Maxim released his grip on me. "There is your proof. She bears the mark." He turned to his other side, gesturing behind him. "And before you stand the Umbra. The king's guard. They serve her now. There, too, is your proof. There is no one above her. The Contessa is no more."

"We cannot say that for a fact!" Marax retorted. "The Contessa comes and goes as she pleases. She may return."

"It matters not," Maxim scoffed. "The Contessa is nothing but a title." He gestured to me. "See the truth before you. And know it."

The psychotic gleam in Marax's eyes intensified. He began to splutter, spittle flying from his lips. "Still . . . still . . . She cannot be crowned! If the prince has perished as you say, she is unwed—"

"We are to be married," Maxim announced, his voice booming through the clearing.

A hush fell over the forest. The murmurs, the dissent, the scheming, it all died. Barrister Corbett's mouth hung open. Maxim glared, daring anyone to object.

Finally, Marax broke the silence. "And now it all becomes clear, *Master Steele*," he sneered. "You have not come to announce that she is our new monarch. You have come to announce that you are! What did you do to The Contessa?"

I gazed ahead. Emotionless. I looked at no one. I cared not for their pathetic quibbling. I cared for none of it.

However, another voice spoke up. Barrister Corbett seemed to have regained his footing. "Maxim, you must admit, this is not the best way to go about such an announcement." He was attempting to keep his tone reasonable. "We have certain standards of etiquette and decorum which we follow. Wouldn't you agree such claims would be better suited for an actual Court meeting rather than this dinner you've arranged? We must go through the proper motions. We must have all the facts presented and investigated."

Maxim was not deterred. "Call your meeting. Hold your investigations. Do as you wish. It will not change the facts. Cling to your etiquette and decorum."

Maxim's chest expanded with his next words. "But know this: no further actions shall be carried out in the name of the Shadow Court. All orders are ceased while your new queen is considered for her coronation. This includes force against the Shadow villages. You are not to implement any action unless it is at her discretion, else face punishment by death."

Maxim looked around the clearing again, and I noticed the shadows in the trees stretch and sway. Then he held his arm out for me. "We take our leave," he finally announced.

As we turned to go, Marax called out, "Then seal your arrangement before the sitting members of the Shadow Court."

I stopped and stared at him. He was assessing me. He had been the entire time.

"Kiss your bride to be," he hissed. "Prove your intention."

"Show respect for your new queen," Maxim growled in response.

"Why should it offend her? Or you?" Marax countered.

"Enough!" Maxim boomed.

And as I stood there, holding Marax's manic gaze, I knew the only thing I would hate more than kissing Maxim was allowing Marax to hold some power over me. He was not welcome to my true feelings.

I placed my hand on Maxim's arm. "Give him what he asks."

Maxim looked down at me. And while he gave nothing away, I knew he was thrown.

I shifted to face him, taking a step into him.

I was a shell. I was hollow and empty inside. I was cold and dark beneath my skin. A kiss was nothing. A frigid and meaningless act. I was already a traitor. The damage had been done.

And if it served as some kind of proof, some sort of test, if it meant that we could then turn our attention to finding Zagan . . . Wasn't that worth it?

There was nothing I wouldn't do to find him.

Maxim gave a slight shake of his head. His jaw clenched. His nostrils flared. And I gave a humorless laugh. *He* did not want to kiss *me*.

Too bad.

I slipped my arms over his shoulders. If he pushed me away, he would make a fool of me.

His cold gray eyes narrowed. He knew he had no choice. He knew it was done.

He pressed one hand to my lower back, the other against my shoulder blades.

Then Maxim leaned down, pulling me into him. The line of my body pressed against his. He stopped just before touching his lips to mine, though. He searched my eyes for some indication that I did not want this from him.

But I closed the mere inches of distance between us. And like the traitor I was, I pressed my lips against Maxim's.

I looked right into his eyes, right into his soul, as I did.

While he took nothing from me, he did not cower. He met me there. An unmoving force. Strong and secure. And I knew a woman in his care would never face danger. But more than that, so much more than that . . .

I finally understood *who he was.*

It took a kiss—the purest of offerings—for my heart to recognize his own.

I was so immersed in what I found in him, that I almost forgot who it was I was pressed against, whose arms I was in.

Almost.

But almost is never completely.

179

The silence was broken by the hem of someone clearing his throat. I pulled back from Maxim then. And I couldn't stop my fingers from touching my lips as I stared into his eyes.

He stared back at me as he always had, as he always would. I doubted the strength of his gaze would ever waver. For anyone.

"I believe this is enough, Marax," Barrister Corbett said. His sense of decency was clearly being challenged.

I turned to the group of men. I gave them all a hard stare. Then I willed the Umbra to remove the hoods of their cloaks. I willed them to exhale the inky brume from their lips, and I addressed the Court members.

"If anyone defies Master Steele's orders, I will be very displeased."

I didn't wait for a response from the Court or a dismissal from Maxim. I didn't care what they decided to do or to believe. I had done my part.

I turned. And I left the clearing in the snowy woods to traverse the dark path through the ice-covered trees.

I could feel the Umbra trail behind me, and I could take no more. Once I was well out of sight, I wished them gone without voicing my request. I couldn't help but shiver slightly when they all vanished from the woods.

Without warning, Maxim grabbed me then and pulled me into his chest, pressing his back against a tree. I opened my mouth to protest, but he sealed his hand over my lips. When I began to thrash against him, he held me tight.

"Shush!" he growled, before craning his neck as if trying to listen to something.

I stilled, waiting to see what he would do next.

180

After a moment, he murmured at my ear, pausing as if listening between each sentence. "They don't believe me. They think I have found a way to imprison The Contessa and that I have brought you against your will. Marax wants to stop us from leaving. He is convincing the others to separate us. He is calling for our immediate execution."

Maxim's cheek brushed against mine, and I fought a shiver.

I didn't understand why it mattered. Why stick around for them? Why not just return to the manor?

As if reading my mind, Maxim said, "I cannot leave from here. This space is warded. We must get to the castle ruins. And none of this matters if they do not accept you as their new ruler. At the very least, they must consider the possibility of it."

He pulled his face back from mine. His eyes searching the forest around us. "Marax is attempting to call upon the Umbra himself." Maxim looked disgusted. "He believes The Contessa has granted him power over them."

I stood there, against Maxim, waiting. The allegiance of the Umbra being tested. Finally, Maxim looked down at me, and he gave his head a slow shake. "He is unable. Your virtue has been proven."

Maxim released his hold on me. My hectic breaths were visible in the frigid air, and I couldn't stop searching his eyes, seeing him in a new light.

The shock of the moment must have flashed across my face because without looking away, Maxim gave one slow nod.

"He didn't know," I finally whispered.

Maxim shook his head.

"You didn't tell him!" I cried. I gathered the skirt of my dress in my hands, feeling as though I needed to run immediately with the knowledge I possessed.

"He did not wish to know, Violet. There was no point."

"No point?!" I looked around as though I could find some explanation for it all. "How can you say that?" I grabbed Maxim's arm, desperately looking up at him, my voice dropping "How is it even possible?"

He looked at my hand for a long moment before staring at me. And the look he gave me made me want to tremble, not out of fright but out of . . . something else. Something that scared me. I pulled back my hand. And waited.

Maxim released a heavy breath, and I could see a lifetime of weariness wash across his face. "Come with me," he said simply.

"I will tell you everything."

CHAPTER 12

"**M**Y MOTHER WAS ONE OF YOUR PEOPLE."

I couldn't keep my eyes off Maxim. I followed his every move while he paced across the sitting room in my quarters, his every shift and expression.

I had not changed. I had not dared to walk away from him. I sat on the settee in the gown and jewels he had chosen. And fires burned on each end of the room—bright and hot.

And still, the shadows filled the space, lining the walls, stretching silently and solemnly as if rapt on Maxim's every word.

"My mother was a Radiant."

I fought not to shake my head. There was not a spark of Light in him anywhere. At least not in the sense I was used to—not in the way I would expect from the child of a Radiant.

Maxim had told me once that all beings carried a certain amount of Light. And I had taken his words to heart. But he was consumed by Darkness as far as I could tell.

However, I said nothing. I would not interrupt. I wanted to hear all he had to say.

So in the Dark Manor, high up on the fifth floor of the ancient and empty home, I sat and listened as Maxim told me a story.

"Her name was Isadora. She sat in the loft of her family's barn one night. She liked to sit there with the hatches thrown open, while watching the starry skies, letting her feet swing from the ledge.

"And her family thought her odd for it. Being of your kind, they could not understand the appeal the night held for her.

"One evening, as she sat out in the barn admiring the heavens, she sang a song. And when she came to the end of it, she found a man standing in front of the barn gazing up at her.

"There was a certain quality to the night, she would often say. The night possessed an allure the day could never match. There was a mystery to it. A secret. The day will show you all, but the night keeps much hidden. The day, she claimed, was prideful. Arrogant. Intent on blazing the brightest and blocking out all else. The night, however, was humble and as a result infinitely more powerful.

"The qualities she found aweing in regard to the night, she could see in the man standing before her. She did not know his identity, but she knew he was someone immense. And when he spoke, she knew his words were the truest she would ever hear.

"He was the night personified.

"He told her that he had left this world long ago. He told her that he had returned for one night. He was walking the forests of the world when he heard her song.

"He looked at her in a way no other had. And he told her he could see her for what she was. He knew—had he been able to stay for more than a single night—that he would love her. And he invited her to walk through the forest with him.

"She spent that lone night with him, never to see him again."

Maxim paused then. And he placed his hands in the pockets of his trousers. He lifted his head to look up at the ceiling. I imagined, had we been outdoors, that he would be scanning the sky—looking for something.

I knew he regretted having to say whatever was coming next. However, he continued without faltering.

"On the next summer solstice, she gave birth . . . to not one, but two children."

Little by little, piece by piece, everything came shattering down around me.

The cobwebs, the dust, and the locked doors—it was all wiped away. And all that had been buried and hidden suddenly lay raw and fragile at my feet.

Something warm slipped down my cheek. I did not dare dab at my face, though. I did not dare move. I kept my hands folded in my lap.

And Maxim's story continued without interruption. "Yet, the two were different. Because while my mother bore the children of the Shadow King, she was also angel kissed. She had been chosen to bear one of your Prisms.

"But the Light and the Dark work in different ways. The Darkness is all consuming. It stretches and expands. It seeps and fills. And it was passed on to both of her children.

"The Light, however, is more brittle, more rigid. It could not be broken. Could not be halved. The essence of Light—both that which my mother had to pass down as well as that from the angel's kiss—would not be fractured. It remained whole, passing to one and only one.

"And passing her very essence onto the one child meant her death was imminent. She lived for a single year with her children before one of your angels came for her. Her child of Light was taken. Promised to be cared for and honored. Fated to be a savior for those of the Light.

"She was told the child of Darkness would go with her to the other side.

"But the Shadow King would never allow such a fate for the woman he loved—even if it had been for a single night only. He saved her and the child from their end. And she was granted a new life . . . in the Darkness, in the night, among the Shadows."

Maxim was quiet then. He stood before the fire and stared into it. I did not speak for a very long time. But finally, when the weight of his words had settled, I rose from the settee.

He turned to look at me. With the fire at his back, deep shadows swept across his face.

I looked at his chest; he watched me knowing where my eyes traveled.

"Not a tattoo," I said quietly.

"No," he confirmed just as quietly.

"Why have you kept this a secret? Why not claim your rightful place at Court?"

Maxim looked off to the side, as if envisioning a different time. "My mother was bestowed the position of Scribe for the Court—an honored and esteemed position. While fulfilling her duties she met a man, a Shadow, one who became her husband.

"He served as the Master-at-Arms. He was a good and noble man. He found a way to use his position to help those who had been forgotten.

"He knew our people had fallen on dark times. He knew the very Court which he was a member of was corrupt. He often vowed to see The Contessa removed from power—her Umbra imprisoned as they should be.

"And he did all he could to right those wrongs without forfeit to his position.

"He said our people were great once. He said we were led by a great king. He believed he was upholding the ancient standards and morals. He often spoke of his belief that the king would return one day, and we would know him because he bore 'the mark.'

"I admired him. I saw what he did for those who were considered lowly. There was nothing more I wanted than to serve my people the way he did.

"When the man who was a father to me was killed, I inherited his role at Court. Although I was still very young, I had proven myself worthy for the title.

"It was just around that time, shortly after his death, when the mark began to form. And my mother revealed the truth of my lineage.

"I was glad for her discretion. Because I was old enough to understand what it meant for me. Mark or no, I was not in a position to battle The Contessa and her Umbra. And I had no desire to serve her.

"What good would it have done to claim my title? To oust myself?

"I saw where I could be of greater service and I chose to keep that part of myself hidden; only in anonymity can the greatest of good be done.

"I was granted access to all of the Court's knowledge and resources. They believed I was carrying out the injustices they ordered. When in reality, I've been doing all I can to help my people. I've been doing all I can to foster a resistance against the Court and to learn of the power I possess—of how I might lock away the Umbra and topple The Contessa.

"I thought perhaps with my . . ." Maxim spent a long moment with his head bent, seeming to have trouble with his next word.

I stood in the dark room with my hands clasped in front of me, waiting. I would give him all the time in the world to finish speaking.

Finally, he looked up at me. "I thought *together*, we might actually be able to right all those wrongs."

I knew Maxim was not referring to the two of us. I knew exactly who he meant.

My chest was heavy with regret that was not mine to claim. Still I had to ask, my words breaking, "Why didn't you tell him?"

There was no defensiveness in Maxim's response, just the simple truth. "It was not something he was ready to hear."

"What about your mother?" I asked. "He should have known—"

"She perished after the man she loved died. She had lost her will to continue. She lived two short lives. One in the Light. The other in the Dark. She is at rest now."

Maxim shook his head. "I knew nothing of her other child while she lived. Before her death, when she revealed the truth of my identity, she spoke of him. She believed he was cared for at the Radiant Court. She believed he would be honored there because of what he was. And she knew she could not make herself known because of what she had become—because of the new life she led.

"After my mother's death, after I had taken my position at Court, The Contessa presented him to us one day. She held demonstrations of his power. His cruelty. He was a Dark, cold individual. And the very few times I was in his presence, I saw no redeeming qualities within him.

"That was, until you arrived. And when he fought the Umbra by my side that night out in the village, when he did what he could to help save our people, I saw . . . the good he was capable of.

"I thought that I could help him. I thought I could help you both. I thought the time had finally come for a new era."

Standing there before me, no longer holding anything back, I saw something in Maxim's face. It was incredibly slight, something I normally would have missed. But just this once, I saw it in the crease at the corner of his eyes and the set of his jaw—I saw regret.

Without thinking, I took a step forward, and I lifted my hand, stretching it in his direction. I felt the need to cross the room. To go to him. To embrace him.

But his eyes flashed, and I froze where I was. I let my hand drop. I did not cross the room. I did not go to him.

It had been a mistake. One I would not make again. There were things, deep things, within this man. Things I should not stir.

He was honorable. And noble. He did not want to compromise his values. Yet, be he a king's heir, a master at his craft, a knight to his people . . . he was still just a man.

He stared at me as he spoke, and I knew what he was doing. I knew he was reminding himself. "I know, more than anything, you wish to find him and bring him home."

Maxim closed his eyes then. "I know you doubt me. You doubt my intentions and my motivations, but if there is one thing I can make you believe, Violet, know that I, too, want to find him. It matters to me as well."

His voice softened as he opened his eyes and said, "Give me two nights to watch over the Court. I must ensure they make no moves against our people in the villages. I cannot leave them unprotected. And during these next two nights, I will scour texts, I will confer with witches, I will do all I can to uncover clues as to where your love may be. Because at this time, I cannot say where he is. I do not know the first place to begin looking."

I closed my eyes then. Maxim's request broke my heart. I could not live through another two nights, not knowing, not taking action. But I understood.

I felt another warm tear slide down my face. Then a gentle pressure on my chin. When I opened my eyes, I saw Maxim standing before me. He had moved silently through the room.

He lifted my face up to his. He wiped his thumb over my cheek. His words were a soft murmur in the dark. "What I can tell you is that you cannot remain so sad for long. Otherwise, I will be forced to spend the rest of my life trying to make you happy."

He leaned his face down to mine, and I could see how clear his gray eyes were as he spoke his final words.

"And we both know . . . I never could."

CHAPTER 13

I WAS ALONE.

I stood in the sitting room with the fire and the shadows.

Maxim left. And I was alone.

I don't know how long I stood there. Waiting. For what, I didn't know. But I was waiting for something.

And finally, something came.

A low shuffling sound from out in the hall. The Crone entered carrying a dinner tray.

I watched her—void of any compassion for her—as she hobbled and shuffled, struggling under the heavy weight of the tray. Her tattered brown robe covered every inch of her save for those gnarled hands.

And I couldn't help it; I wanted to crush her hunched little form. In spite of recent revelations, in spite of knowing that she must have had a good reason for what she'd done . . . *She had stopped me.*

She was the reason we had lost Zagan. It was all because of her.

But I had heard Maxim's words. I knew there was wisdom to them. And so, I did not jump to violence and vengeance. Instead, I realized that I needed to try to learn from the position I was in.

The Crone was ancient. She was powerful. And she had probably seen more than any of us.

Yet, I knew she wouldn't tell me anything. She would ignore me as she always did. And sure enough, as soon as she dropped the tray on the dining table with a loud clatter, she began to shuffle towards the door.

Still, my voice rang out in the room. A futile effort, but an effort just the same.

"Why did you throw up the wall?" I called.

She continued for the door without a word.

"Do you know where he is? What happened to him?" I tried.

Limping and shuffling, her small form continued forward.

"You don't care," I accused. "He cared about you," I threw at her, "but you don't care enough to try and get him back."

She was almost at the door.

"For all I know you were helping Seraphina."

The room became silent at that. Because the shuffling came to a sudden stop.

The Crone paused where she was.

And I found her sudden halt frightening.

195

Why had she stopped? Why was she not limping through the open door to leave?

In that moment, the anteroom somehow became larger—stretching and expanding. And although we stood but feet from each other, a great distance separated us.

The Crone stood there, flickering between the present and the past.

As I stared at her hunched little form in the shadows, as I stood there suddenly frightened, I knew without a doubt that I had uncovered something.

Although she was across the room, I leaned forward, forcing my presence on her.

But the Crone did not turn around. She did not reply.

And in spite of my fear, I pressed on. Staring at her back, I asked, "Did you know her? Seraphina?"

No answer.

"I know that's who The Contessa is. I know she was one of the Originals from the Dark half. And I know she aided the king."

Still the Crone did not respond.

"Did you know her?" I asked again with more force.

Yet there was nothing but silence between us.

"Will she return?" I tried.

Finally, the Crone shifted where she stood, limping to pivot and face me. I knew she stared at me from beneath her tattered robe. I could feel the weight of her gaze.

And although I meant to keep my voice strong, I couldn't stop it from wavering when I spoke next.

"Do you know what has become of him? Do you know how I can get him back?"

In her brittle, ancient voice, gasping for breath, she spoke one word.

" . . . 'relia."

And the stupid child that I was, I did not understand at first. At first, I was angry that she had ignored my questions—that she was muttering nonsense.

But the Crone tried again. She tried to strengthen her brittle voice, gasping for a fortifying breath.

" . . . 'urelia." She repeated.

Her words made me feel like icy fingers stroked my back.

Coughing and wheezing, she tried one finale time. " . . . 'urelia."

I couldn't move. Couldn't breathe. Because I believed I understood what she was trying to say.

A name.

The Crone spoke a single name. And it was a name I knew.

It was the other woman the Shadow King had written of. *Aurelia.* The first Prism. The one betrayed by the Council of Elders. The one that lay dying under the king's care.

Under Seraphina's care.

And I felt cold as I began to understand. I looked at the weak, ancient woman who stood before me—damaged and broken. I felt the far-off crackle of power. And it was so obvious. I couldn't believe I had not considered the possibility. I leaned forward, bending at the waist, clutching an arm over my stomach.

"That's who you are?" I asked on a breath, suddenly finding clarity. "Aurelia?"

I stood there, waiting a lifetime for the Crone to reply.

Slowly. With great effort the old woman raised her arm. She pointed one gnarled finger. And I knew she was pointing beyond the manor walls. I knew what lay in that direction. I knew she pointed at the cliff outside.

The Crone shook her finger, and again she forced the single word, finally pronouncing it fully.

"*Aurelia.*"

I turned my head in the direction of the cliff, envisioning it beyond the walls. Then I looked back at the Crone.

I couldn't help but picture The Contessa with her black billowing dress. "The Contessa," I stated, hating the vision. I cursed her name, vowing my revenge. "Seraphina," I said, calling her by name.

I could only imagine what had happened between the two women after the king had departed.

But the Crone shook her head and waved her finger once again. "Aurelia."

"The Contessa?" I asked.

And the Crone . . . *nodded.*

I became aggravated. "You make it seem as though you're trying to say that The Contessa is Aurelia," I told her.

As I watched the small hunched form of the Crone in the firelight, I heard nothing but the amplified sound of my own breathing. If she spoke then, I did not hear her. I could only see. Because the Crone nodded once more, the hood of her tattered robe dipping and bowing, betraying nothing but infinite blackness from within.

I had been shoved from a cliff and I plummeted, falling endlessly into my own abyss.

Everything shifted. Grinding, crumbling, and then settling into place. And I finally understood. I saw it all play out before me— the scene from the king's journal.

The Council had chosen Aurelia to be the first Prism. To be a savior to her people. And then, in the blink of an eye, they had destroyed her. To spare themselves, they had destroyed her heart, her mind, her body. They took from her. Used her. Left her to die.

But the Shadow King heard her cries. He brought her into his world of Darkness. And somehow . . . *she had lived.*

She did not continue on as a broken, hunched, limping figure of a woman. She did not hide behind a tattered cloak, roaming the halls of the Dark Manor with distant vestiges of power.

No. Aurelia had become an exquisite nightmare, awash in Dark power, surrounded by the Umbra. She had become The Contessa.

The betrayal. The transgression. The deceit.

These things are enough to drive anyone mad. And while I possessed power that ran incredibly deep, I was still just a woman. A woman who could break. And I began to crack.

"How?" I demanded of The Crone. I could feel the shadows in the room stretching and climbing, hovering around me. My voice had grown deep and hollow.

She said nothing.

"How?" I demanded once more.

According to the king's journal, Aurelia had sacrificed her Light for her love—the other Prism, Cortho. And in doing so,

199

she had become infected with Darkness. The king himself had written that she was not long for this world. He believed she was on her last breath. So how then, could she still be here? How could she be The Contessa?

"*HOW?*" I roared at The Crone. The floor at our feet shook and the chandeliers rattled and swayed.

The Crone simply shook her head. She had uttered one word only. And now she was done speaking.

My hands fisted at my sides. I had thought The Contessa was one of the Originals from the Dark half. *Because it had made sense.* It had been a logical deduction. It explained how she controlled the Umbra.

The Contessa couldn't be Aurelia. Aurelia had been a Prism. *A Radiant.*

Except . . .

My skin iced over. And it had never felt as cold as it did then.

I was a Radiant. I was a Prism.

I looked down at myself. At my hands. I touched the dress I wore. The collar. I touched my cheek with my fingertips.

I had become something Dark. Exquisite. Haunting. And the Umbra now answered to me.

I shattered then. Everything that I was. The last vestiges of who I had been, fluttered away like hundreds of blackbirds in the wind.

I had been wrong. So wrong. And this was worse. This was far worse. The violation of it all tore far deeper than I could have ever imagined.

She was a Prism. The first of her kind. And all these years later, she had come for me. We were the same. And why? What had turned her into what she was?

The Council.

Her love . . . her life . . . had been taken from her. *Because of the Council.* She had transformed into something Dark and haunted. *Because of the Council.* She had taken Zagan from me. An unending war between Radiants and Shadows had consumed both sides. Countless lives had been ruined. *Because of the Council.*

Because of the Elders.

I could not hold back the Darkness any longer. I had known it was more powerful than I. I had warned Maxim. I knew I needed to keep it locked away.

But I had reached my breaking point.

I tried. I did. I tried to hold it back. I struggled to stay afloat. I did not want to let it pull me under. But there are some forces greater than ourselves. Some elements are too big to fight.

I stood on an empty beach in the dark, staring down a tsunami.

Everyone breaks. Everyone. It is a universal truth. An absolute with no exceptions. The only difference between us is how we break. And what it turns us into.

Standing there with the black gown trailing at my feet in a pool of darkness, I felt a single rib crack. I looked down at my chest, not in shock or fear. But in detached observation.

Then another crack. Followed by another. I could feel my bones break and reform, knitting together in a shifted fashion.

I realized I was becoming something different. Something greater. It was what I had always been destined to be. And I would fight it no longer.

I was breaking. Shifting. And reforming.

I was immense. I was aweing. I was more than any one person should be.

And it was right.

But a low hum began to vibrate through the room, and my eyes darted to the Crone. "Don't you dare!" I seethed. I shot a pulse of energy towards her, sending her flying into the wall. The old hag was going to try and subdue me, the way she had Maxim once.

And of course. Of course. Low and behold, who should appear at the open door of the suite but the Dark, valiant knight himself. In his hands were old books. No doubt some reading material to make me think I was helping in finding Zagan—busy work.

He looked at the Crone crumpled in the corner of the room and his eyes went wide. Then he looked at me. He looked in my eyes. And I smiled at the fear I saw on his face.

The books in his hands tumbled to the floor as he stepped into the room.

"Violet!" His voice reverberated in my ears with power and authority.

Where he was loud and commanding, I was Dark and silky. "I warned you, Maxim. But you didn't listen. And now it's too late."

Maxim took a step towards me and he raised his hands at his sides. He fought to keep his voice even, conversational almost. "What are you doing, Violet?"

"I'm putting an end to all of this," I told him. "I am going to make it right. And what was taken from me must be returned."

"Let me help you," Maxim countered. "Let's make things right, together." He held out a hand, wanting me to take it.

"No, Maxim. No more inaction. No more waiting. You had your chance. And look at where it has brought us. The time is now."

"Take my hand, Violet," he insisted, shifting closer to me.

I flexed the incredible power I held. I called upon it. I called upon *them*.

And three of the Umbra stepped forward from the shadows, flanking my sides. Maxim's jaw tightened, his outstretched hand fisting.

"You don't need to do this, Violet. Send them away. You have me. I am here for you."

I let out a short huff of laughter. "Oh, Maxim. You are not enough. You never could be enough."

With a shake of his head, the slash of his brow intensified, and the darling fool tried to use the Dark Tongue against me.

I let out a cackle and the fire burning in each hearth extinguished.

Maxim tried again, speaking the same command, only louder.

I took the power of it, took a hold of it, felt the weight of it, and then I threw it right back at Maxim. All without uttering a word.

He fell to his knees before me. His arms pinned at his sides.

In the dress he had chosen for me, with the elaborate collar he had selected for me, my lips a dark plum and my lashes the blackest of black, I walked to Maxim and I knelt in front of him. I caressed his cheek with the back of my hand.

"Oh, Maxim," I sighed. "What could have been." Then I placed my paper white cheek against his and whispered in his ear.

"It never could have been."

I pulled back and raked my nail along his cheek, meeting his eye. I couldn't help but smile at the irony of it all.

All along, I had thought Maxim would be the one to betray me.

I stood and I crossed to one of the Umbra. I placed my lips over its, and I inhaled the brume billowing from its maw. With the caustic smoke choking and burning my lungs, I drew in deeper, fighting past the pain and suffocation. And when I finally pulled back from the thing, I could see tendrils of black smoke wisp from my lips.

I could feel the strength and the power it offered. I understood that I was strong enough to withstand it. And that was the key.

We become monsters by degrees. Little by little. Sip by sip. Everything leading up to this had been merely an exercise in growth and tolerance.

I was ready. I could take what the Umbra had to offer. And I saw that if it did not kill me, it made me stronger. I could feel myself becoming wispy, shadowy at the edges.

And while I embraced the Darkness, I held on to the Light. I knew what a valuable commodity it was. I found a way to grab a hold of them both. Because I needed both.

And that, I realized, was where The Contessa had failed. She had not found a way to hold on to the Light. And she could not obtain her one desire without it.

But I could. I could have what she spent lifetimes dreaming of.

So in a swirl of inky shadows, I left Maxim there on the floor of my quarters while he stared at me in horror, while he witnessed the unthinkable, while I became his worst nightmare.

But he had nothing to fear. I wanted nothing from him nor his people. I had no other use for the Umbra. All I needed from them was the ability to become smoke. To drift away. To reach Aleece.

The Darkness provided the way. The Light provided passage.

It was what The Contessa wanted all along. What she was willing to do anything for. She had wanted to enter Aleece. She had wanted vengeance against the Council. And she had needed my Light to do so. Because I was whole. Complete. I had connected with another.

The Umbra could not enter with me, and I cared not. They had served their purpose; they had shown me the way.

I stepped into Aleece.

CHAPTER 14

~*Violet's Playlist: Seven Devils, Florence + The Machine*~

M Y LONG DARK HAIR SHINED as the strands which had fallen loose were swept up. The dress I wore turned even blacker on my next breath, becoming so dark it absorbed any light which dared touch it.

My nails hardened. Blackening, they shifted into fine points. Claws.

And I walked through Aleece.

It was a beautiful, cloudless day. The sky was vivid blue overhead. The grass at my feet was a lush green. Peaceful. Tranquil.

I stood at the reflecting pond, surrounded by the rolling hills and the wildflowers, the sweet air. I stared ahead. I stared at the heart of it all.

The tower. Soaring to the heavens. Split down the center. One side alabaster, the other side onyx.

The snow-capped cliff climbed behind it, and the sweeping waterfall framed the castle in an air of majesty. The mist rose from the pools at its base, creating a hazy, dreamlike appearance.

I took in the beauty of the scene before me. And it made me sick.

So I blocked out the sun.

It was too easy. I had become too powerful. I had become what the Elders feared. And they had been right to try and kill me. Because now I was going to destroy them.

I would turn their kingdom to dust.

I didn't know why, but for some reason, my ability—that of which I was capable—was somehow infinitely more powerful here in Aleece.

A low faint hum began to vibrate at my feet. Building, growing, stretching. Spreading across the earth. And I called forth the Darkness.

Because it did not live within me only. The Darkness is everywhere. In the brightest of meadows, in the holiest of sanctuaries, the Darkness lurks. Waiting.

It is everywhere because you cannot have Light, you cannot have existence, without it. It lives within you. Within all of us. Everyone carries it.

And for some reason we bury it. We shove it down. We suffocate it.

We are cowards.

I would not deny my power any longer.

I released the Darkness from Aleece. I unleashed it. Shadows coiled from the ground and the air. And I pulled them to myself. I held my hands out to my sides, grabbing ahold of the energy in that plane.

It came so easily then. It flowed through my veins and seeped from my skin.

The Darkness I carried was immense. There was no limit to its power.

And in a move that was too simple, I manipulated the elements. In a rush, black billowing clouds roiled through the tranquil blue sky, smothering any Light.

Aleece was plunged into Darkness.

All hope and beauty bled from the land. Thunder rumbled and lightning struck. The wind lashed across the hills. And without Light, without hope, everything withered and died.

The grass, the wildflowers, the leaves . . . they all shriveled, turning black before crumbling to dust and blowing away. The earth was charred without ever seeing fire.

I looked around as the wind whipped the fabric of my dress. Then step by step, I made my way to the tower.

And with each step I took, I destroyed the home of the Council.

I unleashed more Darkness and a vortex opened in the black sky above. With my next step came a deafening crack that reverberated for miles. The ground shook violently as the barren trees, scattered throughout the land, became uprooted. In a glorious blast of power, they were sucked into the churning sky above.

The black clouds spun, and arcs of lightning forked and veined through the funnel.

Another step.

The water.

With a simple lift of my arms, I rid their world of water. The reflecting pond, the pools, the falls, they were all sucked away. A pounding rush of water cascaded from the ground into the black clouds above.

Another step and I paused. I surveyed all I'd done.

The land lay bare, with no water and no vegetation. But still there were structures. The buildings, the temples, the fountains—they could not remain. I would not permit them. With a deep rumble, with the very earth shaking at my feet, they were all destroyed. The buildings were demolished where they stood, crumbling into rubble. And the tiny fragments that persisted were pulled from the ground into the turbulent sky above to be swallowed within the churning vortex.

Another step and I scanned the horizon.

The dirt. I would not even leave them their dirt. With a succession of thudding bursts, the very dirt from beneath my feet went flying through the air in a violent sandstorm before it reached the vortex and was sucked away.

I looked at the Dark existence. Everything was gone. All that remained was a lightless churning sky above and the dead black land below.

And the Ivory Tower.

It stood there, cleft down the middle, and somehow the alabaster and onyx of each side seemed even starker as it soared from the charred earth. But what was more infuriating was the way the tower shined from within.

I could feel my lip curl as I let out a snarl.

I would snuff out the Light.

I took another step towards it. I would not—could not—allow it to persist. I willed its destruction. I pulled from the Darkness. Shadows swirled around me, collecting in my palms. Sheer power and strength. And I directed the force of it at the tower.

The ground shook. Yet the tower stood fast.

The wind whipped with my fury.

But before I could try again, before I could finalize its destruction, they sent a distraction for me.

Up ahead, walking straight for me, as if from the very center— the very heart of the tower—as if emerging from the cleft itself was . . .

I laughed. The old fools. Did they think this would stop me? Was I to see a vision of myself and feel something from it? Some jarring realization? Some shock of shame?

They had conjured a mirror image to match my every step. Moving closer and closer. I could see the way my black gown billowed behind me. See the black color of my lips and lining of my eyes. See the paper white skin, the shining hair piled atop my head. And the gray crystalline eyes. Lifeless eyes.

I felt nothing. I had evolved from petty emotions.

I continued forward, striding to greet the illusion. When I was several yards before it, I came to a stop. And the reflection halted in synchronization.

I stared at the likeness. It was not perfect, and I was not surprised. It was a pathetic attempt.

I raised my hand; the image did also. I shot an explosive force of power, angered by the illusion, happy to watch it crumple to the ground.

The earth shook and lightning struck. The winds whipped.

It was too easy.

There was only one person who could have stopped me. And they had taken him from me.

And where was the Council now? Where was their army of angels?

I continued forward, knowing I would not leave until the tower was destroyed.

I came to a stop just before the illusion of my collapsed form on the ground. I felt nothing for it. I faced the home of the Elders and took it in. The Light from the tower seemed to grow in intensity. It was so strong, so bright, that I could no longer see the cleft down the middle.

Its spires soared into the sky. One side alabaster. One side onyx. A flare of Light down the center. And a vortex of Darkness churning above.

I held my hands out and with a cry that shook the tower and reverberated all around the blackened land, I unleashed the full potential of my power upon the castle without cease.

A steady stream of power, of Darkness, welled from the core of my being, with no limit to its strength.

Yet still the tower remained.

My arms shook. My jaw clenched. I continued my effort.

I was prepared to stay for eternity if that was what it took. I would not stop.

But at some point, there was a flicker up ahead. Something approached from the east side of the tower—the alabaster side. Slowly. Starting from a great distance away but drawing closer and closer.

And finally, the something took shape. Finally, they decided to face me.

Thirteen white robed figures. They walked in a line. Hoods drawn. One hand outstretched.

They came for me.

If I was meant to be intimidated, I was not. They were laughable. They were sickening. They were no match for me. I could easily crush them with a swipe of my hand.

But first I wanted them to see their home destroyed.

I redoubled my efforts. Driving all the power I possessed, all the power I could draw, directly to the Ivory tower.

Yet there was another flicker, another distraction. However, it was not the same as before. Not a flicker, but a shift. A sway.

It was much darker. Something in the distance. Something moving towards me. From the West side of the tower—the onyx side.

It was too inky to make out at first. But as the something drew closer, it began to take shape.

Thirteen black robed figures. They walked in a line. Hoods drawn. One hand outstretched.

And they, too, came for me.

The Dark half had returned to Aleece. Every last one of them.

They all came for me. Step by step. A line of Light and a line of Dark. The aweing, divine presence of the tower between them.

With each approaching step, I could feel the pressure bearing down on my shoulders. I tried to pull my focus from the tower. I intended to stop the Elders—Light and Dark. With an arcing sweep of my arm, I would fell them all.

But all my power, all my energy, was sucked into the tower. And I was unable to break the connection. Unable to pull free. My eyes widened as I stared at the reverent structure, as I realized I was bound. Tethered.

Trapped. I was trapped.

In that moment, I knew I had been betrayed by this place.

My face contorted in agony. In rage.

I was not destroying the tower with Darkness. The tower was pulling it from me. Stripping me of it. Draining me of strength. Taking from me.

My cry echoed through the raging skies.

And the Originals bore down upon me. One side blinding me with Light. The other smothering me with Dark.

I began to tremble. And then one knee crashed to the ground. I struggled to right myself, to push myself back up. I refused to kneel before the Elders.

But my other knee slammed to the ground. And still my arms were outstretched in front of me. Every bit of the Darkness I directed at the tower was taken from me.

With their slow steady steps, with their outstretched arms, with the Light and the Dark combining . . . I began to drown.

I couldn't breathe.

Finally, they stood before me, still as statues. Thirteen white robes to my left. Thirteen black robes to my right. The Ivory tower directly ahead. The churning dark vortex above. And the crumpled vision of myself at my knees.

The Elders began to whisper. Deep, hollow voices, as if spoken from a great distance. Rapidly overlapping with amplified sibilance.

Then the buzzing, the humming, began to build around me. From one side a bright hot light and from the other its counter. And the two forces were pushing against me, making their way beneath my skin where they mingled and met. Combining into a force that I could not purge. A force that awakened the parts of my identity I had locked away.

I cried out again, but no sound left my lips. The robed figures took a step closer in unison, their hands still raised. I fought, I shuddered on my knees, trying to return to my feet.

Again, they took another step closer, and the power intensified. I fell to my hands as the connection to the Ivory tower finally severed.

They surrounded me.

The pressure. My joints collapsed. My ligaments snapped. Muscles squished. And my bones shattered.

My will was great. But the collective—the very elemental balance of the Light and Dark—was life itself.

I drifted down into the wasteland I had created. My chest and head lying upon the rubble in a gossamer pool of black fabric.

Weak and powerless. Nothing more than a handful of dust.

I lay with my eyes open before the mirror image of myself. My head at her feet, hers at mine. Yin and yang.

And I saw then that the Elders had not sent an image of myself. It was not an illusion. Not an exercise in self-reflection.

My eyes were wide open now. And before me was another person. Another person who lay in a pool of blackness all her own.

Lying before me was The Contessa.

Somehow, she had finally made her way to Aleece. And I had struck her down. Her eyes were not open, like mine. Her eyes were shut. She no longer had to bear witness to the Council's sins against her. She was granted respite.

This was not her downfall. It was mine.

Finally, the Originals dropped their outstretched hands.

They stayed where they were. Unmoving.

Holy relics.

And they looked down at us. They looked at us as we lay upon the broken land.

And something rattled somewhere deep in my awareness. I knew something was off. Wrong.

One of the Elders was different from the others.

Limping and shuffling with arthritic movement, one of the Originals hobbled forward from the line then, shattering the frozen tableau of our gathered forms. She did not wear black like the others. She did not wear white. Her ancient form was hunched in a brown tattered robe.

The Crone.

Yet as she threw her hood back, her posture straightened. It was as if she had been trapped in a cramped space and she was finally able to stretch and straighten her spine. Her long dark hair tumbled down her back as she emerged from the cowl. And her smooth skin plumped. Her gnarled hands unfurled, and she took in a deep breath.

She was no longer an old hag. She was a beautiful woman. And she looked to the tall broad figure next to her.

He, too, folded back his cowl. And I could instantly see what the girl from Maxim's story meant. There was no denying his greatness—the way he embodied the night.

And I could clearly see his sons in his dark chiseled features.

"Dresden," the woman said in greeting.

"Seraphina." He bowed his head to her with dignified respect.

Seraphina.

The king's journal. The Original who had aided him. Maxim and I had thought she was the Contessa. But she had been helping us all along. She had been the Crone.

I remembered another detail from the journal entry. Seraphina had difficulty in our world. She had not been "*sponsored by an element.*" She had struggled to exist in the Dark Manor, and she left from time to time.

She had also watched over Aurelia. And the king—*Dresden*—had tasked her with finding the others.

She looked at the Contessa, lying on the ground, and her brows rose as her clear gray eyes rounded. Her cheeks hollowed. "I failed her," she said. And there was such remorse, such regret, in her voice.

Then she turned her gaze upon the king and bowed her lovely head, her hair tumbling down her shoulders. "I failed you."

The king's eyes drifted over the two girls at his feet. Then he placed his hand on the Crone—on Seraphina's—shoulder. She had no choice but to raise her eyes and meet the power of his gaze. "You did well," he countered.

Although I could feel nothing, I felt the power in his voice, the depth to it, the Darkness in it.

He removed his hand from Seraphina before turning to those in the white robes. His tone was stern. "Call him," the king demanded.

From beneath their white robes came the same hollow, far-off whispers. And then Cord appeared. He stood between the white and black robes with wings of Light and a sword of fire. Tall and broad. His head held high.

He had been summoned. And he appeared. Emotionless. A soldier carrying out his orders. He showed no reaction to the barren ruins of Aleece nor the presence of Dark Originals. His eyes remained focused somewhere in the distance. Waiting for his next order.

The king turned to look at all assembled before him. "Here lies your daughter, Davis. Look upon her. See what you and yours have done to her." Then he turned to Cord. "And here lies your Aurelia, Cortho."

His voice seemed to echo across the barren land. "Your Prisms. Your first and your last, have returned to you." He did not say more. He did not need to. The error of the Elders' ways was laid bare for all to see.

At the king's words, Cord dropped his sword, the fire of it extinguishing. And it clattered against the rocks at his feet. He did not look down, though. Not right away. His eyes remained fixed upon some point in the distance. Or perhaps, some point in the past.

I knew then, there was a reason I had found the king's journal. There was a reason it was the only one in the entire manor. I knew that it had been placed there for me.

Because Cortho, too, was named in the entry. He had been Aurelia's love, her other half, the original Prism. And she had believed he died.

Yet here, now, was Cord. Addressed by his full name.

As Cord stood there expressionless, emotionless, he began to shift his focus. And inch by inch he dropped his gaze until he stared at the crumpled form of Aurelia. He stood where he was, looking at her, for a long moment before he stepped forward to stand above her.

I had only ever seen him stoic and emotionless. But as he gazed at Aurelia, cracks began to form across the facade. He looked as though he was wracking his mind, trying to find something, searching for something forgotten. Finally, something—I didn't know what—passed over his face. It was something that I couldn't understand. I knew whatever it was, it was something raw.

Cord looked down at Aurelia's gown spilling around her broken form. He looked at her as she lay in a pool of darkness. Then he pulled the white robe he wore over his head leaving him in his linen trousers only. And with his massive chest bare, he squatted next to her and covered Aurelia with the white robe.

He paused for a long moment with his hands hovering above her. But finally, with the utmost care, as if handling a broken bird, he picked her up in his arms.

At his touch, her chest rose. The movement was incredibly subtle, but it was undeniable. Her rib cage expanded with a single breath.

Cortho stood, towering at his full height, with Aurelia in his arms.

After waiting countless lifetimes, she had made her way to Aleece. She did not find the vengeance she sought. Instead she found something greater. Something more precious.

She found what was lost long ago.

She had seemed so large before, but now, cradled in Cord's arms, pressed against his chest, I could see just how small she really was.

Although raw and uncertain, there was no hesitation in Cord's movements. And without a thought or a look—without the acknowledgement that anyone else existed—he left Aleece with the girl he had lost.

No one dared to stop him.

With the two of them gone, I knew it was my time. The Elders would turn to me now.

But from my back, I heard a voice. A child's voice. One void of emotion or inflection. And I knew I had heard the little girl speak before.

"Leave us," she said.

After a moment's pause, someone replied, "As you wish, *Oracle*."

Her words were obeyed. All who were assembled, dispersed as if they had never been.

"Rise," she told me.

And I found that I was not dust. I found that my bones were not shattered. I found that I could push myself from the ground.

I lifted my chest. My head. I pushed against the rock and my body rose. I turned to face her.

The Oracle stood in front of me with her long blonde hair and her dingy white dress. And she blinded me with those two beams of Light as she looked at me.

"Kneel."

I did as she commanded. And she lowered herself as well. We knelt together, face to face.

It was only then that I saw the dark clouds had been swept from the sky. It was only then that I realized the wind did not bluster.

But still, there were no trees, no hills, no vegetation or structures. We sat on a barren rock as it orbited through space and time. And from horizon to horizon, I could see the brightest display of galaxies and stars.

In a single blink, the beams of light were gone. The Oracle's eyes became mirrors, reflecting the heavenly bodies surrounding us.

She looked at me with those wide mirrored eyes. And she spoke.

"You have brought it closer and closer. Now . . . *it is here.*"

CHAPTER 15

~Violet's Playlist: Saturn, Sleeping At Last~

I KNELT UPON THE NOTHING I HAD CREATED. A giant, bare rock orbiting through space. All around us, blanketed over us—the infinite light of galaxies and stars.

I watched the vision of it in the little girl's eyes as she scanned the skies. I struggled to find my voice, transfixed by the magnitude of what surrounded us. But finally, I asked, "What is it?"

She looked at me, and I stared at my reflection. It was blurry and distorted. I found myself pulled into the sight, trying to bring the reflection into focus.

Although entranced by her gaze, I still noticed something. Something disturbing. Something chilling. For the first time, her emotionless child's voice took on a tone. In the two words she whispered next, I found a certain disbelief.

I found fear.

"The end."

I paused, letting her words sink in. "The end?" I asked, not understanding.

She silently nodded.

I pulled my gaze away from hers, jarred by the glimpse of emotion. My eyes darted back and forth over the ground before looking up at her again. "I don't understand."

"Look around you. It is gone. It is all gone. Aleece is no more. The Council. The Light. All of it is gone."

"But . . . I . . . I . . ."

"Do not despair," she said, placing her hand over mine. "You have repaired that which was fractured." She looked over my shoulder at the Ivory Tower.

I could see it reflected in her eyes as she said, "You have united the Light and the Dark. Balance is restored."

In her eyes—in those mirrors—I could see the tower as it stood whole. It was no longer alabaster and onyx but ivory. And it shone in the darkness as it soared above the bare rock and climbed into the heavens.

It was all that remained in Aleece. The only thing that still existed. And it was restored.

"You were the only force great enough to call together the Light and the Dark. It was the only way to repair that which was fractured. You did exactly as you were meant to do."

My mouth fell open, but no words came out. I didn't understand what had happened. I knew it was my doing. I knew I had just brought devastation to Aleece. But I couldn't accept it. It was too large of a cross to bear.

The Oracle placed her other small hand on my knee. "It is the way it had to be."

But I could not connect to what I had been just moments ago. It had not been me.

And as I searched for some kind of explanation in her eyes, as I saw myself reflected there, I drew in a breath. My hair was in chestnut waves down my shoulders. My skin was rosy, my lips pink. And my eyes glimmered violet. No longer lifeless. No longer crystalline.

I was not what I had been.

"But . . . you can fix everything, can't you?" I asked. "Make it right? Undo this damage?"

"What has been done, cannot be undone," she replied.

Then the Oracle tilted her head again, searching the clear night sky, the heavenly bodies swirling in her eyes. "There must be change for there to be life. Otherwise, we become nothing more than a picture, frozen in time. A memory."

She looked back at me. "Do not blame yourself. This was your destiny. You were chosen to bring the end."

"Are you saying I never had a choice in any of it?" I asked.

"You had a choice," she replied. "But everything leading up to now has been designed to shape that choice. The moment the Council decided to take Aurelia's life, you were chosen to bring the end to theirs. You were the only one who could."

The Oracle leaned into me. "A prophecy was written for you. You would be made whole. And you would bring an end to the Dark . . . and the Light."

I shook my head, looking at my hands. "I didn't want this. I didn't want to do any of this." In a remark to myself, I murmured, "I was certain the prophecy was about Zagan."

225

The Oracle shook her head as well, her blonde hair swinging about her child's face. "It was never about him. It was always you."

She gave a little sigh. "Yours was the first in a string of foretellings. Now that you have fulfilled it, the others will come to pass. The end draws nigh for many."

She dipped her head to meet my line of sight. And although her voice was void of emotion, I couldn't help but think she was trying to comfort me. "You will continue. This is not the end for you."

"I do not wish to continue," I told her.

I had lost too much. Done too much. I clasped my hands together in my lap and let my head hang forward. It was not fair. How could I bring the end, yet not for myself?

"I don't want to continue if I can't find him," I qualified. "Please," I begged, lifting my head again, "can you tell me what happened to him? Do you know where he is? Is he buried miles beneath the earth outside the Dark Manor? Did he wisp somewhere? If the Contessa—Aurelia—made it here, does that mean he is here also?" I almost leaned around The Oracle then, believing I would see him walking towards us.

But I didn't glance around, I stared at the little girl in front of me and I asked something of her with a desperation that I have never experienced since.

"Please. How do I find him?"

The Oracle shifted forward. "You can spend your life searching the world, and it will be in vain. He no longer walks the world. If you look beyond your own heart, you will never find him."

My head fell forward once more, my shoulders sagging at her blunt words. "He's truly gone?" I asked, unable to accept the notion.

The Oracle paused and I braced myself for the brutal blow that was about to come.

"Not if you look within," she replied.

I lifted my head, seeing myself in her eyes. Her eyes were large, too large, as if they had widened several degrees. And I felt her quiet little girl voice deep within my mind. "That which you seek, seeks you."

The Oracle tilted her head and the stars reflecting in her eyes swirled at the motion. "Go and find your peace, if that is what you wish. You are not finished yet. There is still more for you to do, more to fulfill, but no one can choose for you. If it is peace you desire, then go and find him. You know where to look."

I swallowed and nodded. I understood.

When I was able to find my voice again, I asked, "What will happen to Aleece? And the Council?"

"It is the end," the Oracle repeated. "Aleece is no more. The Light is gone. The Darkness is gone. The Elders have reached their end. And so too, have I."

Before I could close my eyes at the guilt I felt, The Oracle added, "Both the Light and Dark may now rest in peace. Restored. Made whole. No longer adrift, no longer searching."

"My father?" I asked.

"The end comes for him now."

"How much time does he have?"

"It does not work that way." She tilted her head, considering something before reassuring, "You will have a chance to see him again. To say your goodbyes."

"But—"

"All things must face their end. It cannot be escaped."

Guilt. Such guilt filled me.

"In forcing the scales to balance, you have saved your people," The Oracle consoled. "Think of your mother. With balance restored, that which plagued them, is no more. They will no longer suffer from their disease.

"And in bringing Aurelia here, you have saved her too."

The little girl studied me for a moment. "Do you know what happened to her?" she asked.

I shook my head, unsure what she meant.

"She sacrificed her Light for another. More than anything she wished to save Cortho from his end. And do you know why she did not perish after expending her very soul? It was because a few meager threads still connected her to him. After all, he was not entirely gone. Gravely injured, but not gone.

"And as Aurelia lay dying, as the one you call the Shadow King granted her sanctuary, she lived. She lived because somewhere out there, Cortho lived. But it was not enough. While Cortho had her Light to save him, to restore him, she had only Darkness. It filled her. It seeped in and took hold of her heart. Her hatred, her desire for revenge, filled her. It consumed her. And it became her. She grew stronger. Her need for vengeance was enough to fortify her—but only in the darkest of ways.

"The one you call the Shadow King was impressed by her resilience. He allowed her to remain at his Court. She proved

228

herself worthy and thirsty for knowledge. He bestowed the title of Contessa upon her. But he warned her of her lust for vengeance. He warned of the Darkness.

"He knew it all too well. It had become a part of him.

"Yet she did not listen. She could not hear his words.

"And after he was gone, with no one to guide her, her desire for revenge only grew. It fed her, and she became strong enough to release the Umbra".

The little girl placed a delicate finger under my chin and lifted my head. "You set her free. Because of you, she was able to enter Aleece. She was able to follow you in. And she found the one thing that could save her."

"Will she remember him?" I asked.

The little girl looked up at the sky again, studying it. "It is irrelevant," she finally answered. Then she lowered her gaze to meet mine. "A greater question is upon you."

I held my breath, waiting to hear what she would say next, suddenly terrified.

"You may return to your world, knowing you have fulfilled your destiny, grateful for all who have helped you reach this point. You will return whole. You will return with incredible power. Both of the Light and the Dark. You will return with the ability to restore balance to those who still seek it. Yet, will you choose to do so?"

"How can I ever face anyone again," I cried. "How can I ever face myself? The shame I feel . . . The loss is greater than anything I've ever—"

Two small hands covered my own with a searing heat, and suddenly a small glow of light pulsed from between my fingers. "But look at what you are," the Oracle whispered.

Slowly, she began to pull my hands back, and I let them fall away. The gesture looked like the opening of a book. And I stared at what was there.

Light and Dark. Small, bright, twinkling stars glittering in swaths of inky shadows.

As I stared at the sight, a single tear fell into my palm, causing the little specks of light to shimmer and the bands of shadows to sway.

The Oracle lifted her gaze to mine, and I saw myself in her eyes. My skin rosy, my lips pink, and my eyes violet.

"Sometimes, some things need to be broken wide open . . . to discover all that lies within.

"You feel great shame, but why? Can you not see all that you have done? Can you not feel all which you have created? Do you not understand the lives which you have spared suffering through the far reaches of time?

"Shame is too silly and small and lowly for you. For someone who is whole."

"Whole?" I objected. "I will never be whole again. The Contessa, the council, they took that from me."

"As a being, you are whole." The little girl gestured to my hands. "You can see that for yourself. What you speak of is something which lies in here," she said pointing to her chest.

"You have fulfilled your destiny. If it be your wish, go and join the one you seek. You may be at peace."

She cocked her head at me in that unnerving manner. And I suddenly remembered my mother and Elijah discussing The Oracle, in what seemed like another lifetime ago. They had claimed madness would overcome those who met with her.

Standing there, with the cosmos swirling all around us, and those two mirrors reflecting my image back at me, I could understand how it was all too much to take in. I could see the edge of madness just before me.

But I was not one who had anything to lose. That was the difference between myself and all those who had come before me.

I cared for nothing.

The odd little girl in the tattered dress nodded her head and repeated the same six words. "That which you seek, seeks you."

I could only stare at my reflection in her eyes.

The little girl stood. It seemed as if she took great pains in clarifying her comment. "You know where to find him if you truly wish. You have known all along. But you were too full of anger."

She looked down at me, and she placed her small hand on my cheek. She smiled, her face radiating. "This is the end."

Then a howl sounded in the darkness—a single note of mourning. I felt it in my bones.

The Oracles sweet child's face fell at the sound, her features pained, and her tiny, dirty hand clutched her chest.

From the nothing surrounding us, something was approaching. A dark form. As it came closer and closer, it took shape.

A wolf. It was the large black wolf. The one always by her side.

It's shining eyes stared at the little girl as it limped step by step for her. It wheezed with each breath. Each step, a struggle.

It didn't take its eyes off of her.

The little girl stood frozen where she was, her mouth agape, unable to breath, as she clutched her chest, watching the injured wolf approach. And large silver tears began to fall from her eyes.

With the last of its strength, with a final look up at the girl, the wolf dragged its body to her, collapsing at her feet.

The little girl looked down at her wolf.

And the little girl screamed. I heard the tortured cry from deep within my mind.

The ground crumbled away, and I fell from a great height. I tumbled back to where I had started.

I returned to where it all began.

CHAPTER 16

I HAVE TRIED TO SHARE EVERYTHING. I have tried to hold nothing back. And so, I will tell you what happened next.

You may judge me. You may cast your disapproval. You may call me fatalistic or dramatic, weak or macabre. But you will never know. You will never understand. Because you have not lived my life.

Find faults in my choices if you will. But this is what happened. Judge as you like. But know that my story does not require your permission.

Do not forget that you are the one who decided to listen . . .

***

I returned to the Dark Manor.

The Crone, Maxim, the Umbra—they were gone. And I cared not for them. Perhaps the Umbra lurked somewhere upon the manor grounds. Perhaps they would drift free through the night. Perhaps Maxim and the others would have to carry the burden of that evil. It was not my qualm. They would find a way.

I did not care. I had played my part. I had been a pawn and performed my role. I was done. The Oracle had said so. I had been granted permission.

I would find my peace.

I would find my own end. One of my choosing.

I stepped from the bath. I dressed. I brushed my hair until it dried into soft waves. I painted my lashes black and my lips red.

The moment my tasks were complete I turned and walked away. With each slow step crimson rose petals spun and swayed, drifting around me before floating to the floor. I had selected a dress I'd worn once before. One I had tucked away deep in my closet.

I ran in it once. Through the night, over dirt and bramble. Through the cavernous hall of the manor. Down the steps of the abandoned wing. Straight to him.

I had thought I'd lost him then.

This time I knew I had.

With my hair in sweeping waves, my lips stained, and rose petals raining around me, I descended through the dark, empty manor for what I knew was the last time. There was only one place I wanted to be. I would go there. I would lay myself down.

And I would find him.

My body could continue to live in this world, resting there in the haunted wing for as long as it drew breath. My heart could continue to pump warm blood if it chose. My body would be there . . .

But I would not. I would be wherever he was. I would drift and I would find him. I was going to stay with him. I had become too powerful to push away.

My last wish was that those who knew me would not pity me. Because I would be at peace, buried deep beneath the manor. I had found magic and light and love there once. It was a sacred place. And it was where I wanted to lie.

I pushed open the old rotted plank of wood, barring entry to the underground wing, and I took each stone step silently into his sanctuary.

The Darkness, the ghosts, the sorrow of the decrepit wing, the shadows which haunted that hall . . . they all bowed to me.

I was their queen now. I had earned their devotion. They saw the blackness born of my heart and they basked in its glory.

I was adorned with a crown of shadows.

I was determined to shed all which weighed upon me. I was determined to join them, to become nothing more than another shadow which slumbered there.

I walked for a small eternity down the Dark Prince's wing. Leaving a trail of rose petals in my wake. They dried and blackened behind me. I held my arms out and allowed my fingertips to brush the walls of the narrow hall. Willowy strands of light streamed where my skin made contact.

I absorbed the sorrow, the loss, the Darkness. And I cradled it all beneath my ribs.

When I reached his door, I stopped. I placed both hands upon it and allowed my cheek to rest against the rotted wood.

I tried to deny them, but I could not stop the flood of memories. I saw it all—the time I had spent behind this door. It almost brought me to my knees.

But the Darkness, the shadows, the sorrow . . . they soared around me, sending rose petals flying, and they kept me aloft.

After standing there for centuries . . .

I pushed open the door.

And I finally understood what it felt like to have a dagger shoved through my gut.

I had not planned to stop my breath. I had expected to let it continue, uninterrupted. In and out, my breathing would continue without me, rising through the manor in a whisper of silence.

And although I had not planned to stumble or stutter, I found myself choking, which caused me great confusion. It was not supposed to be like this.

I was entering what I considered a sacred place. I should not be choking and spluttering. But my eyes began to rim with liquid at the strangulation.

I had found a peaceful numbness. It had been so easy to take each step with that numbness. But after pushing open the door, I was no longer numb. Hairline cracks began to rupture the ice in my veins.

The walls shook. Dirt and debris rained down from the ceiling. My mouth opened and closed. But no words and no breath escaped my lips.

I was trying to speak out of reflex. But there was nothing to say.

Finally, with a desperate gasp, my breath sawed in and out of my chest as I began to comprehend . . .

I had been so foolish.

So ignorant.

How had I been so selfish? So blind? So stupid?

I clutched my stomach.

And then I fell to my hands and knees.

I squeezed my eyes shut, my head hanging between my shoulders. I knew I was hyperventilating.

Whatever happened, I knew I could not look up from the floor. Because I could not feel the presence of another person.

I knew I was alone in the room.

And yet, there he was, lying on the bed.

Something hot fell across the bridge of my nose. Silent shrieks and wails sounded from just behind me in the hallway as the Darkness there began to churn in a fervor, rattling the doors throughout the long corridor.

A sob escaped my lips. Followed by another. And then another.

I could have done something. There had been a chance.

Zagan had returned.

I imagined him bloody and dirty, smattered with black tar, inky markings swirling across his skin. I could see him tormented, lost to his demons, shaking and shuddering as he pulled himself into the bed.

And where had I been?

At the Shadow Court? With Maxim? In his arms as I declared my devotion to him?

Or a few floors above? Sharing a macabre kiss with the Umbra?

In Aleece? Caring solely about vengeance and punishment?

At the thought, my dress turned black. Each petal was now inky as it bloomed, shriveling the instant it was formed. And a layer of frost scuttled across the walls of the room.

I had never hated myself more.

I picked myself up, stumbling, and made my way to him. Falling at the side of his bed, I threw myself across his chest. There was a faint, impossibly slow beat to his heart. And his ribs barely rose on a breath. But I could not sense him. He was not present.

It was exactly what I had come to do. It was a final resting place.

Yet, still, I tried. Over and over again, I tried. Pulse after pulse of Light, I tried to revive him. Heal him. Restore him.

I tried to connect with him. I searched for some thread to grab a hold of and yank on. I tried to pull him to me. To bring him back from wherever he was.

It was no use.

Finally, I sat back and stared at him. I knew he wasn't there, but I knew I could find him. I held his perfect face in my hands and kissed him through my tears. I stroked the hair off his forehead. I looked at him one last time. And I did not mourn the time I'd had with him.

I cherished it.

No one had seen him the way I had. No one had known him the way I had. I knew that I was incredibly lucky to have experienced him, for however brief it may have been.

I kissed him again.

I wiped my tears from his face, and I picked myself up. I crossed to the other side of the bed. I lay down.

I took his hand in mine. I did not waste time. I closed my eyes and I let myself go. I let myself fall, knowing that I would not return.

I was powerful enough to stay with him now.

But I couldn't drift. I couldn't float. I was so desperate to go wherever the mind goes when we dream, that I could not reach it.

I could not leave my physical body. And the purest sense of panic flooded me. I tried to scramble back. I tried to push away from it.

I squeezed my eyes shut, refusing to open them. I lay absolutely still, denying myself the ability to move. I willed myself away.

Yet the more I fought, the more I realized I was solid. I persisted. I was of this world. And I was not going anywhere.

So instead, I lay there for a long time and just was.

I was in the Dark Manor. In the abandoned wing. In Zagan's bed.

I was right next to him, but I could not reach him.

Yet that was not the worst part of it all. That was not what slayed me. The true atrocity was that I was no longer alone in the room. Another had entered. And with that awareness came an unending well of fury.

How dare another enter this place.

The ego. The gall. The disrespect.

I immediately knew it had to be Maxim. I could *feel* him.

And I knew it was my punishment. It had to be.

I refused to acknowledge his presence. Out of spite. Out of necessity. Out of preservation for my sanity, I squeezed my eyes shut even tighter. Otherwise, I would burn the entire manor and all that surrounded it to the ground.

A hand was on my cheek. I cringed but I did not move. I refused to acknowledge my own consciousness. Instead I told myself it was Zagan's hand. I heard the breath that came before my name and I willed myself to only hear Zagan's voice.

And I adjusted the physical traits so perfectly, that I almost wanted to open my eyes. Because I could almost believe it was him.

"Violet."

It was too bittersweet. It was perfect. I did too good of a job in forcing myself to hear his voice. It was quiet, the air scraping across his vocal cords as if they'd gone too long without use.

"Violet," he repeated.

Perfect. Just perfect.

"Open your eyes."

I almost wanted to smile.

"Open your eyes," he repeated. The wounded sound to his voice was paired with a slight sharpness to his tone, as if he were angered that I did not obey his command.

It was so good I wanted to shake my head in response.

"Violet." Two hands took a hold of my shoulders. And I couldn't stop the tear that slipped from the corner of my eye. Because I had made the touch feel like his.

"You are difficult."

Another tear slipped down the side of my face.

"I know you are awake."

A finger traced my wet cheek, trying to wipe the tear away.

"Your eyes are leaking. Stop this. Why are you not opening them?"

After a moment, after the sound of shuffling, I felt two arms slip under me. He lifted me from the bed and held me against his chest. It even felt like he staggered as he tried to take a step forward. It played so well into the injured vision I had of him.

Maybe Maxim was, in fact, injured. Maybe that was why it felt so real when he took a few jagged steps before finding a jerky rhythm as he carried me out of the room and down the dark hall.

I didn't try to stop him. I allowed him to take me from the underground wing, I allowed him to carry me through the long hall on the first floor, and I even allowed him to take me to the foot of the grand staircase.

I allowed it all because I refused to open my eyes. I refused to acknowledge that I persisted.

And in some morbid way, I was grateful to Maxim. I did not know why he chose to carry me up the stairs, but I knew it was exactly what Zagan would have done. And I was able to continue with my desperate illusion.

Because the fantasy was so wonderful, I did something dangerous then, something that could have been disastrous. I allowed my eyes to flit open, to just barely peek beyond the fringe of my lashes.

And I saw Zagan.

I felt a dizzying gratitude at that point; I marveled in my ability to see what I wanted. "You look just like him," I murmured to myself. "Maybe you always have. Maybe I just didn't see it before."

He looked down at me with black eyes. "You're in shock," he said.

I ignored his comment, feeling like I was in a dream. "Where are you taking me, Maxim?"

"To your room," he said. "I am locking you in there. You are never to leave it again."

I thought about the last time I had insisted on leaving. How Zagan had refused and then relented. He had been right. We shouldn't have left the manor. We shouldn't have stepped outside.

"Alright, Maxim," I answered. "It's what he would have wanted."

"Why are you calling me that?" he growled.

I smiled a sad smile. For whatever reason, Maxim was playing along.

But as he carried me up each flight of stairs, I began to wonder if perhaps this was not a punishment after all. I began to wonder if this was some kind of gift. A compensation from those above. A reward for playing my part.

And what a lovely gift. He staggered the whole way up the stairs, continually righting himself. And his deep voice was strained with every word he spoke. I could not have asked for a more realistic dream. It was the perfect portrayal of Zagan, returned broken and damaged. I could just see him, fighting his way back, too strong to be defeated, too powerful to fail.

Through my suite he carried me, all the way to my bed. And he set me down.

"No!" I snapped. My eyes flashed open, and I stared at him as he towered next to me.

243

"No?" he asked.

"He wouldn't put me in the bed like this!"

I panicked, afraid it was all going to slip away. "He'd run the bath first! He always does! He'd want me to be comfortable! Look at how dirty you are. Look at how dirty you've made me."

Oh god, it was going to slip away. I squeezed my eyes shut, terrified the illusion would dissolve, terrified to suddenly see Maxim.

"You're ruining it!" I cried.

I wanted it to continue. I contemplated living the rest of my life in this charade because as pathetic as it was, as lowly and weak and traitorous as it made me, Maxim was the closest thing I could have to him.

I could feel hot tears begin to slip down my cheeks. And I could just picture him. His eyes darting back and forth over my face. His chest billowing. His shoulders rising and falling. His jaw clenching.

"Stop that!" he bellowed. "What do I have to do to make you stop that? I can't stand it!"

I squeezed my eyes tighter. "Don't yell at me!"

He began fuming, mumbling under his breath. "I suppose next you'll try attacking me. If I had learned anything, I would have searched you for weapons . . . witless, asinine woman . . ."

I could hear a growl of frustration rise from his chest. Then after a moment's deliberation, he finally snapped, "Stop this now or you will leave!"

I clapped my hand over my mouth at the pain his words caused.

After a pause. After a breath. After several breaths, once he'd regained control, his voice dropped. Softening ever so slightly. Begrudging.

"Tomorrow," he said.

I did not believe I had any heart left to break. But when I heard those words, a little piece of mine cracked.

And that's the thing about a heart: as long as one beats, there is always more to break.

I was right to begin with. This was my punishment.

But why would he say that? How would Maxim have known?

I couldn't help it. I opened my eyes, squinting at him, hoping to still see Zagan.

He looked down at me. Then he looked at himself, at his bare torso, his arms. He balled his hands into two fists and the ridges and planes across his abdomen and chest—his shoulders and arms—bunched and flexed beneath his skin smattered with blood and dirt and tar.

I could see the doubt on his face, the disgust. I could see how he glanced back at me, how he did not want to taint me—sully me.

Maxim would never look at himself like that.

He would never look at me like that.

And I began to shake. My chin began to tremble. I did not want to allow myself an ounce of hope. Of possibility. Because if I was wrong. If it was taken away from me . . .

He turned to leave. My hand flew into the air and captured his wrist. He stopped and turned to look down at me.

"Zagan?" I asked. It was the faintest of whispers. The sound barely existed. But it was enough.

He looked down at me and his chest expanded. Then slowly. So slowly. And carefully. So carefully. He folded himself onto the bed. Next to me. Against me. He gathered me in his arms. He held me against his chest. And he pressed his lips to my forehead.

The room was dark and quiet. The manor was dark and quiet. The grounds were dark and quiet. There was no fire in the hearth. No sunlight pouring through the windows.

We sat in the dark quiet room.

And he held me.

Zagan held me.

CHAPTER 17

H E SLEPT.
His arms were wrapped around me, holding on to me tightly. And he slept.

I was glad for it. Elated that his large frame took up too much space beside me. Elated that I was tied up in him.

And I wanted to stay there. I did.

But I couldn't.

I did my very best to slip out from his hold. It took some time; I had to go slowly. Because although he rested, although his breathing was even and slow, his arms were incredibly tense. They were locked, caging my body against his.

And I knew, even in sleep, he was not about to let me go.

Once I finally slipped free, I changed out of the dress I wore. I chose a white gauzy nightgown in its place—floor length with full sleeves.

I had known the choice was rather cliché and wildly sentimental. But I didn't care.

I stood there in the dark room, and I looked at Zagan. I looked around the room.

It was difficult to believe, after everything that had happened, but all was calm and settled. Centered. The space around us as well as the space within.

Save for one thing.

There was still something I had to do.

And I could not rest until the task was done.

It had started slow and low while I lay there with him. Then it had grown. A single Dark thread. A single Dark connection.

I could feel it out there. It was why I had not slept. It was why I couldn't stay with him. And it was why I could not stop myself from crossing to the window.

I watched, scanning the manor grounds. They began to appear—one by one—out there in the night, while he slept.

Their eyes were on me. Waiting for me. And maybe ... perhaps ... waiting for him too.

I knew then that they could not be allowed, and I swore I would never let them reach him. Never again.

They had filled him with so much Darkness. They had tortured him, haunted him.

And yet, somehow, he had fought them his entire life. Never giving in. Never surrendering.

They were the last thing standing in the way.

And while I knew they waited for me, I could not cut the tether that connected us. I could not free them to wander the night.

But I knew something else. I was sure of it. And, so, I did not fear the Umbra. Because I did not need the Heart of Darkness.

I could lock them away. *I could feel it.*

In spite of all that had happened, I was not free of the Darkness. It still lived in me. It always would.

True, I had been drained of my power in Aleece. But the Darkness, like the Light, was a part of me now. I could never truly be rid of it. Already, since I'd returned to the manor, I had felt it growing, slipping and sliding through my veins.

Yet it was also different now. I did not believe it would consume me now. I felt as though it was a part of me and only that—a part of me—not some driving force to which I would become lost.

And with my newfound assurance, with a balance of power, in the delicate white gown—I walked out to meet the Umbra.

And still, I was fearful. I had done great things. Great, but terrible. I knew the power I possessed was dangerous.

But I had to try.

I knew this would be a final test. And I knew I had to be stronger than the elements I possessed.

I made my way down the main staircase, through the silence and darkness of the manor, and I opened the front door. In the cold night air, I walked across the front lawn, through the leaves and bramble, to climb the trail leading up to the cliff.

I went to greet the Umbra.

I went to bring them their end.

I did not share my intentions, I kept everything secured and tucked away. I carried it all within. And so, the Umbra did not fear me. I called them all to stand before me upon the cliff's edge.

They obeyed, towering in front of me. And they waited. Watching. Their lifeless, reflective eyes, staring back at me. Dozens of them.

The air was cold and cutting up on the cliff. I could feel it slash at my skin as I stood before them.

Tall gaunt figures in black billowing robes.

I called to them, demanding their obedience, their loyalty. I accepted responsibility for them. I was their master.

Then I called to the Darkness. I pulled it from the skies high above and the earth deep below. I drew it to my hands, to my very bones.

This entire time I had believed I could have one or the other. The Light or the Dark. It was only then, in that moment, that I realized I could use both at the same time. I could be both.

So, up there, on top of the cliff, I called to the Light as well. And with the balance of power I possessed, I opened the earth. I created a chasm beneath the cliff once more.

Yet this one did not gurgle and belch with sulfuric acid. This one was silent and dark. All consuming. Not a gateway to hell, but an infinite void of nothing. A black hole.

I was certain—I somehow knew—that it was not something I would ever be able to do again. Every power, every force I had come up against . . . each entity had deposited something. And piece by piece it had all collected somewhere deep within, coalescing into something greater than I.

Everything that had touched me, everything which had slipped under my skin, now knitted together for one incredible moment of power. I would never be this strong again.

I had one chance.

I would not fail.

Zagan had come back to me. I had to make certain I would never lose him again. I had to make certain he was freed from the Darkness.

This was my offering. This was the heart I would cut from his chest. Not a red, pulsing, bloody heart that would harden and freeze into a glittering gem.

But a black heart. One that would dissolve away into inky tendrils of smoke. One that haunted him his entire life. One that caused him to see himself as a monster in the night.

I would cut out this heart, and unlike Entropy, I would not await its return. I would lock it away, never to be found again.

This was my offering.

I understood then what he had been doing when he went after the Contessa. He had not left me. He had not forsaken me. He had not chosen revenge over me.

He had put me above all else. I understood that now.

Because now that was what I was doing for him.

Suddenly, without warning, I stepped towards the Umbra with my arms opened wide at my sides. I pushed them back. And they began to fall.

I forced them to plummet into the abyss below, their ghostly figures plunging silently through the air, black robes flitting around them.

Many did. My will was great.

But those closest to me, stood their ground, refusing to be locked away. And in their large animal-like eyes, I saw an image of myself as they took my head with the claws they had for hands.

I pushed harder. I pulled power from the cosmos. I sent more Umbra off the cliff.

But still I met resistance.

And then they came for me. They no longer flew backwards, sucked into the event horizon. Now they floated to meet me. And as they came, they opened the gaping holes where their mouths should be, and they breathed into me.

I began to drown in them.

I would have to fight them. I would have to maintain the opening below while willing them off the cliff. And at the same time, I would have to fight them. I would push every last one off.

But before the first advancing Umbra could swipe at me, a sword sliced through the air at my side, decapitating it.

With honed precision Maxim flicked his weapon about to behead the next. I could not grab his arm and wrench it down, I had to keep my hands stretched at my sides as I struggled to keep the chasm open below.

"Stop!" I shouted over the gusting wind. "You will only cause them to resurrect! I need to send them into the void. I need to lock them away."

Each word was a struggle. It took all I had to maintain the chasm, every ounce of my strength and focus.

"What the hell are you doing here, anyway?" I gritted. *Why was he always showing up when the stakes were high?*

I couldn't voice my thoughts any further, though. I fought to send more Umbra off the cliff, leaning forward, leaning into them.

Maxim looked at my face, looked into my eyes, looked at my hair flying around my shoulders in the wind, my white nightgown whipping behind me . . . and he was shocked at my appearance. Shocked at the words I'd just spoken.

He probably thought he would have to fight me. And with the quick glimpse I had of him, I saw the special shackles clipped at his belt, the ones he bound me with once before.

I realized that was probably why he'd come. Maxim had decided to do his best to imprison *me*.

Based on our last encounter, I couldn't blame him.

But Maxim was too noble. That had always been his problem. He had tried to protect me from the Umbra instead of letting the thing take me out. So someone beat Maxim at his own game. Someone else grabbed a hold of me.

A hand slid around my throat from behind. A sword thrust against my neck. Everything in me screamed to fight back and get free.

But I had to maintain the steady stream of power. I had to give my full strength to the void and the Umbra. I *knew* I could not break that connection.

Maxim's eyes widened in the instant I was snared, and I knew whoever held me was not working with him. But Maxim could do nothing about it; the next tall gaunt figure was upon him.

The Umbra grabbed Maxim. He had no choice but to fight it. Luckily, he understood, and he did not immediately try to take the thing's head. Instead, he went for the knees.

At my ear, I heard the voice of a madman. "I served that bitch for years. I'm not about to crawl before another." The sword dug into my neck. "You are going to choose me. It is my turn to rule the Court. You will wed me. And you will kneel to me. Serve me as I wish."

His tongue swiped across my face, from my chin to my cheek. "Or I'll kill you right here."

Marax.

For a split second, my eyes drifted down to the mangled gate in front of the tree tunnel. And I cursed the Archangels for destroying it.

Marax was an idiot. A child who thought he could play with grown-ups. I would have put an end to him right then and there, but I had to aim every ounce of my strength and energy and focus on the Umbra.

I struggled to keep the void open. I shook with the effort. And the sick bastard behind me thought it was because of him. He thought I quaked with fear. And I could feel how much he enjoyed my perceived fright. He was disgusting.

Worse, he didn't seem to care about the fact that the Umbra were advancing, or that Maxim was battling them.

Did he even see what was happening in front of him?

His stupidity ran so deep, it actually made me angry. Did he think all he had to do was make his demands and I'd oblige? He'd be better off killing me.

And yet because of the precise moment he'd chosen, he had the upper hand; he began to drag me from the cliff.

I fought to stand my ground. I struggled to hold open the chasm below. And I watched Maxim do his best to topple the

Umbra. But neither of us could stop Marax from pulling me away.

With each shove from Marax, I was yanked back foot by foot. A fresh stream of blood ran down my neck as his sword nicked my skin there each time.

And with every blow, I could see Maxim inch closer and closer to the cliff's edge, the Umbra's claws coming dangerously close to his throat several times. All the while, he was immersed in those black acrid fumes.

We weren't going to make it.

We would try our best. We would not give up. But we weren't going to make it.

Goosebumps broke out over my skin. Yet it was not the realization of looming defeat which caused them. I felt the sudden chill because just then the temperature on the cliff plummeted, and ice skittered across the grass at our feet.

Over the bluster of the whipping wind, I heard something. A tinny sound. The sound of steel scraping over frost.

But that was not all. There was something else. Something steady and low, like a heartbeat. As it grew, I knew exactly what it was.

The thump of footsteps. Unhurried.

He was coming for me.

And Marax had no idea what lurked for him in the shadows.

There was a crack followed by an immediate scream. The sword at my neck slipped, hanging over my shoulder at a limp angle. Zagan had snapped Marax's arm.

I felt Marax's body yanked from mine just before he went flying through the air, landing in front of me among the Umbra.

Zagan appeared from behind me then, emerging from the shadows. And step by unhurried step, he headed for Marax. No shoes. No shirt. Just a pair of black pants.

His lack of clothing was somehow much more menacing than any armor could ever be. The muscles along his back and arms bulged with his quiet rage. He was too large for his body.

And there was something deeply chilling in the way he dragged his sword along the ground at his side, as if it was something he had no need for.

Marax looked up at him with sheer terror, throwing his one good arm up in front of his face.

I fought to focus. I fought to maintain my control. My arms remained stretched at my sides. And Maxim continued to battle the Umbra. He had managed to keep himself upright, but his clothing was riddled in tears and shreds. One large gap over his chest revealed the mark at his heart.

Three crescent moons intertwined—the same exact mark that pulsed on Zagan's chest.

I held on, fighting harder. Refusing to let go.

Suddenly Zagan stopped where he was. He seemed to realize there was more to the situation than Marax alone. He seemed to snap out of his fervor.

He saw Maxim battling for his life at the edge of the cliff. He saw me struggling to control such intense amounts of power. And he saw the danger, the dire need to push back the Umbra.

I had thought I could do it alone. I had thought I would imprison the Umbra, sending them to their end without hurting any more people, without putting anyone else in danger. It was what I'd wanted.

But we so rarely get what we want.

I don't know why he did what he did then. I don't know what compelled him. But Zagan walked forward towards the precipice. He stood among the Umbra. And because he did not try to fight them, those claw-like hands did not come for him.

Instead, he threw his head back, dropping his sword, and his fists clenched at his sides. His chest began heaving as those black, acrid fumes billowing from the Umbra were drawn to him, swirling around him and seeping into his skin. Inky marks began to appear all across his back and arms, shifting and swaying.

I felt the Umbra . . . *weaken.*

I didn't have the strength for it, but somehow, I managed to grit four words from between my teeth. "What are you doing?!"

Zagan didn't answer. His body shook, and his muscles bulged beneath the black marks floating over his skin.

"He's absorbing their power!" Maxim shouted as he spun, battling for our lives. "Push harder, Violet!"

My heart gave a surging pump. Zagan was helping to lock away the Umbra. He was giving us a fighting chance.

But at what cost? He was going to drown himself in evil.

I pushed harder. Shoving more of them over the edge.

I wanted to shout at him to stop. I didn't want this for him. But I could not speak. Every ounce of what I was went into the inescapable black hole.

And that was when Maxim stumbled. He had absorbed the Darkness, the caustic poison, the evil. And I knew he was at a breaking point.

He went down to one knee at the very edge of the cliff. A claw-like hand arced through the air. And a spray of blood flew from Maxim's neck.

He collapsed where he was.

I did cry out then. And I was terrified it was too late. Squeezing my eyes shut, I knew this could not go on a single moment longer.

With one final push, with everything that I was, I forced the last of the Umbra off the cliff. It did not matter if they were standing erect or lying on the ground, every last one fell.

When I opened my eyes, I knew I had to break my connection with the Umbra. I knew I would be sucked in after them if I didn't. I could feel the pull. I had to close the fissure.

I took a lurching step forward, unable to stop myself. I tried to close the void. I tried to sever my connection. But it was more difficult to sew shut the chasm than it had been to open it.

I stared at Zagan, afraid he would be pulled in as well. Every muscle in his body was straining, and his shoulders were drawn back.

He was trying to fight the pull, too.

My eyes darted to Maxim; he still lay on the cliff's edge. It was a relief to see him there . . . but I had no idea if there was a chance he might be caught in the tow, pulled over.

And as I stared at Maxim, as I fought to close the void, I saw something from the corner of my eye.

A dark form stumbled through the night.

I watched, unable to intervene, as Marax ran at full speed towards Zagan's back.

I wanted to stop him. I wanted to shout at Zagan. I tried to yell out, but instead I took another lurching step forward, being dragged into the black hole.

I was losing strength. I could feel the edges of exhaustion rushing towards me. With one final surge, I tried to close the chasm.

Marax crashed into Zagan.

And the two of them flew forward. They were too close to the precipice. And the pull from below was too strong. They both began tumbling over the cliff's edge.

And I watched as they began to fall.

It was happening all over again. I knew, this time, there would be no coming back. There would be no wisping from the pull of the event horizon.

I would lose him for good.

I could not save him.

But . . .

Someone else could.

An arm swung out. A large strong hand covered in the sticky tar-like blood of the Umbra clasped around Zagan's forearm. Holding him there.

And with his throat slashed open, with Darkness coursing through his veins, with black eyes, with the very last of his strength—Maxim pulled Zagan up, dragging him back onto the cliff.

The final sound to pierce the night was Marax's scream as he plummeted into the void.

Then with a silent clap of thunder, the abyss below sealed shut, disappearing from existence.

I staggered as the last of my strength left me.

I watched as Maxim's eyes rolled back in his head, and he collapsed onto his chest.

And I watched as Zagan fell to his knees, holding his head in his hands.

CHAPTER 18

I SCRAMBLED OVER TO ZAGAN.

He thrashed his head violently, squeezing his temples as if trying to hold himself together. I grabbed his shoulders, but I instantly drew my hands back. His skin was so cold, it burned.

Black marks pulsed over his torso and arms like dark parasites crawling just below the surface. And I could have sworn I heard the shrieks and wails living inside his head. There was so much Darkness churning within him, I wasn't certain if he would ever find his way through it.

I tried again to touch him, wanting to take some of it from him, wanting to soothe him. But as soon as my hands landed on his back, he threw his arms down and whipped his head up to stare at me. His eyes were black and cold.

He was angry. Furious.

I backed up. He staggered to his feet, and he came for me. His normally fluid motions were jerky and slow. And I could see he struggled. I could see a war raged within. Somewhere, deep inside, he fought for control.

I couldn't stop my eyes from growing wide at the sight of him. I honestly didn't know what he would do. And for the first time, I was scared.

He cornered me. Forcing me against the oak tree.

"You don't understand," I tried, shouting to be heard over the wind. "I knew I could do it. I had to. It's over now. It was the last thing standing in the way, and now it's all over."

He didn't hear me. The Darkness filled him, leaving little room for anything else. Those wailing, screeching shadows flexed and shifted around him.

His chest heaved against mine as he pinned me to the tree. I stared into his maddened black eyes, terrified of what was coming.

His voice was frightening, layered and cold. "You leave me no choice—"

But he did not finish his sentence, because a noise was carried on the wind then. The sound seemed to echo around us. Although quiet, it was a sound that somehow pierced his madness. It stopped him from continuing, and it caused his head to tick to the side. It caused him to freeze where he was.

It was a single gurgled breath.

I was trapped in Zagan's eyes. I did not want to look away from him. I was afraid I would lose him if I did. But I had to glance over his shoulder. I had to look in the direction of the sound.

I knew the timing was awful, I knew it was asking too much, but I silently pleaded with him.

In a motion that looked like it took all his strength, Zagan ripped his gaze from mine to look back at Maxim.

When he turned to me once more, I could see the promise of punishment in his eyes. He grabbed a hold of my wrist yanking me from the tree, and I instantly found myself swept up in chaos and shadows as he wisped me from the cliff. Without another word, he threw me towards the bed in the master chamber, up on the fifth floor of the manor.

I took a few stumbling steps as he disappeared.

But he was not gone. A moment later Zagan returned placing Maxim on the bed. He stalked over to me in the cavernous, dark room with those slow, jerky steps—the war continuing to rage within. He battled for self-control.

Towering over me, forcing me to look up at him, he could barely speak. But with black eyes and black marks shifting over his skin he ordered, "Help him."

Then he gave a single shudder and was gone.

I froze where I was for a moment, knowing I needed to go after him. Knowing he needed me. But then Maxim gave another wet gurgle.

"Shit!" I snapped.

I ran out of the room down the hall to the opposite wing. I tore through my quarters collecting towels and a sheet, before racing back to the chamber.

I set everything down on the bed to look at Maxim. The gash at his neck was deep. Under any other circumstance, I would have reasoned that he just needed time to heal.

But I bit my lip and I shook my head. Like Zagan, he, too, had dark marks forming and shifting over his skin. He was drowning in the evil of the Umbra. I could see it all across his chest and arms, and I was afraid it was impacting his ability to heal from his wound. His body was racked with a violent spasm.

I knew Zagan had been living with an excess of Darkness for years. I knew he had a certain tolerance for it. But Maxim . . .

"What do I do?!" I asked him.

His eyes fluttered, but they did not open.

I needed the Crone. I turned from the bed.

"Seraphina!"

I didn't know what to do other than try and call for her. I ran to the doors of the chamber, beckoning. I shouted her name over and over again. But there was no reply, no scraping sound of a bucket, no hunched form limping through the room.

I had to do what I could. I took the towels to the large bathtub that sat near the fireplace, and I ran them under the water. I went back to stand over Maxim. I pulled the last remaining threads of his shirt from him.

I did my best to clean his wound.

I tried to speak to him as I dabbed the towel over him, using his name as much as possible. His body convulsed again. Without a thought, I sent a pulse of energy to the fireplace. Light and heat sprang to life in the room.

"They're gone, Maxim. You did it. The Contessa is gone. The Umbra are locked away. Your people will be safe. You did it. You have worked so hard for them. And . . . Maxim . . . I'm sorry. I'm so sorry for what I did to you. For the things I did and said. Please. I just, I need you to get better. Okay? Okay, Maxim?"

I looked down at him, at his big body, and I felt an incredible pang at how vulnerable he was. I had never seen him as anything but strong and certain.

"Maxim, listen. Your people still need you. The Shadow people need you to lead, okay? It's you who needs to do it. You are their true leader. You've proven that. You need to get better."

I said something then. Something true. A foretelling. It wasn't an attempt to fluff his ego or lure him back to consciousness with false promises. It just was.

"You are the Shadow King now."

I knew it was not Zagan who would fill that role. That was not something he would ever want.

It was Maxim. It had always been Maxim. And I was terrified he would not live to finally claim the crown.

I couldn't help but think of the first time I had felt the Darkness from the Umbra creep through my body. The burning of it, the slow death of it. I hated that Maxim was experiencing it.

After a final pat to the slash at his neck, I ripped the bed sheet into strips. Then I tried to gently wind them around his neck. It was such a pathetic attempt at helping him, but I didn't know what else to do.

Without any thought to the action, I pushed his hair back from his forehead wanting nothing more than to comfort him.

At the touch, his eyelids twitched. Then he tried to take another breath, but he was met with more wet gurgling.

"Shh, it's okay," I murmured, brushing my hand across his forehead again.

And again, there was movement under his eyelids.

"Just relax," I encouraged. "It's all over."

But with a few slow blinks, Maxim began to open his eyes.

He looked up at me, focusing on me. After a moment, his lips began to move but no sound came out. I smiled at him, holding back tears, wanting to reassure him.

"Don't talk," I told him, trying my best to keep my voice even.

He reached his hand up and touched my cheek with his fingertips.

With the touch, I felt a pang of something. I swallowed at the sharpness of it. And out of reflex my eyes flashed to the opposite end of the room. Because what I'd felt was the cutting sting of jealousy. And it had not come from me.

I could see him there, shaking and shuddering, standing in the shadows. Watching me. Watching Maxim's hand on my skin. I didn't know how long he'd been there. He must have just arrived, otherwise I would have sensed him.

My heart stopped. I couldn't breathe. I wanted to explain or reassure or . . . *something*. I wanted to go to him. I needed to.

But Maxim gave another wet cough, gurgling and choking. I looked down at him, taking his hand in my own.

"Shh," I soothed. "Take it easy. It's okay. It's all okay. Just relax." I brushed the hair from his forehead again. "Everything's okay," I promised.

I spoke slowly. "We're all going to be okay."

I glanced back at the other side of the room where Zagan had been a moment ago, terrified I had just spoken a lie.

***

It didn't take long for Maxim to drift into sleep. And although it sounded all wrong, although he struggled, he was managing to breathe.

I didn't want to leave him alone. It felt cruel. But there wasn't more I could do for him.

Maxim seemed to be managing, somehow. He was not battling the Darkness the way Zagan was. The power of the Dark energy seemed to settle into him, absorbing little by little at a much faster rate then I'd seen in Zagan.

And I wondered if that had to do with the sharp control Maxim possessed or his strength of character. Or maybe it was because, as the other son of the Shadow King, he did not have to reconcile the Dark with the Light the way Zagan did. Maybe it was because he possessed only Darkness to begin with.

I didn't know. And it didn't matter. Whatever the reason, I was glad for him.

I silently left the room. I was still in the white nightgown, and I knew I needed to change. But every minute I had waited had been too painful. I couldn't spare a moment more.

I went to go find Zagan.

I knew he was angry with me. I knew he was furious that I had left the manor. That I had driven him over the edge once more. That we were in this unending loop.

I swore as I swept through the frigid dark halls that it was the last time. I would never leave the manor again, if that was what he wanted.

Everything was finally solved. There was nothing left standing in the way.

At least, that was what I told myself.

Down on the first floor, I passed over the slats of moonlight which poured through the windows of the long hall. And I made my way to the boarded-up door at the end of the corridor.

We had been through this all before. I'd run from him. He'd left me.

Neither would happen tonight. I would not run tonight. And I would not let him leave. I was prepared to stop him if I needed to.

Out of nowhere, his arm snaked around my waist, shoving my back into his chest. His other arm banded across my sternum. He grabbed my chin in his hand, forcing my head back against his shoulder. His lips were at my ear.

"I am a curse," he seethed. "I am your punishment." He pushed me forward, keeping his arms wrapped around me, pressing my chest into the wall, pressing his hips into mine.

"I warned you. Time and time again, I warned you. Why did you never listen?! I tried to save you from myself!"

He leaned into me. I could feel his lips smashed against my cheek as he spoke. "You have no idea the impulses I have when it comes to you. The things I want to do to you. To force you to submit to me. The ways I want to ensure that you will never—ever—let another man touch you."

He paused for a long moment, and when he spoke again the pain in his voice was like a knife to the heart. "You should be with him. He is the one you deserve. You should be with him."

He jerked my body into his as he made an icy promise. "And I will never let you."

At his words, something shifted into focus. I suddenly saw all those nights I'd spent with Maxim. And I realized what they'd done to him.

I had thought Zagan came to collect me in a psychotic rage because of the way he would find me: broken and battered. But now I realized the totality of it. I was kept from him. I was with another man. I was with Maxim, pressed against him, my body pinned beneath his.

And Zagan had been unable to get to me, shut out. It was only then when I realized just how cruel it had been.

His head dropped onto my shoulder. "I can't let you be with him. He's better. He's what you deserve. If I was anything more than a monster, I'd free you. I'd leave so you could be with him. But I can't."

My body shook at his words. Not out of fear, but out of my own battle I fought. There was such an overwhelming desire to let him have his way, to give him that release, to relent to him.

But I couldn't. This couldn't be the way of it. I could not—I would not—allow this to continue.

He had to understand.

"You. Do not. Listen." My words were low and controlled.

"*I* have warned *you*," I told him. "I have told you. Truthfully. That I choose to be with you. I have told you that I am strong enough to leave if I choose. You have not believed me. You have

271

never believed me. You are going to be sorry. You have asked for this."

Maybe it was wicked. Maybe it was a bad idea. But I was going to put an end to this. Tonight.

With a speed at which even I was surprised, I rolled off the wall forcing his back into it. At the same time, I threaded my arms under his before flinging them out, freeing myself from his hold.

I ran down the imposing hall, through the swaths of moonlight, knowing it would incite a predatory instinct in him, knowing he would come after me.

I flung open the rotted plank and rushed down the stairs, glancing over my shoulder. Just as I turned the curve, I saw his silhouette take shape at the doorway. He was taking his time, knowing there was nowhere for me to go.

I hastened to his room, scrambling to the far wall, backing myself in the corner. I adjusted the metal I held behind my back, getting ready to use it. Again, I watched his outline appear at the door, filling the frame. He shook his head once before silently crossing to stand before me.

His eyes were black, and an icy chill poured from him. But the dark marks shifting and pulsing under his skin had begun to settle. And I knew it was because he had held me.

He placed his hands against the wall at my shoulders, caging me there, and he leaned his face down to mine. "Say it." His voice was full of anger and darkness, yet somehow it was still a caress that traveled down my spine.

"No," I told him.

His breathing quickened, and the muscle under his eye ticked. His jawline was too sharp, too defined, the tendons in his neck strained against his skin as he tried to hold himself back.

He reached forward to grab the front of my nightgown. "Say it," he repeated.

I shook my head.

He tore the flimsy fabric of the gown, ripping it down the front, flinging it off my arms. I stood in front of him with only a thin scrap of white cotton hugging my hips. I raised my chin in defiance, my hair shifting around my shoulders and chest.

"Say. It." His voice was layered with restraint. He was at a breaking point.

I tilted my chin higher, my neck straining as I stared up at him. "No."

He shook. He raised one hand from the wall, about to touch me, about to grab me. Then he gave his head a violent shake. He began to take a retreating step.

He was going to leave.

He was going to leave before he could do anything to me. And he would probably stay away for as long as he could.

From behind my back, I raised the manacles I'd snatched from Maxim. I snapped one on his wrist. In a continuous motion, I ducked under his arm and spun around his back. Then I shoved his chest into the wall while grabbing a hold of his other arm, yanking it back. With my heart racing, I clasped the other end of the cuff over his free wrist.

His arms were bound behind his back.

A pause. A moment of confusion. Then he roared my name, and the walls in the room shook. "Violet!"

I had carried the cuffs with me, afraid he would try to leave. I had hoped they could prevent him from wisping away. So far, they seemed to be working.

It may have been too wicked. It may have been a bad idea. But I was putting an end to this tonight.

I grabbed his arm to spin him around and face me.

He shook his head, his eyes crazed. "You do not know what you're doing!" he thundered. "You are making it worse! I will not be able to control myself! Get away! Now!"

I shook my head at him. I set my jaw. I could feel my lips purse in defiance. "I'm not going anywhere. And neither are you."

Towering over me with his hands bound behind his back, the muscles all along his arms and chest and abdomen bulged. He took one menacing step into me.

"Free me," he seethed. Then he took another aggressive step, forcing me back.

I gave my head a slow shake.

"Then say it," he gritted. With another step, he backed me against the bed. "Say it. Tell me what I need to hear. Or free me to go."

"Free yourself," I countered. "*You* say it. *You.* Admit to yourself that I choose to be with you. Admit it, and I'll let you go."

"Violet," he hissed, "What you are doing is very dangerous."

"You have no idea," I countered. I ran my hand over his trousers, feeling just how hard and bruising he was. His nostrils flared at the contact as he drew in a sharp breath, and his jaw clenched. He took several more breaths, his shoulders heaving as he stared at me with those black eyes.

"Do not do that again," he warned.

I placed both my hands on his chest. I couldn't help but notice how fair and delicate they looked against his skin. I could also see that the dark marks were continuing to settle and more were fading. Except, of course, for the three crescent moons intertwined over his heart.

I traced the brand with my finger. Then I raked my nails ever so lightly down the ridges of muscle along his torso. In a continuous motion I brushed my hands over his shaft again, slipping across the fabric of his pants.

He threw his head back, letting out another roar of frustration. He pressed his body into mine, groaning. "Free me."

"All you have to do is say it," I repeated. "Acknowledge that I choose to be with you."

He took one final step into me, and I was forced back onto the mattress. He fell on top of me grinding his hips into mine, his wrists still bound.

My head fell to the side and I couldn't stop a moan. The sound seemed to incite him even more. He bit my neck before sucking on my pulse point. I stabbed my fingers into his hair. A flare of energy burst through the room.

He pulled back from me, staring down at me with a streak of blue running through his right eye, and he snarled, "Release. Me."

"Not until you finally admit the truth to yourself," I panted between breaths. "Not until you see me for who I am."

He looked like he was about to explode with rage again. But before he could let out a bellow of frustration, something glinted in the cold darkness of his eyes—something calculating. The muscle in his jaw ticked, and I suddenly became nervous.

275

But all he did was kiss me. He began to move his lips across my chin, down my neck, over my collar bone and breasts, down my stomach. He stopped at the thin cotton waistband, though.

He paused and he looked up at me with so much possession then. And I could also see him promising his revenge. Then he placed his mouth over the delicate fabric right at my very center, his hot breath instantly making its way beneath the material.

I couldn't stop from arching my back as he sucked at the fabric, right where I was hot and swollen. And next he did something truly villainous. He pressed his tongue into the cotton.

I hated him for it.

I let out a cry, running my fingers through his hair, rolling my hips up to meet him. And yet, I tried to push him away at the same time. But my resistance lacked any true desire, any true force. He began a steady rhythm, sucking and pressing, his hot breath, his hair brushing my thighs.

It was incredible torture because it wasn't enough. I knew I would die right there in a single burst if I didn't get more from him. And yet somehow, at the same time, I loved the agony of it.

I reached down to slide the small scrap of cotton off.

But he pulled back. He rose above me to stand at the foot of the bed, looking down at me spread out beneath him.

"Free me now, or let me leave," he insisted. His voice was so low it made me shiver.

"Admit that I choose you," I begged.

His eyes narrowed, and his lips pressed into a thin line. He was being so stubborn. I released a tormented huff.

I sat up in front of him, my chest tight and hot, rising and falling rapidly. My hair tumbled around my face and shoulders. I ran my hand through it, pushing it back.

I wasn't giving up, though. I rose as well, standing on the mattress. I met him eye to eye, looping my arms around his neck, my head a few inches above his. I stared at him. I gave him a kiss. Deep and long. One that lasted forever.

Then I leaned down to reach for his trousers. I let my hair brush against his skin as I undid his zipper, allowing his pants to fall to the floor.

At the same time, I gave the delicate fabric at my hips a tear. One side, then the other, before letting it fall away.

He groaned, compelled to lean into me. While still standing on the mattress in front of him, I wrapped my arms around his shoulders, pressing my breasts into his chest, feeling him shudder against me. I ran my hands all over him—his back, his shoulders and arms, his chest and neck, through his hair.

"It's so easy," I whispered as my lips grazed his temple.

His eyes slid shut at the contact.

"It's so simple," I explained, rubbing my nose along his cheek. "All you have to do is open your eyes and see the truth of it."

He inhaled. He leaned into me. He brushed his face against my hair.

And when he picked his head up, when he opened his eyes again, they were electric blue.

He stared at me, struggling, needing . . . wanting to believe. And finally, with difficulty, he acknowledged me for who I was. His voice was low and dark, a whisper in the room.

"*You choose me,*" he admitted at last.

The room was absolutely still, absolutely quiet for a moment. I began to smile with pure joy—

But goosebumps broke out over my skin as all the energy in the room funneled to one point. I felt the jolt of latent power an instant before he used it.

Zagan's shoulders jerked. And with incredible strength, with undeniable power, with a ferocity, with a refusal to be kept from what he wanted . . . he broke the bonds at his back.

He grabbed my arms from around his neck holding both my wrists in one hand. His other hand snaked around my waist, pinning me against him.

Black veins forked through his eyes, mingling with the blue. My mouth dropped open in shock.

He leaned his face into mine, speaking as his lips hovered just above mine, and he promised punishment for my sins.

"Now you are going to pay."

***

He did not hold back. He did not need to. He understood that now.

He slammed his lips over mine, plunging, delving, taking whatever he wanted. It was not the gentle kiss of a lover. It was unadulterated possession.

I couldn't breathe. I gasped at the ownership of it. I breathed *through* him.

He kept my wrists squeezed in his grip, and he took one swift step back, forcing my legs off the mattress, forcing me to wrap them around his hips.

Without letting go of me, he threw me down to the bed, following after me. With his free hand he covered my breast.

I couldn't gasp at the touch, because he swallowed any sound I made.

I tried to pull back, I tried to regain some semblance of control. But he gave my wrists a bruising jostle, holding me in place.

Then he tried to touch me, tried to glide his fingers between my legs. But I was too hot, too swollen, too drenched. And the pain, the torture on his face was unbearable. He could not take another second of it.

He never cursed, never used profanity, but he swore at the feel of me. "Fuuuuuck!"

He had my wrists pinned at my chest. "Let me go," I breathed, I begged, I sighed.

"Never!" he vowed.

And he tried to shove into me. He tried. But in spite of how slick I was, he was too big, too aroused, too swollen.

I let out a cry, and it only incited him more.

He thrust again, forcing himself into me, demanding I accept him. But still, I was too tight. Again and again he wedged himself, sliding deeper a fraction at a time. And with each forceful thrust, I cried out time after time as wave after wave built.

And I drove him to another kind of madness.

With a final, total shove, I couldn't stop myself from convulsing around him. I cried out, not thinking I would ever be able to stop.

He stilled, watching me, straining not to let each squeeze take him over the edge. Not to let the sight of me, destroy him. Wanting to hold on to his control.

Once I'd stilled, once I was panting and heaving beneath him, once I'd completely drenched his shaft, he adjusted his grip on my bound wrists.

But he did not release me. Still he held me there, my hands pinned down, refusing to let me go, refusing to free me. And he began his tormenting assault.

Slowly, so slowly, he began moving his hips in long strokes. My head fell to the side and I moaned in agony. I knew I was not going to be able to take it. I knew he was going to draw this out. He was going to get some kind of pleasure in the way he had full control over me.

And when he began to build his rhythm, when he began to let go, drawing out the incredible pressure, when he knew I was getting close to falling over the edge . . . he stopped.

He switched to shallow strokes, barely penetrating me, forcing me to writhe under his hold, begging him to let me go, my hips trying to rise to meet him.

"Say it," he supplicated. "Say it."

"I want you," I cried. "I'll always want you."

With one last forceful thrust, he shattered my world. I splintered into pieces. A burst of power struck the room with an invisible bomb blast.

And with each clenching squeeze around his shaft, he could hold back no longer, he threw his head back to bellow his release. His own energy funneled through the room, mingling and combining with mine.

And then slowly, little flecks of Light began to take shape in the cold air, followed by currents of Darkness. Floating and glittering. Tiny stars drifting through gossamer swaths of shadows.

With a few languid lasting thrusts, he looked down at me. He still held my wrists in his grip, they were still pinned against my chest.

His words were low and quiet, barely audible. "I don't understand what you do to me." He absently brought my hands up in his grip as he rubbed at his chest.

His eyes creased at the corners as he stared at me, trying to figure it all out. Then with a look of confusion he whispered, "You are so beautiful, it hurts me to look at you."

I lay under him, my hair fanned out around my face, my skin rosy and dewy, and I knew my violet eyes glittered. I smiled at him.

With my hands over his heart, I looked down at my own chest, at the glimmering, silver outline of three crescent moons. When I looked back up at him, I placed a hand against his cheek and whispered to him.

"I understand."

He gave me the softest kiss then. I had never experienced anything so sweet.

With another smile, I pushed against his shoulder as I rolled on top of him. I sat up, straddling him, my knees bent at his hips.

I placed my hands on his pectorals. And still, after all this time, I was in awe of how big and broad and strong he was, how perfectly defined every inch of him was, how lethal. I could feel the incredible hum of power beneath my touch.

And it was tamed. Eased.

Because of me.

My hair fell around my face as I looked down at him. I leaned forward and it brushed against his shoulders.

With the simple contact, with the sight of me on top of him, he let out a groan. And I could feel him harden, needing so much more. His hands came up to grab my waist, lifting and then wrenching me down onto him as he bucked his hips.

He still wore the shackles on his wrists. But the bonds were broken now.

Never to hold him again.

CHAPTER 19

IT TOOK THREE DAYS FOR MAXIM TO GET BETTER.

I did what I could to make him comfortable, to help however possible. But it seemed that what Maxim needed most was sleep.

When he was able to speak, I asked if there was someone I should get, someone who could help him heal. But he insisted he would be fine. He insisted he just needed a little time.

So I did what I could during the few hours each day when he was awake.

And the rest of my time—the majority of my time—I was in the abandoned wing with Zagan.

I was not pushed away. I was not left behind.

We spent our time down in the Darkness and the shadows . . . together.

He continued to grapple with the Darkness. He continued to fight all he had absorbed up on the cliff's edge.

And although he was still buried away in a deep, dark hole, he was not alone. He did not try and take me to my room; he kept me down there in the manor depths with him.

While I missed the amenities in my suite, I only really cared about being with him.

Besides, Maxim was up on the fifth floor. And I knew Zagan needed a little distance.

I knew there were some wounds knitting shut, and I knew they were still raw. So we kept to the depths of the manor. And it wasn't long until my blanket and pillows covered his bed.

When I did venture out, when I ascended the stairs to spend time with Maxim, to check on him, to keep him company—I went alone.

I said nothing to either of them about what lay between them. I knew that was not something I should touch. But I worried for Zagan.

I finally had him, actually and truly, with nothing standing in the way. And I was afraid. I did not want him to slip through my fingers once again.

But they had to talk. They had to. So on the third night they met in the sitting room just beyond the foyer.

And Maxim shared everything with Zagan. The two of them talked for a long time, locked away on the first floor of the manor while I sat at the very top of the staircase. I perched with my knees pulled into my chest, my arms wrapped around my legs. I watched the candles flickering against the crystal in the chandelier above. And I waited.

I was concerned. I didn't know what this would do to the two of them. I knew better than to wish for sunshine and roses.

When the door to the sitting room finally opened hours later, I rose to my feet and silently descended the stairs. But when I reached the foyer, aglow with more candlelight from the chandeliers and sconces, I found Maxim alone.

He stood there in a pair of Zagan's pants and one of his black shirts. And Maxim looked very different from the way I was used to seeing him.

The shirt he borrowed was untucked, the collar open, and the sleeves rolled up. I was even surprised to find that Maxim's hair was not styled back as he normally wore it.

Seeing him recovering in the bed was one thing. Seeing him up and about in anything less than an impeccable suit was another.

He didn't look the same as Zagan, he would never look the same as him, but now more than ever the similarity was striking.

"Where is he?" I asked.

Maxim looked down at me and I could see the weariness in his eyes. "He will need some time, Violet."

I nodded. "Are you . . . alright?" I asked.

Maxim dipped his head. "I will be fine."

I bit my lip, knowing there was so much I needed to say to him, so much I owed him. We hadn't talked about anything serious while he convalesced. Any conversations we'd had were light and frivolous. I hadn't even mentioned all that happened in Aleece.

"Maxim—"

He shook his head. "Another time, Violet."

He looked at me. Looked at my hair. My skin. My eyes. "I'm glad you're well. And I'm glad he has you."

I opened my mouth, about to reply. But Maxim stopped me, and the slash of his brows deepened as he looked at me with sincerity. "It isn't necessary," he murmured.

I nodded once again, seeing the truth of it.

There was no need to insult his strength, his pride. Maxim was a powerful man; he was going to be just fine.

"I don't think she'll ever return," I told him, wanting to give him something, knowing he knew exactly who I meant. "Not as she was anyway."

I looked down at my hands, feeling incredibly vulnerable. "She wasn't who we thought. She wasn't Seraphina. She was Aurelia. She was the first Prism."

I chanced a glance up at Maxim, and his brows lifted, taking in what I had to say, understanding the gravity of it.

"But the Umbra are gone," I continued. "Marax is gone. Everything you've wished for . . ."

"There is no elation in this," Maxim replied. "It is not a victory. It was something that had to be done. And many were hurt along the way.

"You may not see them now, but the damage results in scars. And we will always carry those with us. We have paid a high price to right the wrongs."

Maxim paused, then he gave me a final look before uttering, "Goodbye, Violet." And he turned to leave.

"Maxim, wait."

He stopped with his back to me.

"You could stay here," I offered. "You don't have to go."

Maxim shook his head. "No, Violet. I couldn't."

But instead of striding down the hall, he pivoted back to me, and he held out his hand.

After a moment of uncertainty, I raised my own. Maxim held my hand in his, firm and secure. His voice was low and quiet, and his words were slow and heartfelt. "I *am* glad for him. I *am* glad he has found you."

With a bow of his head, Maxim did turn to leave then. He took a few swift strides down the hall towards the front entry before disappearing into a wisp of darkness. The shadows lingering at the edges of the candlelight seemed to sway and bow before him as he took his leave.

CHAPTER 20

"**G**OOD GOD, WOMAN! Where have you brought us?"

Although we were facing the large steel door—the only one in the tiny alley—Zagan did not focus on it. Instead, he eyed the foul, urine-soaked dumpster, and his lip curled. However, when yapping sounded on the other side of the metal track, his attention was drawn back to the door.

He narrowed his eyes.

Maxim, on the other hand, stood strong and silent, betraying nothing. As I gave another look his way, though, I realized something was off. When I glanced at his chest, I noticed there was no movement there. And I had a strong suspicion he was holding his breath.

"It'll only be a minute," I promised. Then I banged my fist on the door. Incessantly. After all, Zagan and Maxim were not the only ones who wanted to get away from the fetid smell.

When the door began to slide open there was the familiar screech of metal scraping across metal. And we were welcomed by the blaring sound of a television.

The woman stood in her robe and curlers not even bothering to look at us. Her face was turned to the T.V. in her shabby sitting room. Next to her stood her mangy little mutt aiming its shrill bark at us.

Zagan looked down at the little beast and bared his teeth. The dog immediately let out a whimper before retreating to its bed.

It was enough of an oddity for the woman to rip her gaze from the television. As she watched the little mongrel cowering on its pillow, she began to turn to us. She muttered her displeasure as she shifted around, and her cockney accent grated on my ears almost as much as her dog's yapping.

"Piss off! Bunch of knobheads and muppets—"

When she laid her eyes on Maxim and Zagan, her mouth dropped open, and her cigarette clung to her bottom lip while a curler full of frizzy red hair fell in her eye.

I didn't bother with an explanation. I just tucked some bills in the pocket of her robe and made for the elevator with the two men following me.

I could understand her response. Zagan and Maxim had already been dominating figures. But with a little more Darkness, a little more power . . . it was impossible for them to fully contain what they were.

The Dark energy—the strength they possessed—was overwhelmingly evident.

Three days had passed since Zagan and I had last seen Maxim. While I knew it wasn't nearly enough time to completely come to terms with all they'd become, it had been a start.

I honestly didn't know how I did it. But somehow, I had managed to convince them both to take a visit to D.I. with me.

Yes, I was just that good.

And maybe, possibly, theoretically, I might have just, in the slightest way, stretched the truth a bit on my motivations for coming.

I glanced at the two of them as we rode the elevator down into the club, and I hoped with all my heart that I would be seeing more of them together.

I could see the outward differences. Maxim wore a crisp white shirt with a perfectly tailored suit. The collar of his shirt was open, and the scar at his neck was visible.

His hair was combed back. His head high. He looked refined as ever. But the scar did something. It hinted at something. And I doubted anyone would want to cross him.

Zagan, on the other hand, was less formal in boots, black pants and a black jacket. He had a mark visible at his neck as well, but it wasn't a scar.

Creeping up his neck from under his jacket collar was an inky symbol that looked like a tattoo.

Although most of the marks that had slipped and shifted across his body after our encounter with the Umbra had faded and disappeared, there were still a few that were scattered across his skin, frozen there. Not all had vanished as they normally did. And I didn't know if they would take some time, or if perhaps they never would.

Regardless of what either of them wore—regardless of the features marked upon their skin—there was no denying the solid frame and raw power they both possessed. There was no denying that these were Dark men . . . sons of the night.

When the elevator door finally opened, we made our way through the bustling club. With every being we passed, conversations paused mid-sentence. And it was impossible to ignore the eyes that landed on Zagan and Maxim.

I had to remind myself that I was used to them. But for others, their presence was jarring and commanding and inundating. People had no choice but to pause and take notice.

After a moment, though, after those in the club had a chance to assess the newcomers and determine they weren't a threat, the debauchery of the place continued.

As I made my way to the bar with Zagan and Maxim, it wasn't difficult to find exactly what I was looking for.

It wasn't difficult at all.

I saw a dart land right in someone's backside. The male, who was undeniably attractive, reached back in surprise to pull it out. Initially, he examined the little dart in anger, but as he inspected the barrel, he held it closer, squinting slightly. And then his frown turned into . . . *a smirk.*

He looked back in the direction the dart had come from. When he spotted Lilly, he raised a brow and gave his chin a lift before tucking the small dart in his pocket with a wink.

I didn't understand what was happening. She and a few of the Fatales had little guns that they were shooting at people. And I couldn't imagine why her victim had been happy about it.

I tapped one of the bar tables in front of us. "Here's good," I said.

Zagan and Maxim both stood there, waiting for me to take a seat. "Why don't you two sit and I'll go grab some drinks," I suggested.

"Violet, no."

"That is unadvisable."

They began to voice their protests at the exact same time.

I held up my hands. "It's fine. The bar is twenty feet away," I told them, taking a step back. "You can see me the whole time. I'm not going anywhere."

With another retreating step, I admitted, "I'm just going to say hello to Lilly."

I didn't wait for permission, I turned on my heels and wound my way through the club, dodging the occasional dart that flew by.

I gave my shoulders a little wiggle as I walked, doing my best to shake off the Dark energy that had been coiled so tightly around me.

Lilly spied me as I got closer to her group at the bar. She saw me wiggling my shoulders, and without hesitation, she began to do the same. It was as if she were joining me in some little dance. The only difference was she looked incredibly sexy doing it.

I immediately stopped the little shimmy which only caused her to go at it harder. Once I reached her, I looked at the gun in her hand and raised a brow.

"The darts have our numbers on them," she explained with a giggle. Then she took aim and fired off another round.

I couldn't help but smile at how much fun she was having.

"How's everything going?" I asked as I leaned against the bar next to her.

She twisted around to grab a shot glass and downed the clear liquid in one smooth gulp. "Oh, you know," she replied vaguely.

"Yeah," I agreed.

I didn't want to dance around things, though. I wanted to say what I had come to say. "Look," I started, "I don't know if this is worth anything, but I want you to know I'm sorry. I care that things I did hurt you. I want you to know if there's anything I can do to make things right, I will."

Lilly paused her marksmanship exhibition to look at me through her feathery lashes. "Don't sweat it, Violet. Things have a way of working themselves out. We're cool in my book. I never know what's going to happen when you're around." Her eyes glimmered as she smiled. "So anytime you wanna hang, I'm down."

She twisted around again to grab two shot glasses this time. She handed one to me and clinked it with her own before uttering, "From one serious badass to another."

I took the offering, swallowing the liquid all at once. I instantly began coughing and spluttering. In between heaving breaths and tears, I exclaimed, "What is that?! Kerosene?"

My mouth was on fire. My esophagus was on fire. And a little bomb went off in my stomach once the liquid touched down.

But an instant later, I did have to admit that my veins began to warm, and I felt lighter. "You know what?" I amended. "Don't tell me."

Lilly gave a little giggle, then she turned completely to face the bar. She put down her . . . *dating gun* . . . and we both leaned our forearms on the bar top.

With a sigh Lilly looked at me from the corner of her eye. "You know I really hate dealing with all the serious stuff. I mean, why bother? Why not just have fun?

"But you should know," she continued, "Evelyn is pretty pissed at you. She blames you for setting off the Book of Prophecies."

Lilly rolled onto her hip, resting against the bar, to look at me fully. "Is that true? Did you, you know, like, start it?"

I shrugged, not even bothering to wonder how Evelyn knew it was me. "Seems so," I told her truthfully.

Lilly's eyes widened at the admission. "You're lucky the beings in this place don't know that. If they knew who you were, they'd want your head. That book is fucking fat. And most of the shit in there is bad news."

I released a long breath, staring ahead into the mirror behind the bar. Long waves of chestnut hair, fair rosy complexion, and clear violet eyes.

"That sucks," I admitted.

"Yeah," Lilly agreed.

"I can't do anything about it," I told her.

"Yeah," she repeated.

We stood there, side by side at the bar for a minute. Lilly had rolled forward, resting her arms on the bar again.

"Well," I finally began. "I did bring you something. A peace offering," I explained.

"Oh, yeah?" Lilly asked in surprise. "What is it?"

"It's over there," I said. Lilly turned to look into the crowd. I nodded in Maxim's direction. "I told him you're interested in establishing an alliance between the Fatales and the Shadows."

Lilly bit her lip as she shook her head. "Ooh! You saucy little minx! You know, I've always said the way to a girl's heart is through her panties."

She bobbed her head back and forth as if considering. Then her lips curled into the cutest, most devilish smile I'd ever seen. "Your peace offering is accepted. But he's gotta put out."

I held up my hands, unable to contain my laughter. "Whoa. I got him here. Whatever happens beyond that is between you two."

Then I leaned into her and held my hand up to cover my mouth, whispering, "But he really loosens up if you get a few drinks in him."

Lilly's eyes widened, and she gave a solemn nod.

I didn't know if anything would actually happen between them. I doubted so. But I hoped Maxim would get the chance to enjoy a fun night out.

And hey, Lilly could do her worst.

Lilly picked up the dart gun from the bar and handed it to me. "I hate how much I love you!" she squealed. "I'm going to freshen up!" Then she planted a kiss on my cheek before sauntering away.

I stood at the bar watching her pass the table where Maxim and Zagan sat with an exaggerated swing of her hips and a wink that involved the entire side of her face.

Maxim had noticed the gesture—it would have been impossible not to—and he wasn't very successful in hiding his exasperation. Then his eyes narrowed on me, and his lips thinned.

I did my best to look as innocent as possible.

I wasn't getting any more involved with whatever was going on between the two of them. And I shifted my gaze to meet Zagan's eye. I had felt him watching my every move.

I lifted a shoulder and flashed my own devilish smile just for him.

I needed him to remain relaxed. Because I wasn't done making amends. I had seen another person I needed to speak to. And Zagan wasn't going to like it.

I held up a finger. *One more minute*, I mouthed.

He began to stand, and I shook my head, motioning for him to stay seated. *It's okay*, I mouthed.

He didn't look happy about it, but he stayed at the table.

I left Lilly's phone-number-gun on the bar, and I made my way through the crowd of people to a table filled with seven men. They were all wearing an absolute bare minimum of clothing. I knew it was because they "ran hot" or whatever. I didn't care. There was just one I was interested in speaking to.

Hellion saw me approach and he stood from the table the moment I neared. He moved a few spaces down and took a seat at an empty two-top. I pulled out the opposite chair and sat without invitation.

"He's going to lose his shit," Hellion rumbled as I settled in front of him. His eyes were staring over my shoulder, and I knew he was watching Zagan.

"He's going to be just fine," I countered.

Hellion shook his head. "Not from the looks of it."

"Give him a minute," I assured.

After a moment, Hellion raised a brow and tilted his head before moving his eyes to mine. "I guess you know your man."

"I guess I do." I pushed my hair back from my face, and I met Hellion's gaze with nothing but confidence. "I want to make things right," I told him.

It seemed those six words were ones I was repeating a lot lately.

Hellion shook his head. "We're in a big mess. Things are . . . not good. And the way I figure it, you owe us. Apparently, you triggered something and now all the prophecies in the book are coming to pass."

Apparently, the Fatales and the Dragons had been chatting.

I wondered how long it would be before word got around. I knew secrets were like dandelions—traveling easily in the wind.

"I might have been able to look past that," Hellion continued. "I might have reasoned that you're just a kid. You didn't know any better. But you took the stone. I want it back. You owe us.

"If you want to make things right—that's how you do it. Return the stone. Otherwise, we're enemies. And if I see you or yours anywhere outside this neutral space, I'm coming for you. And I'll be finding a way to settle this debt."

Hellion eased back in his seat, all stone-cold business. I could see how he must intimidate people. I could see how he would have anyone quaking in their boots. But I didn't buy his tough guy routine for a minute. He may have been rock hard on the outside, but I knew there was a soft, gooey center in there.

As I looked at him in his ripped jeans and stubble covered jaw, I absently wondered if he had a mate. If he did, I was willing to bet he fawned over her.

I stopped myself from smiling. Instead, I leaned onto the table with my own hard, cold stare. "Technically," I told him, "I didn't take the stone from you. I took it from the Fatales."

Hellion tilted his head to the side, and I could hear his neck crack. "We let them take it," he rumbled. "We all but put it in their sexy little hands."

"Why?" I asked.

"None of your fucking business," he replied. "But after we followed them to wherever they were taking it, we would have gotten it back."

His eye—the one I had seen Lilly throw an axe into—twitched. "In my book, *you* owe us the stone."

I didn't back down, I didn't cower. I kept my face blank. I betrayed nothing. Finally, I spoke. "Fair enough. I'll see what I can do."

I didn't know if there was any way of getting the stone back. But Entropy was one crazy bitch. If she cut out her husband's heart once, who was I to say she wouldn't do it again, or at least aid someone else in the act. At the very least she'd probably spill some cryptic secret about it that would make sense eventually.

And then there was Zagan. He made getting the stone back seem like he'd hardly have to break a sweat.

Maybe I could get Hellion that stone. But even if I never did, I wasn't concerned about bumping into him. I had no doubt the dragon pack was fierce. I had no doubt that I'd seen only the barest glimpse of what they were truly capable of.

But I doubted his threat was sincere. And even if it was . . . I could hold my own.

I gave Hellion a nod. Then I stood and left the table.

I could see the tension in Zagan's face ease with each step I took towards him. When I was in arm's reach, he stood from the bar table and grabbed me, pulling me into him.

"I can't take anymore," he growled.

"Don't worry, I'm all done here, big guy." I patted his chest and flashed him a smile. I could feel his body tense at the sight. And I smiled even wider. I would never stop loving the effect I had on him.

I looked at Zagan and tilted my head to the side. He nodded in response. We were both ready to leave.

Maxim shifted as if about to get up, but then he paused suddenly. And a look of confusion passed over his face.

He reached back to his shoulder and gave a little jerk. Then he held his hand up in front of his face to inspect the dart he held. His eyes narrowed on me.

I shrugged. "Um, about that . . . You know, not only does Lilly want to discuss a possible alliance, but she is also worried about the, uh . . ."

I looked around the club. "The dragon pack. They're really mad that the Fatales stole the stone from them to begin with. I told her I was sure you would be willing to stay, just to, you know, keep the peace and everything, keep a look out, make sure everyone stays calm."

I shrugged. "What do you think?"

Maxim's shoulders twitched, and his nostrils flared. Again, he reached behind to his shoulders, and again, he pulled free a dart.

"Oh, ha, ha . . ." I tried lamely.

Maxim eyed me, eyed the bar and its patrons, then eyed the Fatales. "If that is the case, I will escort them to their home now."

I turned to look at the Fatales. Lilly had rejoined them and it seemed she was using most of her remaining darts on Maxim.

"Uh, yeah. Okay," I agreed, knowing full well the Fatales were not going anywhere. "Go let them know," I encouraged.

Maxim stood. But before he could turn, before we could say our goodbyes, his hand whipped into the air behind his back. In one fluid motion, he slammed another dart down on the table. This one hadn't even landed. Maxim had plucked it out of thin air, without looking.

I desperately tried to hide my smile.

But it was impossible.

Maxim shook his head, yet still he turned to leave—to escort the Fatales home . . . or so he thought.

He was just that good of a guy.

Zagan and I made our way to the elevator, ready to leave. He looked down at me, questioning.

My eyes widened as I shrugged, and I pinched my mouth to the side. "He needs to have a little fun."

"*Violet* . . ." Zagan chastised.

"Trust me. He's going to thank me."

CHAPTER 21

BACK AT THE MANOR, we had barely gotten to sleep when there was an aggressive banging noise somewhere above. Crumbs of dirt sprinkled down on us from the decrepit ceiling. I sat up in Zagan's bed, thoroughly annoyed.

"What is that?" I snapped.

"Banging," he supplied.

I shot him the evilest of eyes.

He looked at me and one side of his mouth twitched. Then he sat up and swung his legs off the side of the bed.

I leaned over and grabbed his arm, pulling him down onto the mattress. I put my face next to his and threw a pillow over our heads.

"Nope. No. No way, tiger. We are ignoring it. I don't care what it is. I don't care if the manor is falling down. We are pretending we don't hear it."

I refused. I was not leaving the bed. I was also not letting Zagan leave the bed. Too many things could happen. Too many things could go wrong. I would not chance it. No fucking way.

Random, unexpected pounding could not mean something good.

The distant booming sounded again. More crumbling dirt and flecks of rotting wood smattered down on us.

"And I'm telling you another thing," I hissed under the pillow as I tried to wiggle the debris off my body. "This place is getting renovate—"

Zagan covered my mouth with his own, rolling over to lay across me, my pillow shield falling to the side.

More banging sounded. Louder and faster.

I twined my arms behind his neck, pulling him closer.

Then a loud, low chime rang through the manor.

"Is that . . . Is that . . . a *doorbell?*" I asked.

"I wouldn't know. I've never had guests," he replied.

He rolled off me then to stand and yank on his trousers. "It will be fine, Violet," he said over his shoulder. "I will come right back." Then he took two swift strides towards the hall.

But there was no way in hell I was letting him out of my sight. I grabbed my robe and had it slipped over my arms in one fluid motion. Then I jumped onto his back before he could get away.

Zagan's arms slipped under my thighs in a graceful movement of reflex. I draped my arms over the front of his chest.

He shook his head as he climbed the stairs with ease. "I never would have thought I'd compare my *wife* to a lemur . . . yet here we are."

My breath hitched at his comment, at what he called me. But I didn't let that stop me from defending myself. "I'm coming with you," I replied. "It's the only way I know you won't do anything stupid."

"Hmm. That could be my daily greeting to you," he countered.

I laughed at his ear, pressing my face into his neck.

Sunlight flooded the long hall that lined the first floor, pouring in through the windows. I did not squint or recoil at the sudden brightness. Instead, I felt warm and bright myself.

And because of his comment I held my left hand out studying the black diamond as it glittered on my finger. Zagan leaned his head to nip at my wrist.

I wasn't the only one who seemed to transition. I could feel a certain warmth from him too. His skin seemed to tan the slightest bit, his hair lightening just a few degrees.

But the entire time we made our way down the hall, the pounding and chiming continued. I envisioned the gate out front at the entry to the tree tunnel. I could see it mangled and bent, left where it was after the Archangels had blown it open. And once again, I made a mental note to have it fixed ASAP.

I cringed. I actually cringed when Zagan walked right up to the door.

"Wait! We need to get weapons," I urged. I tried to scramble down from him, but he tightened his grip on me, holding me in place on his back. And then he did the worst possible thing.

He opened the door.

I tensed as the towering entry swung inch by inch. And then I froze for a moment, not truly believing what I saw. I was convinced it was a trick, some illusion to lure us out of the manor.

"Mom?" I asked. My eyes widened at the man standing beside her. "Dad?"

"Hello, Violet." While my mother's greeting was warm enough, she did clear her throat. And I knew she was uncomfortable with our frivolous welcome, not to mention our attire—or lack thereof. I was, after all, still on Zagan's shirtless back in nothing but my robe.

I wiggled my butt, desperately trying to get down. Finally, Zagan loosened his grip, allowing my feet to touch the floor. Clutching my robe closed and tightening the belt, I stepped around to stand at his side.

"I wasn't expecting you," I stammered.

I looked back and forth at my parents in disbelief. I had tried several times over the last two weeks to get in touch with my mother at the Radiant Court. I had continually been told that she was "in a meeting" and that she would call me back.

I had actually planned on having Zagan take me there after sunset. I had been determined to see her.

"Come in, I'll be just a moment," I said, beginning to retreat into the foyer.

"We can't stay," my mother replied. "We came to say goodbye."

I stopped and took a step back to the entry. "Goodbye?" I echoed.

"Your father has an idea for how we can bring home the Prisms trapped in the fire realm," she explained. "The ones I hid there," she added.

As if I could have forgotten that little tidbit.

"We are taking a team of Angela in an attempt to bring back the others. Elijah has volunteered to lead it."

My eyes roved back and forth between my parents, completely caught off guard. "How dangerous is it?" I finally asked.

My mother's response was stark. "I would say our chances are fifty-fifty. It is possible I may not be able to bring any of them back. And . . . it is possible none of us will return."

I stood there with my mouth agape, my eyes still darting between the two of them. My mother no longer appeared ill. She no longer had a sickly tinge to her skin. Standing there in the sunlight she radiated as she always had, her hair glinting, her eyes sparkling like the ocean.

She wore her green dress—a warrior's dress—and her archery bow was secured at her back. The gold cuff that was wrapped around her arm glinted with each subtle shift and sway.

And even my father's white kaftan, which I had always seen as a peaceful, neutral garment, took on a new life. It was now a practical piece of clothing for comfort and ease of movement.

And my bones suddenly felt very heavy seeing him there before me.

While he didn't appear any different in the way he dressed, I could see he had aged. My entire life he had always looked the same. But now he had aged.

He was still broad, still strong. His gray hair, gray cropped beard, and weathered features were the same. He was still handsome, fit, distinguished. Clearly capable. Clearly powerful.

Just less so than before. Deep lines now ran through his face, and his hair had thinned. I suddenly found it difficult to take a breath.

He took a step forward, holding his hand out to me. I looked at it for a moment, and then I took it. His grip was warm and solid.

I was going to fall apart. I was going to break.

He was going to bring back everything from Aleece, everything I had left there, everything I'd thought I'd been pardoned of.

Somehow it had not followed me. Somehow, I did not carry the burden of it all when I returned.

And when I was in Aleece, I was not his daughter. He was not my father. Those roles did not take shape there.

He was one of the cloaked Originals, and I was . . . the one who fulfilled the prophecy.

But now, with him standing here in front of me, I was Violet. And he was my father.

I began to shake my head, knowing I could not cope with it.

Yet he smiled at me, and I could see a certain relief, a certain weight drift from his shoulders. "You are radiant, my dear. You look . . . *radiant.*"

My chest heaved, "Daddy, I—"

"None of it was because of you." He squeezed my hand in his and I could still feel the strength. "I know it's difficult to see that. But we made our choices. This was all our doing. And you—my daughter—had to pay a high price because of it.

"We are the ones to apologize to you." Then he stopped himself and cleared his throat. "I," he corrected, "I am the one who must apologize to you.

"Violet, I disagreed with that fateful decision the Council made long ago. I dissented. Yet it matters not. It does not erase my guilt.

"You see, we are not individuals. The Council was a collective. We spoke as one. And my opinion was outweighed. I am so very sorry."

His grip tightened around my hand as he shook his head and stared at me. "Had I known my own daughter . . . Had I known it would be you . . ."

His chest puffed on a long inhale. "It was always you," he murmured. He squinted, taking me in. "How could I not have seen it?"

I didn't know what to say. I didn't know how to feel. I felt a desperate need to beg for forgiveness. But I knew that was not why he was here. I knew that was the very thing he sought for himself.

I squeezed his hand as tightly as I could. It was all I could offer. Words failed me.

After a moment, I cleared my throat, asking, "Should you be going on this . . ." I didn't know what to call it.

"There is nothing more I wish to do," he answered. "I would like to try and atone for what I have done, in whatever manner I may. And to do so while assisting your mother . . ."

He looked at her with such pride, such love. "Well, there is nothing more I wish to do."

"But," I objected, "how can you? I mean how—"

He looked back and forth between me and my mother. "Unlike the others, I have a very strong connection here. Because of the two of you. While my time might be limited, I am tethered here. For now."

I swallowed, nodding. Then I blurted, "We should come with you. To help." I glanced up at Zagan to gage his reaction.

He gave a single nod. He would follow wherever I went.

But my mother stepped forward, coming shoulder to shoulder with my father. "I should be able to take the Angela through because of the abilities they possess, because of the manner in which they can bend the light. I should be able to take them, and they should be able to return. At least in theory.

"But those who are trapped . . . they will be very difficult to pull out. It will already be perilous. The two of you would be two more we have to fight to bring back.

"Your offer is appreciated beyond words," she noted. "But it will be best if you stay. We simply came to say goodbye."

Her eyes lingered on Zagan. And although she did not speak any words, the look she gave him, the smile she gave him, held her heart.

I looked at my parents and a tear slipped from my eye. "This is so sudden. I should . . . We should have . . ."

I knew my father had limited time, and now my mother was going to put herself in a dangerous situation—one from which I did not know if she would return.

Immortals die. They pass on to the other side. I had always known this. But being faced with it. Discovering that it was coming closer . . .

My father looked at me with his piercing clear eyes. "Are you well, Violet?"

I nodded. I looked up at the clear blue sky above, and I nodded. "Yes, daddy. I am."

He looked into my face. He saw the truth for himself. And he smiled.

"Will I see you again?" I asked him.

He took a moment to contemplate, glancing to the sky as well. Then he met my eye and murmured, "I believe so."

I said goodbye to my parents. I wished them well. Knowing my mother, knowing my father, and knowing Elijah . . . I had a feeling their chances were good.

CHAPTER 22

A Little While Later

~Violet's Playlist: Hanging By A Moment, Lifehouse~

EVERYONE BREAKS.

Everyone.

It is a universal truth. An absolute with no exceptions. The only difference between us is how we break.

And what it turns us into.

I have learned, though, that sometimes it is not a violent break. Sometimes it is gentle.

I have found that sometimes it is not a sudden break. Sometimes it happens gradually.

And sometimes—often times—it is for the better.

I knew the time I'd had with Zagan was over. I knew the beginning was over.

The tortured son of a forgotten king haunting a forgotten manor . . .

314

The naive girl chasing Shadows . . .

We were no longer those people. We would never be those people again.

It was time to begin something new.

I made it my mission to clean the manor. To restore it. It would probably take me centuries. But I had vowed to make progress, little by little.

I skipped the first floor, since Maxim had it cleaned. I decided to go through the rooms floor by floor to evaluate and get a general idea of what would need to be done.

In one of the third-floor rooms, I found another massive bookshelf that had collapsed. I was curious if there were additional journals or something noteworthy hidden beneath it. If so, I wanted to share any personal mementos with Maxim.

When I attempted to lift the casing, though, I knew it wasn't going to budge.

I needed help.

So I made my way down to the abandoned wing to look for Zagan. I absently wondered if he really would let me renovate his hall.

I would wait. I wouldn't push. It was his space, and I respected that. But maybe I could sneak in some new floors or something.

True, I no longer focused on the icy chill and rotted wood frames. I had grown accustomed to the Darkness that lingered here. And my presence was no longer a disturbance.

The Darkness did not chase me. The ghosts of the manor did not wail and sway. They were at peace.

And I realized so, too, was I.

I opened one of the decrepit doors in the hall and stepped into the room with the piano. Ever since our final encounter with the Umbra, Zagan had been spending a lot of time in here. He would sit for long periods with the red glow of dying embers, with the shadows, with the dark notes floating around him.

I knew it was a way to release all he had absorbed up on that cliff, a way to cope, a way to exorcise his demons.

And whenever I wanted to find him, I'd look here first.

I gazed around in the Darkness. I did a slow circle in the center of the room, glancing over the shadowed corners and the crumbling rock walls.

But I couldn't find him. He wasn't here.

And then I thought I heard something. Something unfamiliar. I was confused for a moment, unsure if I was imagining the sound.

I paused. I held my breath. I tilted my head.

I could hear something. Faint but steady. It was music. And it was coming from somewhere . . . *above.*

Was I imagining it?

I allowed my fingers to sweep across the top of the piano next to me before making my way out of the room. I began to walk down the hall. But then I picked up my pace as I traveled through the Dark Wing of the Dark Prince, unable to stop myself.

I took the stone stairs two at a time. And by the time I burst through the rotted plank at the top, I found myself running through the long main hall of the Dark Manor.

I found myself running over the slatted moonlight which glimmered across the floor as it shone through the windows lining the hall. The music was louder up here.

It was real.

And I was drawn to it. Nothing could have stolen my focus in that moment. The closer I drew, the more certain I became; I somehow knew the song.

Errant notes floated around me, seeping into my skin.

But this song was layered and complex. At the heart of it was a melody I knew. Yet this melody was being presented in the most incredible wrapping. Dipping and swelling, the highs and lows came together to create something complete. Soaring notes were intertwined with poignant pauses of silence.

I rounded a corner and stopped at an open door just as the last note drifted through the space between us.

The first thing I noticed was the moonlight. It spilled through the open windows, seeming stronger and brighter in this room. The curtains had been pushed to the sides, and they swayed in the hint of a breeze.

He stood from the piano to face me.

Somehow, I had become breathless. My chest rose and fell. I stared at Zagan. "You're not . . . *downstairs.*"

He stood there, taking me in. And I saw a certain light in his eyes. One that had never been there before. Or at least, if it had, I had lacked the ability to see it.

"No," he affirmed. There was so much certainty in the set of his shoulders, so much strength and reassurance. He looked larger than I'd ever seen him. He didn't just take up the space around him, he filled the entire room.

A few more of the inky marks had faded from his skin. But there were others that had begun to darken, solidifying their place on his body. A mark on the other side of his chest. The one stretching up his neck. One at his shoulder. Another at his hip, creeping up from the waistband of his pants.

Black tattoos—maybe Maxim would call them scars—reminders of all he was, all he possessed, and all he'd been through.

But *they* did not cover him; *he* wore them.

I looked at the piano, pointing a shaking finger at it. "That song . . ."

It was one I had on a playlist. Nothing special. Just a song.

But I knew the lyrics to it. It was about changing and truth. Falling in love. Letting go.

I had never thought much of it. But hearing it through him, with all the layers and depth surrounding the simple melody . . .

I looked back at Zagan, my head tilting, not quite understanding.

He was on the main floor of the manor. In the piano room with the air drifting through the windows and the moonlight pouring in. And he played something.

The notes were not haunted. I was not awash in sorrow. There was life in what he played. There was a promise of tomorrow.

Still, I pointed at the piano. "That song . . ."

He gave a slight shrug. "It was time for a new one."

His words were not lost on me, yet I couldn't help but ask, "What are you doing up here?" Without realizing it, I had taken a step towards him.

His hands which had been resting at his sides opened, and he held them out, looking at them. His broad shoulders rose, his lungs filling. And with a long low breath, the muscles all across his shoulders and chest relaxed.

He dropped his hands to look at me. And still I had somehow managed to take several more steps towards him, until I was standing just before him.

I had to look up to watch his face. And as I tilted my head back, I felt something shift and settle somewhere beneath my ribs. Because as Zagan looked down at me, his features were relaxed. And there was the barest upturn at the corners of his lips.

I didn't know if I would ever see a dazzling smile from him, one that would bring me to my knees, but that wouldn't stop me from spending the rest of my life trying to coax one from him.

Finally, he spoke.

"This is a curse, Violet Archer. You have been cursed with me. Through this life and the next."

His words were simple. He spoke a simple truth. There was no regret or pity in his low voice. Just truth. A truth that made my skin warm.

I smiled at him. And after a moment, I shook my head, softly disagreeing with him. "No."

"This," I said, waving my hands between us, "this isn't a curse. This," I said, waving my hand between us again, "this is love. The gods have blessed me, Zagan Black."

He looked at me, taking in my hair, my face, my neck and chest, before meeting my eye again. And he slipped his hand over mine.

We left the room with the piano and passed through the Dark Manor. The space was dim and full of slumbering shadows, but it glittered in the moonlight. Out the grand entrance and down the lawn we went, drifting over the weeds and bramble. My hair danced behind my shoulders as the breeze shifted.

The towering entrance to the tree tunnel sat before us, silent and still. We walked soundlessly into the darkness of the space. The branches and leaves of the oak trees were woven so tightly in the canopy above—no light would ever get through.

Except . . .

As we walked, the wind rippled across the branches overhead. I looked up, and I saw the tiniest spots of light begin to pierce the canopy.

Another gust of wind swept through the tunnel then, sending leaves spinning around us. We stopped where we were. And one by one, the oaks on either side lifted their branches revealing the night sky above. I turned, drawn to the Dark Manor then, and I could see an enormous full moon filling up the sky and floating just above the manor.

Like a halo.

The cobwebs had been cleared from the façade, and here and there hints of light winked through the unobstructed windows. A burning fireplace in one room. A lit chandelier in another.

The shadows remained. And so, too, did the Darkness and the ghosts and the sorrow. They were a part of this place. But they were at peace now.

And there was Light now, too.

There was balance now.

Deep within, in the hidden depths of the manor was the abandoned wing. I knew it would never actually be renovated. I knew it would always be there—a silent dark heart.

But I knew, *I knew,* we would not dwell there any longer.

And I did not contemplate the end of our time down there for a moment more because my view of the manor was suddenly blocked. Zagan stepped in front of me, leaning over me. And I couldn't help but let out a little sigh.

He took each side of my jaw in his hands, tilting my head up. "Do you want to turn back?" he asked. His deep voice was a rumble that sent a shiver over my skin despite the temperate night.

I closed my eyes and rubbed my cheek against his palm where he held me. I paused a moment to savor the feel of him. With the next inhale that I took my chest expanded, pressing against his. I opened my eyes at the jolt which shot to my very center from the intimate contact.

I ran my hands up his arms to grab his wrists, and I took a few steps backwards, retreating from him. I bit my lip, trying my best to stop the smile that was beginning to curl at the corners of my mouth.

"I'll go with you," I told him. "But you'll have to catch me first."

"Violet . . ." he warned, my name a dark purr on his lips.

I turned and began to run through the tree tunnel. My hair streamed behind me and moonlight shimmered around me.

I glanced over my shoulder and saw Zagan coming for me. His dark hair was swept off his face as he jogged after me with ease, his every movement perfectly honed, slicing through the night air like a predator intent on his prey. His eyes sparked—electric blue.

He was coming for me . . .

He always would.

EPILOGUE

"WHY DO YOU KEEP PUTTING THIS OFF? It's been over a year. You've done everything but make it official. It's time."

He paced in the canvas tent. The small lantern flickered, and the shadows which occupied the space shifted and swayed. Although his spine was straight and his broad shoulders thrown back, I could see the hesitation in his eyes.

But finally, Maxim spoke.

"There are still a few buildings to renovate in the commons and some positions at Court which need to be filled. It would be prudent to postpone."

I rolled my eyes. "You're crazy," I told him. "The commons are beautiful. Everyone is in adoration of what you've done. And all the important appointments have been filled—to everyone's approval.

"You have done an amazing job, Maxim. Your people are proud, as they should be, of the new era you have all worked so tirelessly to create. You have resurrected this place. And you have done well."

"We," he corrected.

I gave a half nod, half shrug, not agreeing with him. Zagan and I had helped him whenever we could, but Maxim had been the driving force behind the restoration of the Shadow Village.

I wasn't about to argue with him, though. I needed to get him out of the tent. "*We* have done well," I agreed for his sake. "Now . . . *it's time*."

Maxim's pacing slowed. Then he stopped altogether. He came to stand before me, towering over me, and the dark slash of his brow intensified.

He took my hands in his. "I do not enjoy speaking these words aloud. However, I feel I must say this once." His gray eyes seemed to glint in the dim light as he looked down at me. "I appreciate everything you have done. I consider you a friend. And I would be the less had I not been granted the fortune to know you."

I blinked. "My god, Maxim . . . You've really turned soft. I don't know if this is such a good idea anymore. There's still time to cancel."

Maxim gave me a smile. I couldn't help but grin back before giving his hands a squeeze. "I adore you," I said simply. "You are a brother to me. And we *all* are better for knowing you."

With a heave of his chest, he released my hands and looked me over. "He is lucky to have you."

I couldn't help but feel a slight pang at his words. I couldn't help but think of all we'd been through. I bit my cheek, and I murmured, "Thank you, Maxim."

He shook his head. "Don't, Violet."

"What? I didn't say anything."

"Don't," he repeated. He looked down at me with such intensity, searching my eyes, reliving the past as well. Finally, he said, "You made me realize there were things I didn't know I wanted. That was all. It was never anything more than that."

I met the power of his gaze, the certainty of it, and I nodded.

Then I gave a sigh of understanding, I let out a breath, finally letting go of the past. And I realized there was one final offer I needed to make. One last gesture to right the wrongs.

"Maxim, I really do want you to know that we can take up residence elsewhere. You can reinstate the Dark Manor if you prefer. I don't think you've given it serious thought. There's still time. You can hold Court there if you wish. I . . . I know how special it is."

Maxim walked over to the tent flaps to peer into the night. He assessed what lay before him, and I couldn't help but cross to stand next to him, wanting to take in the view myself.

We stood in the same tent, in the same field, in the same village, where we had met once before. Only this time, we were not surrounded by a bleak land and the shambles of an abandoned village. We were not surrounded by tragedy and hopelessness.

Because the shops, and homes, and buildings which lined the little valley had been restored. Businesses had been established. The cobblestone road now extended down into the abandoned part of the village, complete with gas lanterns that flickered in the snowy night.

And in the middle of it all, Maxim had established a commons where the heart of the Shadow government operated—the new Shadow Court.

The field in which we stood had become an expansive park, where events and activities took place. There were fairs and markets and friendly tournaments. And the reason for it all stood beside me.

He gave a nod, acknowledging all the hard work that had gone into the village. "This is the new home of the Shadow Court. But thank you for the offer, Violet. Truly."

I looked at the valley and then back at Maxim. "I suppose so. Time to make it official, then." I held my hand out to him. "Shall we?"

He straightened, seeming to grow taller and bigger, demanding more space, the shadows of the tent coalesced around him. Then he offered his arm, and we stepped out into the night together.

It was peaceful. Calm. Solemn.

A layer of white snow covered the ground and large flakes drifted from the sky.

We walked through the snow to the back of the gathered crowd, where Zagan stood waiting. Far ahead, I could see the makeshift stage. And between us and that stage was a sea of people, who had all come to celebrate this special night.

It was the winter solstice, the longest night of the year, an evening especially full of power and beauty for the Shadow people. I could feel the energy of it vibrate around me—the magic of it.

Maxim gave a slight bow and released my arm. Zagan nodded.

He was tall and strong. He possessed a honed control these days. And while he stood there, calm and balanced, I could see tension at the corners of his eyes. I went up on my toes to give him a kiss on the cheek and murmur at his ear.

"It'll be fine."

His lips thinned and his nostrils flared, but he nodded.

The three of us took a moment to stand where we were at the back of the gathered crowd. Then, in a deep, loud voice Maxim began to chant. As he did, a hush fell upon the crowd.

One by one they turned, laying all eyes upon Maxim, before joining him in the elemental prayer. And hearing the call of her people, the full moon rose above us, larger and brighter than I'd ever seen.

The last few snowflakes fell across the land. Maxim's people parted before us. An aisle to the stage had been created.

With Maxim and Zagan at each side, we walked through the crowd and up onto the stage. Our silver robes shimmered, reflecting the moonlight. They had been spun from moon flower silk, especially for this occasion.

Once we had taken our position upon the stage, Maxim took a moment to stare out, taking in the sight of all those assembled before him. Then he removed his cloak and knelt.

The mark on his chest, the three crescent moons, shimmered beneath the light from the night sky. And a deafening roar swept through the crowd.

I took Zagan's hand in mine and gave it a squeeze, releasing a small surge of energy, trying to ease his tension. He drew in a breath and looked down at me before letting go of my hand. He removed his own cloak, baring his own mark. It, too, glinted in the moonlight. And a hush fell over the crowd once more.

Then Zagan stepped behind Maxim and draped his cloak over Maxim's shoulders.

Another roar filled the night.

The king of the Shadows had been crowned.

One of Maxim's people had told me it was important that I be there to give my blessing as well. And although I didn't really see how . . . there was nothing I would not do for Maxim.

So I stepped up to him and placed my hand on his shoulder while he knelt—my offering of support and approval.

Maxim bowed his head, and I couldn't help but smile.

This was how it should be.

Then the stage became flooded in celebration. One by one, people began to file on the stage to congratulate Maxim. He was nothing if not noble and gracious, greeting everyone by name.

As discreetly as I could, I gathered up Maxim's discarded robe and crossed to the back of the stage where Zagan waited.

Throwing the cloak over his shoulders, I pulled up the hood for him. "Come on," I whispered, drawing my own cowl. And we slipped away.

Two shadows in the night.

Maxim would understand the crowd was too much for Zagan. And I knew Maxim would not miss us. I knew he would be entertaining his people until the sun rose.

We made our way through the deserted street with Zagan slipping his large hand over my own.

And at last, all was settled. The Shadow people had their king. The Radiants, too, had a noble leader. My mother had stepped aside. She was still working tirelessly to return all the Prisms who were hidden away.

Elijah had remained with those who were lost, refusing to leave until they could all get out safely. And I wished him the best. He had made mistakes. Grave ones. But I knew he believed he was doing what was right at the time. And I was not one to cast stones.

I hoped that he would find what he was looking for. I was certain he would.

The book of prophecies was in full effect, many finding that their end was near. But I was learning that that was not always something to fear. All stories must end. And they all reach their conclusion in different ways.

New ones begin.

I looked up at Zagan as we walked down the street, and I smiled at him. "What now, husband?" I asked.

He stopped in the middle of the snowy street with the lanterns flickering around us. Then he drew back his hood and pulled me into his arms. The slight upturn at the corner of his mouth transformed into a full-blown, heart-stopping smile.

I was certain I'd lost my breath.

He leaned down, grabbing my hood by the sides, placing his face in front of mine and whispered, "Whatever you like . . . *wife.*"

***

Printed in Great Britain
by Amazon